Murder in Montague Place

Murder in Montague Place

Martyn Beardsley

ROBERT HALE · LONDON

ISBN 978-0-7198-0704-6

Robert Hale Limited
Clerkenwell House
Clerkenwell Green
London EC1R 0HT

www.halebooks.com

2 4 6 8 10 9 7 5 3 1

Typeset in 10.75/14pt Palatino
Printed in Great Britain by the MPG Books Group,
Bodmin and King's Lynn

TOM PRIKE WAS one of the best attic thieves in London. He should have been – for three years he was under the wing of Dark John, the swarthy Cumbrian who ostensibly hawked cutlery about the streets but was regarded with a certain amount of awe by fellow criminals and officers of the law alike for his ghost-like ability to enter and leave apparently secure premises. The only thing he could not escape from was the bottle, and strong spirits brought about his premature demise during the hard winter of 1843.

A year later, Tom Prike was making his own way in the world. He was fourteen, but in his over-large, threadbare coat, ragged trousers tied at the waist with string and hems in tatters from dragging along the ground and with his slow, hunched-over way of walking, from a distance he might have been mistaken for an old man. When working, though, Tom was as lithe as a cat, as dextrous as a watchmaker. Burgling the houses of the well-off by stealthy entrance via attic or garret windows could be a very lucrative business, but it was clear to see that Tom Prike had not made his fortune from it. That was because he was a freelancer, employed by others to perform tasks they knew he could do better than they. They kept the majority of the haul and he received a cut. It was a pitiful amount and grossly unfair, but it was the only way he knew. Those who called upon his services had the intelligence – the best places to rob, the safest times. Tom had no handily placed contacts, knew no servants with inside information. It was easier for him to wait for the jobs to come to him.

Which is why Tom Prike was loitering in Russell Square. It was late afternoon, the winter sun sinking behind tall, elegant buildings and the temperature plummeting. Every now and then a shiver ran through his whole body, which he did his best to hide. It was important to maintain the air of one quite content to sit on the freezing pavement in the gathering gloom, doodling in the dirt with a stick. He had his eyes on a house across the way in Montague Place. The family were visiting relatives in Blackheath; one of the servants should have left a window open on the uppermost floor at the rear. He could not see this from where he waited, but when all was clear a light would appear in the top floor window facing the road, and this was Tom's signal. The attic of his target house, he knew from an earlier scouting mission, could not be directly accessed by climbing – but it could be reached by starting his ascent at the house next door, whose first floor was scaleable. Tom's fingers were becoming numb and white. He put one hand in his pocket for warmth, but continued to scrabble on the ground with the other: he had to keep up his act or risk being moved on. He knew a bobby passed through Russell Square approximately every fifteen minutes on his beat, and must be due again soon.

Tom swapped the stick to his left hand and warmed his right, and then became aware of his growing hunger, too. He was well used to going without meals, but if a faintness came on because of it, that, combined with the increasing stiffness in his limbs and hands would put the whole job in jeopardy. This would not be an easy climb, and speed would be required because even the rear of the house was overlooked by several others. As time passed, he began to wonder whether it was such a good idea, whether he shouldn't just put it off for today and head for Rawbone Sal's doss house in St George's-in-the-East. Sal could always be relied on to let him sit by the fire for a bit and maybe even spare him some scraps to eat. But then, at long last, like a beacon on the shoreline guiding a ship safely home, a candle flickered into life in the little third floor window of the house Tom was watching.

He raised his aching backside from the hard ground and felt his knees creak as his legs straightened. But suddenly he was down again. The policeman had returned, striding out of Southampton Row, his bull's eye lamp lit. His route did not take him past the spot where Tom Prike was sitting – the youth made quite sure of that – but there was still just enough light left to make him visible, and it would only take one glance in the right direction. Tom bowed his head and concentrated on making circles in the road with his stick, but out of the corner of his eye he could see the dark figure moving through the square and the beam from the lamp flicking this way and that. The peeler should have turned right for Woburn Square – but he did not. He paused, then turned left, towards Tom Prike. Tom continued to make meaningless marks with his stick, head down. It was a reasonable enough ruse when it was light, but as darkness came rapidly on it looked less and less convincing. It was too late to employ a new strategy now. The policeman's clumping feet came to a halt about twenty paces away, and the bull's eye flashed in Tom's direction. But the yellow beam continued to move until it fell on the door of a lawyer's office. The officer approached the door and tried the handle. Satisfied that all was secure, he turned his back and marched away towards Woburn Square.

Tom threw down his stick and made his move.

The house adjoining his target had a narrow gap between it and the next one. Not wide enough even to be called an alley, but just sufficient for a scrawny lad to slip through and reach the back of the buildings. Here, after a brief pause to reassure himself that there were no servants in the shadows having a crafty smoke or taking a break from their labours, Tom climbed onto a metal bin. From there he was able to grasp a drainpipe. This being a posh house, it was freshly painted and shiny. Tom preferred to work shabbier buildings since rusting, rough-surfaced pipes provided a better grip. This one was not only smooth, but wet with condensation on the verge of turning to frost, and he needed to take extra care as he began to shin upwards. Luckily, he only needed to ascend one floor before he was able to haul himself onto a flat roof. He just had to traverse this and then there was another drainpipe providing direct access to the attic window, which was his goal. He crouched down before crossing the open space, for there was a light in a window on this floor. Anyone in that room might see him pass by it. He could see no one inside from his position – but not knowing was dangerous for someone in Tom's profession. Lesser practitioners might have scurried past and hoped for the best, but that was not Tom Prike's way. He crawled soundlessly across the lead-covered roof until finally he could press himself against the wall beside the window; then he inched his head closer to assess any dangers which might lurk within.

And danger did lurk within – but not in a way he could possibly have imagined.

Tom Prike spied two people inside that room and quickly jerked back his head. Not because he feared he had been spotted – he knew he hadn't – but because he recognized one of the occupants, and it was not at all who he might have expected to see. Thoughts of robbing the next door house were temporarily forgotten, and he leaned forward again to weigh up this development. He couldn't hear what was being said, but judging from the angry expressions and jabbing fingers, some sort of heated dispute was taking place. Tom became totally absorbed in this scene, certain that things were about to come to a head. But when they did, everything happened so quickly and violently that he could barely take it all in. A knife appeared – long-bladed, viciously sharp-looking. There was a flailing of arms, a tangling of bodies, a silvery blur. And then a powerful spurt of red. It was dark, almost purple in the candle light, and it continued to gush freely in a pulsing sort of way such as Tom had never witnessed before. His eyes were wide; his strength deserted him; he began to shake – and this time it was not from the cold. He was witnessing a man's very lifeblood drain away faster than he could have ever thought possible – the blood drenching the clothes and soaking the carpet. Tom Prike was sickened yet mesmerized, gawping.

And then something made the assailant look up at the window.

Tom pulled his head back in an instant, but one image remained graven on his mind: the eyes of the killer looking directly into his own. He did not stop to consider how likely it might be that a person inside a lit room would be able to really see or recognize someone in the darkness outside. He did not even bother with the drainpipe, but leapt into the darkness from the edge of the roof, stifling a cry of pain as his feet hit the hard ground below. He tumbled head-over-heels, crashing into some unseen obstacle, then jumped to his feet and, ignoring the pain in both ankles, fled into the night.

I

G REAT SCOTLAND YARD, the Back Hall. Early evening, and the end of a long shift. Sergeant Raddle fussily tidied his desk in the reception area. It was cold. Eye-wateringly cold February air seeped under doors and through the gaps in ill-fitting casements. A small cloud billowed from the good sergeant's numb red nose as he walked over to the open fire and gave the glowing coals one last poke. Straightening up, he glanced at the big, walnut-encircled clock face high on the wall behind his desk then strode back to his post: slow and erect, boots echoing authoritatively off the stone floor of the foyer. The debilitating chill even held back the elegant minute-hand of that stately timepiece, robbing it of the strength to make that one last effort to reach the black XII at the pinnacle of its journey and mark the end of his duties for the day. Or so it seemed.

This public entrance to the Yard was busy. Usually, this was one of the quieter times, when people were more interested in home and their evening meal; but there had been a quarterly meeting of senior inspectors on the first floor, bringing not only them but their attendant lackeys to the building. Additionally, the Whitehall Division in which the Yard lay had been conducting a round-up of bail-jumpers and those with outstanding peace warrants against their names – quite possibly with the sole intention of impressing the said inspectors from all the other divisions. The meeting had just broken up, so small knots of senior officers in fancy uniforms loitered in conversation before going their separate ways; moving between them and around them were beat constables leading bedraggled prisoners to the cells and travelling in the opposite direction were men and women of a more cheerful demeanour, making their way from incarceration and back out into the world. Yet another category of person populated the lofty foyer of Great Scotland Yard: the general idler to be found in all public places. The lost, the confused, the cold seeking warmth, the anonymous passer-through. Sergeant Raddle kept a particular eye on these people. It was not unknown for pockets to be relieved of their contents even within the walls of this venerable establishment.

A rush of icy air around Sergeant Raddle's ankles drew his attention to the big double doors. A lady. An attractive lady very obviously in distress, no less, hovered half in, half out of them, unsure of herself, eyes darting this way and that. Sergeant Raddle admired her beauty but wished she would either come or go so that the doors might be properly shut ....

He eventually caught the eye of the distraught woman, who responded by hurrying towards him, her luxuriant fur-trimmed coat swishing across the stone floor. She opened her mouth to speak, hesitated, then finally launched into her overture.

'I ... I *hardly know where to ... something has happened ... my husband....*'

Her voice was uncomfortably loud, and uncomfortably close to the borders of hysteria for Sergeant Raddle's liking.

Among those congregated in the Back Hall was a rather stout man, largely plainly dressed but with a blue and white checked waistcoat just visible beneath his winter garments. He was in conversation with another, and even though he was able to keep up his end of the discussion and his associate believed he had his full attention, his alert eyes had taken in this unfolding scene at the duty sergeant's desk.

'There, there, madam,' Sergeant Raddle was saying in a practised, avuncular manner. 'I'm sure we can find a solution to the problem, whatever it might be.'

'I need ... I have read about those people – like spies....'

Spies? Sergeant Raddle's heart sank. *Spies?*

'Someone is spying on your husband, madam?'

She put a hand to her brow. Her striking blue eyes momentarily swam with salty wetness but she staved off actual tears in a manner admirable to Sergeant Raddle. 'No, no. Those policemen who are *like* spies, but—'

'I can assure you, madam, that *none* of our officers would resort to spying, whatever your husband might think!'

The loiterer who had picked up on this encounter paused in his own conversation, and seemed to be considering whether, or when, to approach. His companion had now followed the direction of the first man's gaze, too.

'You don't understand!' said the woman in almost a sob. 'What I need is one of those new types of policemen – not a spy, but—'

'A *detective*,' announced the onlooker finally and boldly. He had appeared silently, unnoticed, almost as if materialized by a magician. He was of about medium height and in early middle-age, with dark, searching eyes, which, it was possible to conjecture might in certain circumstances be used as instruments of intimidation, but which in this case twinkled with confidence and sympathy. He touched the woman lightly on the arm.

'A detective officer,' he repeated, quieter now, and more confidentially. 'That's what *you* need, unless I'm very much mistaken.' He raised his hat. 'Inspector Bucket of that department.'

The exasperation drained from the woman's face. 'Yes, a *detective* officer – that's it!'

'The detective force is not *new*, madam,' Sergeant Raddle informed her. 'It must be at least two years since—'

'Two years is new enough in the Lord's great scheme of things, Mr Raddle,' exclaimed Mr Bucket. He looked up at the clock, even though he knew exactly what time it was. 'Upon my soul, Sergeant – this is dedication beyond the call of duty. Mrs Raddle will wonder what has become of you!'

While Sergeant Raddle was expressing his ready agreement with this statement, Mr Bucket added, in an affable aside to the lady, '*And Mrs Raddle ain't one whose nerves can stand much of that sort of wondering, madam. Unlike Mrs Bucket, who possesses a deal more phlegm, if you'll pardon the expression.*'

And so Sergeant Raddle was finally released from his duties and hurried to get his heavy winter coat.

'Now then, madam,' said Mr Bucket. 'It don't take neither a spy *nor* a detective to see that you are greatly troubled by some very pressing matter. One to do with your partner on life's journey – and what could be more pressing than that? Explain all, and let me see if I can be of any assistance.'

'There has been a death, Mr Bucket. A horrible murder – *and my dear husband has been arrested as the culprit!*'

'And needless to say you are convinced of his innocence.'

'I am *certain* of his innocence, sir! I know it as a fact.'

Mr Bucket transferred his hat to the hand which already held his stick, freeing the other to thoughtfully stroke a luxuriant dark side-burn. 'And when might this murder have occurred, madam? For there ain't been one in the Whitehall Division that I've a-heard of.'

'I believe the murder to have taken place yesterday at a house in Montague Place near the British Museum – a businessman was stabbed to death. My husband was arrested just this afternoon at our house in Russell Square. I'm afraid I don't know about your police divisions or which one it falls under, Inspector, but I do know that a man from this office, not in uniform, was brought in to help with the investigation. My husband was taken away while I was out and I neither saw the officer nor was able to determine his name.'

The lady was quite tall; fully as tall as Mr Bucket. Whorls of straw-berry-blonde hair floated beneath her hat like summer clouds; her complexion was very fair, yet with a natural blush to the cheeks and very full lips; her eyes were of a particularly luminous shade of blue. As she gazed openly at Mr Bucket her long lashes fluttered agitat-edly – perhaps a little too much for his liking.

'If this is another detective officer's case I cannot rightly inter-vene …' Mr Bucket began.

Her eyes widened and sparkled ever bluer; the long lashes flut-tered faster. 'But sir, there has been a terrible mistake and I implore—'

'But I *can* make some inquiries and satisfy both of us that all that is being done is above board and fair and square, as you might say,' Mr Bucket hastened to add, again patting her arm. 'If innocent your husband be, and I have no reason to doubt *your* good word, then all shall come clear in the fullness of time. For now, we must be patient and strong. Strong and patient – *that's* what we need to be. Now, my dear, let us begin with your name ….'

She held out a pink, slightly plump little hand for Mr Bucket to shake. 'Mrs Eleanora Scambles. My husband is Jonathan Scambles – Doctor Jonathan Webster Scambles. He has a practice on Tottenham

Court Road. It is a very successful practice, Mr Bucket. A celebrated author and a member of the cabinet are among his patients, so you can see that if news of this dreadful error gets abroad—'

'*Strong and patient*, Mrs Scambles! I shall do my best.' He gave a slight bow. 'That's all I need. Until next time, Mrs Scambles.'

'Thank you so much, Mr Bucket.'

With a resigned dimming of her azure gaze and further swishing of her furs, the woman turned and ventured back out into the gloom and the chill air of Whitehall Place.

Mr Bucket wasn't the only person to have observed her departure.

A person, unnoticed by Mrs Scambles and lingering at some distance behind the inspector's back, had been leaning against a wall, flipping through the pages of the *Morning Post* – but his eyes had strayed a little too often in the direction of the two figures in earnest conversation. Whether it was Mrs Scambles' beauty or something else which had attracted his interest was difficult to say. The great double doors had barely stopped swinging from the lady's departure when he folded up his paper, tucked it under his arm and was swallowed up by the darkness outside.

II

IT WAS GORDON'S second full day as a detective officer, and if anything he was feeling more daunted by the challenge that lay before him than he had been on the first. The previous day, he hadn't known quite what to expect, and anyway, he had been buoyed by the excitement of joining a service whose mystique had excited him ever since he had first read about it. *And* he was to be under the tutelage of one of its most illustrious members, to boot. But that first day, the occurrences of which he was supposed to be assimilating but which had dissolved into a maelstrom of strange experiences, a bizarre new language, rules, regulations and an apparently endless parade of barely believable characters, had provided him with such sensory excess as to keep him awake until the early hours of the previous night and had woken him this morning long before his usual hour.

'Look'ee here, now, Mr Gordon. Most of these places is low lodging houses frequented by a certain type of lady and a host of magsmen, dollymops, bit fakers and the like. Not *all* are of that persuasion in these parts, to be sure. See that gent crossing the street there?' Mr Bucket jabbed a sturdy thumb in the direction of an insignificant little fellow who was passing them in the opposite direction – someone towards whom Gordon could swear he had not even glanced while he had been talking to him, and thus someone whom it seemed impossible for him to have even noticed. 'A poor clerk: shabby-smart black attire. Stooping posture from hour after hour sat bending over a desk. Poor souls – could never do it myself – rather be a felon. And inky fingers. They never seem to be able to get it *all* off....'

To have seen ink on the man's fingers from that distance was impossible. Gordon refused to believe it, but—

'Gotta be able to *read* people,' continued Mr Bucket. 'Many a face you'll come to know, but many you won't and you gotta come to recognize the *type* at the very least.'

They were walking along a frost-whitened mean side-street somewhere between Drury Lane and the Strand, with no particular purpose in mind other than to 'Have a little look-see' as Mr Bucket had put it when they had set out from Great Scotland Yard an hour earlier. How anyone could ever come to know his way around these labyrinthine streets, alleys and courts without soon becoming hopelessly lost was completely beyond Gordon. He marched briskly to keep up with his chief, which helped to warm him against the bitter cold, chafing his face and numbing his hands and feet.

'Quiet at this hour,' Bucket muttered. 'Most of these folk is night-owls. But see here – if it ain't Cock-eyed Joe!'

A sallow, gaunt man of about fifty had just emerged from a door on their left. He had no obvious optical deformity – but then Gordon was already learning the futility of trying to read too much into these enigmatic London nicknames.

'Mornin', Mr Bucket.'

'What brings you out at this early hour, Joe?'

'Belly's right bad, Mr Bucket. Gotta take somethin' for it – can't stand it no longer.' He spoke with a grimace, slightly bent over, one hand clutching his abdomen.

'There's a good chemist's shop in Oxford Street, Joe. You want to try some of his rhubarb and magnesia. Inspector Stope's missus swears by him.'

'Nah, I'm off to the Wellington for a pint. Beer flushes your system out good and proper if you only takes enough of it, and that's a known fact.'

Mr Bucket raised an eyebrow but let this piece of questionable medical advice pass without further comment. 'Joe here's a smasher, ain't you Joe.'

Joe's eyes turned to the pavement by his feet and he began to move on. 'Gave that lark up months ago, Mr Bucket,' he mumbled as he wandered away.

'*Smasher?*' Gordon queried. It sounded like some sort of tough, but Cock-eyed Joe certainly didn't look cut out for that sort of work.

'A receiver and passer-on of base coins, that's what the likes of Joe is about. He was never a very good one but he always got by in the business. And still does, despite what he says.'

Gordon hesitated as he watched the man walk away, before stating what seemed the obvious question. 'Then ... shouldn't we arrest him?'

'*Gotta catch 'em at it*! That's the law, that is. Inconvenient at times, but nothing to be done for it.'

Their meandering route took them north-east to the vicinity of Lincoln's Inn, and upon hearing the bells of some nearby church chiming ten o'clock, Mr Bucket cast his eyes around until they alighted upon a coffee stall. 'Ah – time for my morning constitutional!'

They stayed there for a few minutes drinking surprisingly good coffee from cracked china cups, and while Gordon warmed his hands at the coffee man's charcoal burner, Mr Bucket kept up a running commentary on the theatre that was London as it was enacted before their eyes.

'And who might that red-headed fellow crossing the street be but Ginger Jem! Never looked this way, but he spotted us all right. Look – he's stopped to look in the cat's meat shop and in a second he'll set off – but away from us instead of towards us as he was originally proceeding.'

Sure enough, Ginger Jem casually sauntered away – Gordon would certainly have never have noticed anything untoward about him, let alone that his behaviour showed him to be avoiding them.

'Inspector Stope has a peace warrant out against Jem,' Mr Bucket commented with surprising indifference. Gordon could now understand why their smasher was left unmolested, but surely if this man had a warrant in his name...?

Mr Bucket read his thoughts. 'That ain't no reason to spoil a nice coffee stop on a perishing morning like this.' He leaned his stick against the coffee man's stall and wrapped both hands around the steaming cup. 'Jem ain't hard to find, and Billy Stope will pick him up with no difficulty in his own good time.'

After a moment's silence, Mr Bucket turned his penetrating gaze on Gordon, and for a moment he got some idea of what it would be like to be a criminal trying to hide the truth from him. 'So, Mr Gordon. New to police work *and* to this fair city?'

'I had never even been to London before I joined the detective force, Mr Bucket.'

'*Never?* I never heard of such a thing! Why, everyone's been to London at some time or another – especially men of your standing.'

'I grew up in Ringwood in Hampshire, and purchased my commission with the Cameronians before I had time to do anything with my life. Indeed, I only returned from overseas service little more than a year ago.'

The inspector opened a couple of buttons at the top of his great coat and delved into a pocket, producing a small notebook whose pages he began to flip through. 'James Alexander Gordon, of that ilk. Seventh Earl of Drumnadrochit, no less.'

'I shan't inherit that title until my father passes away,' Gordon corrected him – though he was sure that Mr Bucket knew that perfectly well already. He fully expected him to make some further mention of his father, since the infamous case for which his name was now forever associated had been the talk of the London papers for some months. But the renowned detective resisted the temptation – if indeed there was one.

'Well, now,' commented Mr Bucket as they drained and returned the cups and resumed their perambulations. '*Named* like a Scotchman, *father* a Scotchman – yet lives in England and talks like a true blue-blooded Englishman ....'

Gordon couldn't help smiling at the inspector's straight-speaking inquisitiveness. Coming from some it might have seemed offensive, but Mr Bucket, he was learning, had a disarming way about him.

'My father settled in Hampshire after a spell in the West Indies. I've only ever been to Scotland to visit relatives. Are you a Londoner, Mr Bucket?'

'Born in Battersea, live in Pimlico and rarely had cause to stray further afield than Hemel Hempstead in the far north, where my brother and his good lady live. Spent a time in the army myself, to be sure, but never sent to serve in foreign fields, as you might say.'

'Really? Which regiment?'

'Funny you should ask that question, Mr Gordon, because thereby hangs a tale, as they say—'

But just then their attention was diverted to the strange and disturbing cry of a woman. They were by now on Great Queen Street and both turned their heads in time to see a maid come careering precipitously down the steps leading from one of the better class of houses, waving her arms wildly in the air and continuing to pour forth the same anguished but indecipherable utterances. She stopped at the bottom of the steps and pivoted aimlessly this way and that, clapping her hands to cheeks completely drained of colour.

'*Dying!*' was the first intelligible sound to come from her lips, aimed at no one in particular as they approached. '*The missus is barely clinging to life – won't somebody assist her?!*'

Her plaintive screeching was so piercing as to be almost painful on the ear, and the detectives quickened their stride – Gordon had already learned from his chief that it didn't do for policemen to run, except in pursuit of an absconder.

'I'm Mr Bucket of the Detective, I am. And this is Mr James Alexander Gordon of that ilk, my promising new sergeant. What seems to be the matter, miss?'

The maid half-sobbed and half-gasped a torrent of jumbled words by way of explanation as they followed her through the hallway and into the parlour, and there they saw, groaning and writhing on the floor, a woman of about forty years, clearly extremely handsome despite the facial contortions she was engaged in. During the course of her agonized struggles the lady's crinolines had ridden up somewhat, exposing the whole of both legs from the knees down. Gordon barely knew where to place his gaze, but couldn't help noticing that she had very fine calves, for which observation he felt, under the circumstances – or indeed any circumstances – mightily and professionally ashamed.

'Has madam taken anything, eaten anything untoward?' Mr Bucket asked the maid calmly.

But though she was still on her feet the maid was in little better condition than her mistress, and neither Gordon nor the inspector could make out a word of what she was saying.

'Now, now, my dear,' Mr Bucket admonished her in a firm but

kindly way as he took hold of her shoulders. 'For the good lady's sake you must compose yourself sufficiently to provide us with an answer – or who knows what might happen to her for the delay?'

In reply, the distressed girl pointed towards three glass domes on a table in the centre of the room. *'Gone! Theft!'*

Mr Bucket raised a fleshy finger to the side of his nose; his keen eyes moved from the domes to the woman squirming on the floor and back again, then narrowed like those of a cat closing in on its quarry.

'Stuffed animals of some kind?'

The maid could only respond with a no doubt unintentional sound which was a cross between a sob and the mucoid snort of someone with a very heavy cold, which Gordon found none too appealing coming from a member of the fairer sex. She did, though, manage to shake her head.

Now Mr Bucket's eyes lit up. Somehow, he had it!

'Ferns!'

'Aaaargh!' came a wail of acknowledgement and misery from the floor.

Thinking the poor woman may have inadvertently eaten some sort of plant which had proved injurious to her health, Gordon suggested summoning a doctor.

Mr Bucket leaned closer to him and spoke in a confidential tone. 'This here ailment seems to be of what you might call a hysterical rather than physical nature. Mrs Bucket's eldest sister is similarly inclined when confronted by adversity. *Ferns*, Mr Gordon! A recent but very popular pastime among the ladies. Mrs Bucket herself has taken an interest in that direction – though I am doing my best to dampen her ardour on account of the great expense involved. Some very rare and sought-after specimens about. First time I've come across a theft of same, though, I do declare.'

In the meantime another maid had arrived with some smelling salts, and Mr Bucket was finally able to interview the lady of the house while Gordon examined the transparent domes and the general area around them in the forlorn hope of coming across some clue which might help them to identify the perpetrator of the theft. As might be expected, there were some imprints on the glass made by the fingers of, presumably, the thief – but nothing which would help them identify him or her.

'I was hosting a meeting of the National Truss Society for the Relief of the Ruptured Poor, of which I am the treasurer,' the lady of the house was explaining to Mr Bucket now that she had revived somewhat and settled herself into a chair.

'A *very* worthy organization,' Mr Bucket commented solemnly. 'My own father suffered from that very complaint owing to the merest slip of the foot while moving a chest of drawers. I do declare there are many who would suffer agonies without the support of the kind which you ladies generously and selflessly offer.'

Some colour returned to the lady's face and she allowed herself a modest smile. 'Well, I do hope you and your officers are able to shed some light onto this matter....'

'The entire and considerable resources of the detective force shall be directed towards a resolution of this case,' Mr Bucket assured her. Gordon was not convinced that the inspector was, at that point, quite as committed to the matter as he made out – but he was subsequently to discover that his words would be closer to the mark than either of them then realized.

The detectives left the lady in much better spirits than they had found her, and when their shift was over they adjourned to the Ten Bells in Craven Street, near to their Great Scotland Yard base. The Bells, as Gordon's colleagues called it, was an old-style public house with sanded floors and spittoons. The ceiling was low, and there was a particularly large fireplace opposite the bar. It had well-worn but comfortable-looking settles on either side of it, but the blaze from the fire, which was so well stoked up on this cold night, was such that few could remain in close vicinity for very long.

'Don't go imagining that this kind of alcoholic occurrence happens at the end of every day, Mr Gordon of that ilk,' Mr Bucket was at pains to explain. 'Because it don't. Only now and then, when the mood takes us – ain't that true, Blackie?'

Sergeant Blacksnape nodded. There were five of them sitting round a table in a corner of the pub. Daniel Blacksnape was a wiry Tyneside man whose thick accent, Gordon had noticed, was apparently a source of amusement and jest to the Londoners among them.

Inspector Billy Stope sat on the other side of Mr Bucket; the two of them clearly went back a long way, well before the formation of the detective force of which they were both original members. Stope was a physically imposing man, tall and broad, with a heavy brow and massive hands, which looked as though they could easily crush the pint pot he was holding. His belly was of equally impressive dimensions and his breath had a sort of husky wheeziness to it, though Gordon had little doubt that Billy Stope would not be found lacking if called into action. He had heard the odd person refer to him as 'Flash Billy' – though in hushed tones as though afraid it might get back to him. Gordon could now see how it might have arisen. Although largely dressed in the usual generally sober way of a detective officer, there were one or two little touches such as his rather gaudy black and red checked waistcoat and the ostentatiously large and ornate tie pin with what looked like a diamond at the centre of it, which perhaps spoke of a certain level of vanity. And on a couple of occasions Gordon had witnessed him insist on buying rounds of drinks for people who had greeted him in passing, yet with whom he seemed to be only loosely acquainted.

The final member of the little party was Misty – it was all he was ever called within Gordon's hearing and he never did find out any other name for him. He was a quiet, reflective sergeant who had grey hair yet appeared to be a little younger than the still-dark Mr Bucket. All detective officers were either sergeants or inspectors, and all experienced men – except Gordon. They were considered to be the elite of the Metropolitan force, hand-picked for the work, and here he was, feeling not a little proud to be one of them. Especially here, admitted to their inner social sanctum. That feeling lasted, though, only until Danny Blacksnape made a comment. The evening had hitherto been nothing but convivial, and Mr Bucket had just been amusing everyone with the story of the stolen ferns and the swooning woman, when out of the blue Blackie, whom Gordon had observed to be inordinately fond of his rum, piped up, 'Mr Gordon, I hear that your father is a very close friend of the Chief.'

The 'Chief' was Commissioner Sir Marriot Ogle-Tarbolton, to whom the Detective Department was directly answerable.

'That is not quite true.'

'Is it not, man? Only I thought it were a bit odd on account o' yer 'ould man's brush wi' the law, like ....'

'Now then, Blackie,' Mr Bucket interjected matily, clapping his colleague on the shoulder with a big paw. 'No need for all that, particularly since Mr Gordon's pa walked out of court without a stain on his character.'

'Aye, but we arl know—'

'It's actually my grandfather,' Gordon said. 'He served in the same regiment as Sir Marriot Ogle-Tarbolton's father. And yes, without that connection I should certainly never have gained admittance into the Detective Service. I'm equally sure that if I don't come up to scratch I'll be got out as quickly as I was got in.'

'And I ain't seen no danger of *that* as yet,' Mr Bucket remarked before taking a sup of his beer.

'But 'e still got straight in in the first place – *straight* in, mind – when some of us had to serve ten year before—'

'Now's a good time to shut yer gob, Blackie,' muttered big Billy Stope suddenly, in a manner which even intimidated Gordon despite it being directed at his antagonist. 'The drink always gives you a bit of bounce and it don't sit well with yer. It really don't.'

Blackie was about to counter this, but the strains of a popular ballad began to echo around the room and took the sting out of the bad feeling which was arising among their group. Through the haze of tobacco smoke Gordon could make out a little old fellow with a single but very prominent upper front tooth, leaning with his chair on two legs, back propped against the wall, crooning away blissfully. Soon others joined in, and the evening turned into an impromptu variety show with various offerings from around the pub. Mr Bucket himself eventually rose to his feet and gave a solo rendition of *Take, O Take Those Lips Away* to the great approbation of all. Gordon had thus far only thought of him and as a private and undemonstrative man, so he was surprised by both the ease and confidence with which he gave his performance, and the clear and steady tenor voice, which effortlessly reached every corner of the room. The argument was forgotten, and it was a very advanced hour before they vacated their seats – not drunk, Gordon reflected, though certainly somewhat merry.

Billy Stope and Mr Bucket were walking out arm-in-arm just ahead of him and he overheard some of their conversation.

'So, *you* have some stolen ferns to investigate while *I* have a murder, eh?' said Stope.

'Murder?' queried Mr Bucket.

'Have you not heard? To tell the truth your ferns will take a lot more investigating than my murder – I've already made an arrest. A doctor, of all people.'

'Oh, *that*. Yes, I've already heard about that. A *doctor* taking a life instead of preserving one! What's the world coming to? Can it really be so, Billy?'

'Everything points to it – much of it circumstantial – but to top it all there's a piece of cast-iron evidence to put him right at the scene.'

'Sounds like you're in luck, Billy boy. What little gem might that be, then?'

'Little gem?'

'The evidence!'

'Oh, that ....'

Mr Stope seemed to hesitate, and Gordon hoped that Mr Bucket had not overstepped the mark. He had already learned that officers were *very* protective of their cases and how it was considered to be particularly bad form for an 'outsider' to stick his nose in. But the dilemma was circumvented by Sergeant Blacksnape's loud and by now rather slurred northern tones.

'Ever seen a corpse done in something horrible?' he asked Gordon in a kind of leering way. 'You'll see *lots* of 'em in this job, man!'

Before he could answer, Mr Bucket interposed. 'Seen one, Blackie? Has he *seen* one? Why, he's been responsible for dozens of 'em!'

'Eh?'

'Mr Gordon here was a captain in the 26th Regiment of Foot. Very warm work in China, so I hear, eh, Mr Gordon?'

'At times, Mr Bucket,' he replied, allowing himself a slight smile at Blacksnape's sullen expression.

'Away with you, James Alexander Gordon of that ilk,' the inspector said, prodding him in the chest with his formidable fore-finger. 'Early start for you and me tomorrow, and no mistake.'

They all went their separate ways. Mr Bucket headed south to Pimlico and Gordon towards Westminster Bridge and his rooms across the Thames in Kennington. But he had not gone far when a figure suddenly darted from the shadows of a narrow lane to his right and barred his path. He instantly took half a step back and raised his cane – but in a second his brain had had time to process what was before him, and he recognized this as a small figure in a passive rather than an aggressive posture. There was little illumination from the gas lamps at this spot, and all Gordon could make out was the dirty face of a boy who could have been little more than ten years of age.

'Mr Bucket?' came a quavering voice. The lad was shivering from head to toe, and Gordon could see from his outline that he wore no great coat but only a jacket. It made him wonder how long he had been waiting there in the freezing temperatures. He turned to look back, but Mr Bucket had disappeared from sight.

'He has gone home. May I help? I'm his colleague.'

The boy shook his head. 'Tell Mr Bucket Tom Prike sent me 'cos 'e wants to be left aht of it. Tom says to tell Mr Bucket to let the doc take the rap – *and if 'e don't, 'e must watch 'is back.*'

Gordon was about to probe the boy about this curious message, but as soon as it was delivered he vanished silently into the night.

III

A FIGHT SPILLED OUT of a gin shop at the end of Great White Lion Street. Feebly illuminated by a solitary gas lamp, labourers in their dusty and discoloured fustian roared and set about each other over some obscure dispute. Fists flew, shillelaghs flashed, heads were locked under arms, all to the accompaniment of shouts, curses, grunts of pain.

This was Seven Dials.

People passed close by, indifferent to the fracas. One group of children chased another whose leader was waving a hat wildly in the air as if it were some kind of trophy. A man led a donkey cart laden with vegetables from Covent Market and steered his beast slightly to one side of the melee, puffing on his pipe and casting only the merest glance. And a tall man in black skirted the mob as if they existed only in the imaginations of others. This pedestrian stood out because of his gentleman's garb, with a smart frock coat and a top hat of the finest hardened silk. Even his stick had what looked like an ornate silver handle. He turned into narrow Little Earl Street, and approached a run-down building with broken windows, which housed a beer shop.

The light from the few oil lamps inside were so dim that his entrance was barely noticed. He stood for a moment, observing. In an alcove to his right was a Lascar sailor slumped across his table. The visitor might have taken him to be in a drunken stupor had he not detected the sickly sweet smell of opium from his pipe, the stem of which still adhered to his gaping, drooling mouth while the bowl rested on the table, twitching slightly each time the man exhaled.

The visitor's gaze moved round the room, and finally settled on the General. The General was, among other things, an occasional trainer of prize-fighters and was once a pugilist himself – in the vicinity of Seven Dials it was said that he once beat Joe Jullocky, the Manchester Mangler, for the middleweight championship of All England. The General had since lost much of his hair (and shaved the remainder) together with most of his teeth, while gaining enough bulk in all the wrong places to turn him into a heavyweight. But he still looked like an active enough man, and his thick neck, wonky nose and cauliflower ears, together with his reputation, were enough to dissuade all but the most foolish or inebriated of potential adversaries. And the General appeared to be in a pugnacious mood today. The visitor observed the old fighter approach a big man talking to four companions seated round a table on the far side of the room. He tapped the burly man on the shoulder, and the visitor, even in this poor light, could see the look of fear on the seated man's face when he saw who had come to call. He immediately and ardently stated his case – presumably his defence – and threw his arms out in a desperately submissive, beseeching gesture. But the General was not so easily placated, and the big man was encouraged to leave his seat. He was rugged-faced, broad-shouldered and a full head taller than the man who now ushered him towards a door.

While the big man's companions slipped hastily away, the visitor headed for the door through which their companion and the General had gone.

'I thought you wuz an *hon'rable* man, Michael.'

'I *am*, General. For God's sake, ask anyone!'

The smartly dressed interloper could hear it all. He had silently slipped into the dim corridor where the discussion was taking place, and stood in the shadows, invisible. The General's tone was calm – yet all the more full of menace for it. The other man had a strong Irish accent and his voice dripped with terror.

'But you and me 'ad an arrangement.'

'I needed the money *desperate*. I knew I could get it back so it ain't like double-crossin'.'

'It ain't *like* double-crossin', it *is* double-crossin', Michael. Yer know I can't let it go.'

The General took a step closer to Michael – who made a sudden bolt for the door. The observer pressed himself back against the wall, and saw a flurry of fists. There was a high-pitched whistling sound as the air from Michael's lungs was forced at high velocity through his pain-constricted throat, and then a heavy thud as he collapsed, writhing, to the floor. Several more rapid blows quickly followed. The visitor stepped forward into the glow of a solitary candle in a jar on a windowsill.

'Very efficient work, General.'

The General, who was stooping over his fallen victim, twisted round as suddenly as his bulk would allow, rising as he did so. ''Oo are you, then – a peeler?'

'I'm your guardian angel.'

'You're a damned nosey bugger 'oo's seen too much, that what you are!'

The General began to lumber forwards. But the other man pulled on the silver handle of his stick and whipped out a long, thin sword blade. 'I'd run you through before you even got close. But there's no need – like I said, I'm your guardian angel. You can only benefit from my visit.'

The General lowered his fists. 'Stop talkin' in riddles an' tell me what yer wants.'

'My employer has got a job, and pays well.'

'*Who the hell are yer?* Ye'r dressed like a gent but yer don't sound like one, despite yer fine words.'

'It's to do with the murder in Montague Place – poor Edward Mizzentoft. Some say you did it.'

'That doctor done it.'

'But did he? I hear you had good reason to kill Mizzentoft. I hear you had warm words with him on the day he died. Maybe the police are wrong about Doctor Scambles.'

'He's as good as swung for it, so what's it to anybody?'

A sudden gust of cold air blew through a hole in the window frame where the wood had rotted away, causing the candle on the sill to gutter and almost die. When it flared back to life it highlighted a livid, recent scar across the bridge of the General's nose.

'People are asking questions, turning stones over and looking underneath. If Scambles is released, things might come out which the person who is paying me – and who is going to pay you – would rather not.'

'Nobody won't be payin' me, 'cos I ain't gettin' involved.' The General began to walk towards the door, but the visitor raised his sword so that the tip was level with the old fighter's face.

'But you *are* involved. Like I say, people are talking. Your name has been mentioned. If Scambles gets off it will be *you* the police come for next. My employer has contacts. Believe me, we could make the mud stick as far as Mizzentoft goes. I'd say it's a question of risk the noose, or be well paid for an easy piece of work.'

There was a long silence while the General's brain clunked into gear. 'What piece of work?'

IV

A SUDDEN STRONG GUST of the coldest wind Gordon had ever known – and he had endured a Chinese winter out in the field – almost dislodged his top hat. When he looked at his fingers after rearranging it, he saw that they were coated in frost crystals from its brim. The temperature, albeit probably some way below freezing, was no lower today than yesterday but this wind made things feel ten times worse. Gordon's toes felt as though they might snap off, and his nose ran so freely he found himself checking his handkerchief to see if it was bleeding.

'Chilly work, eh, Mr Gordon?' Even Mr Bucket spoke through gritted teeth, as if his jaws were frozen together.

'Indeed. Perhaps our man has remained indoors.'

Mr Bucket smiled, no doubt, Gordon thought, at his naivety. 'They don't have the liberty of staying indoors, Mr Gordon. If they don't go out to ply their trade, they don't eat. Some might not even be able to afford a room for the night.' He stamped his feet a few times and flapped his arms about him, and then took Gordon by the elbow and they set off. 'But a turn around the block won't do us any harm. He's just as likely to be on Regent Street or Pall Mall as here.'

Mr Bucket had received reports of a group of pickpockets working in this area, led by a character known as Johnny Stovepipe, a habitual criminal nicknamed after his usual form of headwear who had recently been released from a three-year sentence and was apparently active again.

'He won't make it easy for the likes of us,' Mr Bucket remarked as they trudged round the corner of the Haymarket into Coventry Street. 'Odds are it'll be transportation for him next time, and he knows it.'

Ahead, they saw two little girls sitting on an upturned wooden packing case at the end of an alley. They looked so alike that Gordon had little doubt but that they were sisters.

'*Pretty flowers! Two bunches a penny!*' cried the older of the two. The younger one clutched a large bunch of violets but merely gazed vacantly at the icy ground, shivering violently. Their faces were white and pinched, with dark smudges beneath the eyes. Although bareheaded, they were at least wrapped in shawls – but then as the detectives drew closer, Gordon saw to his horror that neither of them was wearing shoes.

'Mr Bucket!' the older girl exclaimed upon spotting him. Even the younger now looked up and raised a feeble smile.

'Why, Annie,' said Mr Bucket as if he were their uncle on a family visit. 'What pretty flowers you have today – Mrs Bucket's favourites!'

'You said lavenders wuz 'er favourites last time we 'ad some!' the younger girl piped up innocently, and received a nudge from her older sister.

'Very changeable in that respect is Mrs Bucket, Elsie. Can't hardly keep up with her, and that's for sure.'

The older girl handed him a little bunch, and although the transaction took place quickly, Gordon noticed that he gave her far more than the penny asking price.

'Such little things, and *barefooted*. I don't know how they can survive!' he commented as they walked on, glancing back over his shoulder at them.

'They don't all … ' Mr Bucket replied. But Gordon could tell he was somewhat distracted, and the reason soon became clear when he spotted a crossing sweeper working on Piccadilly Circus who looked no older than the two girls they had just met, and called him over. 'Here, Harry. Now here's a sixpence for you, and a few more pennies for some coffee. That's for you – and Annie and Elsie over there.'

'Righto, Mr Bucket,' said the boy.

'*And mind you give it 'em, Harry,*' Mr Bucket warned him, waggling his forefinger like a teacher's cane. 'You know I'll know about it if you don't.'

'Mr *Bucket*!' replied Harry, as if dismayed that his honesty should be thus questioned.

'Seen anything of Johnny Stovepipe?'

'Johnny's in Newgate, Mr Bucket.'

'Not any more he ain't.'

'Ah, din't know.' He quickly skipped off in the direction of a coffee house across the street.

'And mind you takes the cups back.'

Although Gordon was paying attention to all this, he still couldn't get the image of the two little frozen, shoeless girls out of his mind. And Mr Bucket seemed to be aware of how much it had affected him.

'You feel as if you want to save 'em all,' he mused. 'I know I did – and still do, make no mistake. But you *can't* save 'em all and it would drive you mad to think like that. But you *can* get to know one or two and do what you can. That's the best way, that is, Mr Gordon of— *Wait a minute!*'

Gordon followed his eyes, but could see nothing out of the ordinary – just what he had already learned was a typically animated, hectic London street: the constant clatter of hansoms, broughams, tradesmen's carts and omnibuses on the cobbles; the cries of the street hawkers and the general throng of pedestrians.

'The lad looking in the milliner's shop. Now what does a lad like *that* want with a milliner's shop, eh?'

Gordon had to admit that he might have looked out of place had he actually gone inside, but....

'And who's he standing beside, eh?'

It was a well-dressed lady apparently discussing the wares on display with a friend; they were seemingly oblivious to the youth beside them.

'See that?' cried Mr Bucket almost to himself. 'He fanned her!'

Gordon was thrown into confusion. He wasn't sure what he was supposed to be looking for or why, and all that had apparently happened was that the young man who had aroused Mr Bucket's suspicions had raised his hand to lift his hat and scratch his head.

'*Fanned?*'

'When he raised his hand he felt the outside of her pocket for something worth stealing. Because he's stationed himself so close it didn't arouse any suspicion once she saw him scratch his noggin. Get ready to act fast, Mr James Alexander Gordon of that ilk!'

31

'Is *that* Johnny Stovepipe?'

'No, but ....'

Mr Bucket's searching gaze was roving up and down the street. '... *That* is!'

'The young man by the knife grinder? He's wearing a *billycock* hat....'

'Our 'Johnny's in a cunning disguise, to be sure. But it's him all right, that's who it is. And look – *she's* in on it, too. *Get ready, sir!*' Mr Bucket pulled his hat down tighter and clutched his stick like a knight in armour about to charge.

A perfectly decently attired woman now also approached the shop window on the opposite side to the youth. She appeared to greet the two women, but evidently more as a stranger than an acquaintance. As she did so she dropped one of her gloves. At the very same moment that this distraction occurred, the youth's hand shot into the pocket of the woman nearest to him and back out again, and he immediately set off along Piccadilly in the direction of Hyde Park Corner. Now Johnny Stovepipe was walking towards him, and although they passed without acknowledging each other there was a barely perceptible brushing against one another and a subtle move-ment of arms and hands.

'Whatever was taken, Johnny now has it,' said Mr Bucket said, setting off after his man with Gordon hurrying to catch him up. 'Most come quietly, but Johnny won't. Not this time.'

They hurried their step, and when Johnny, who was about twenty paces ahead of them, turned off Piccadilly, Mr Bucket exclaimed, 'Keep on his tail, Mr Gordon. I'm a-going to try and outflank him, as my old colonel used to say.' And with that he headed off up Old Bond Street.

Johnny had gone up Dover Street. There was a side road off to the right but he passed that, sauntering at a very leisurely pace, presumably so as not to attract attention. There was another turning to the left further ahead, and Gordon's instincts told him that he would take this. But before he had a chance, the unmistakable figure of Mr Bucket suddenly appeared from the opposite end of Dover Street. Gordon saw Johnny's step falter and his body tense. He suddenly spun round and began running in Gordon's direction. He quickly stepped into the middle of the street and stretched his arms out wide.

'STOP, POLICE!' he cried for the first time in his life – and how strange and unconvincing it sounded coming from his lips. But it made Johnny veer into the side road he had originally passed, and off Gordon went in pursuit. Mr Bucket, who was able but clearly not the swiftest of men, instantly drew his rattle from his pocket, and its eerie and surprisingly loud *clackety-clack* rang in Gordon's ears as he pounded after Johnny Stovepipe. He was fast. Gordon was keeping up but not gaining on him as they hurtled down the alley and out onto Old Bond Street. It was teeming with people and traffic, but Johnny barged through the crowds and shot straight across the road, dodging between two carriages, one of whose horses reared up in fright and jerked the vehicle across Gordon's path. It only cost him a second or two, but it was enough for Johnny to extend his lead and Gordon just caught sight of him disappearing down another narrow lane. He renewed the chase with something of a heavy heart because he knew the advantage was now with Johnny. Mr Bucket's rattle called out loud and clear again just behind him, and people stopped to stare as the detectives charged into Burlington Street. Johnny had already vanished and there were several turnings he could have taken. But now there came the sound of another rattle from an alley to Gordon's right as if in answer to that of Mr Bucket, followed by a cry of 'STOP, THIEF!' Gordon skidded on the icy path and almost fell as he turned sharply into this thoroughfare. There, ahead of him, he saw a constable in uniform wrestling on the ground with Johnny Stovepipe. The constable's rattle, which in the violent struggle he attempted to use as a weapon, was knocked from his grasp and went clattering across the cobbles; in the confusion Johnny broke free and was about to escape when his path was blocked by two men who had come running out of a shop, alerted by the noise. It was the shopkeeper in his apron and a very smart-looking and fairly elderly – but tall and well-made – gentleman. The latter laid about Johnny with his stick while the shopkeeper made a grab for his arms. As he closed in, Gordon saw Johnny reach into his pocket, and at the same time heard Mr Bucket, fast coming up on his shoulder, shout a warning.

'*Watch out for his life-preserver, gents!*'

Sure enough, in a flash Johnny had whipped out what looked like a leather strap with a heavy lead ball attached to the end, which he lashed at the old man. The ball hit him on the forehead with a sickening crack. He turned and reeled away clutching his wound, blood seeping freely through his fingers. Johnny wound himself up to take another swing, this time at the shopkeeper, and Gordon saw his chance. He charged and drove his shoulder into the boy's ribcage. Gordon knew from the way he felt his chest collapse that it was a damaging collision, and he heard Johnny grunt like a stuck pig. The force of the collision caused them both to tumble to the ground in a tangled heap. Gordon found himself on his back with Johnny virtually on top of him, and though the crook gasped for air and grimaced with pain, he raised his fearsome life-preserver ready to lash it down at the sergeant. At that moment a shadow came over them both, and a police truncheon prodded the end of Johnny Stovepipe's nose, pressing it flat against his face and jerking his head back.

'Now, Johnny. It's all up for you, don't you see?' said Mr Bucket soothingly, as if to a cornered, wounded animal. '*You* want the beak to know you came along all nice and calm like a good fellow. That's the outcome *you're* hoping for, I can tell.'

This brief interruption gave Johnny enough time to assess his new situation, and the fight suddenly went out of him like a pricked balloon. He petulantly tossed aside his weapon, and bowed his head to his heaving chest, muttering and cursing under his breath.

The injured old man was assisted to the nearby house of a doctor, while their little party trooped southwards in the direction of Great Scotland Yard with the uniformed constable keeping a firm hand on Johnny's shoulder. It was a sight which drew stares all along the way and Gordon thought he had rarely felt more self-conscious in his life than after this, his first arrest. The better class of person, he noticed, tended to look their way but make no comment. The lower orders stared openly and seemed unable to resist expressing their opinions – though judgements were divided. Some declared their approbation, while others hissed, '*Shame!*' and much worse in their direction.

It was only when they reached Whitehall that Gordon remembered something that the events of the morning had temporarily pushed from his mind. 'I had a curious encounter last night just after we parted, Mr Bucket.'

'Well, Mr Gordon of that ilk, we all had a fair amount to drink. No need to say more of it ....'

'No – what I mean is, a youth approached me with a message for you.' Gordon told him what had been said.

Mr Bucket suddenly brought their little procession to a halt and asked Gordon to repeat what he had just told him. 'Exact words, Mr Gordon,' he said. 'Pray, make sure you give me the *exact* words.'

'He said that the message was from someone called Tom Prike. He evidently didn't bring it himself because he wanted to be "left out of it".' The precise message, and I can remember most of his words quite clearly, was *Tell Mr Bucket to let the doc take the rap, and if not he must watch his back.* Who is this Tom Prike?'

'A young fellow who passes the odd snippet of intelligence my way. Not like him to be shy, though. Not at all ....'

They continued on their way again and were soon close to the station, and as they turned from Whitehall into Great Scotland Yard they almost bumped into a woman coming the other way: tall and extremely pretty, yet with a troubled, disconsolate look in her vivid blue eyes. When she saw them, though, her expression brightened.

'Mr Bucket! They told me you could not be contacted ....'

'Mrs Scambles! I do still rather have my hands full, madam.'

'I see. It's just that—'

'I did inquire after ... shall we say, the case in question. As I warned you, my dear, I'm afraid there seems to be little I can do. Nothing untoward a-going on there as far as I can see.'

'But there has been a new development!'

'Is that so?'

'Someone got into my house yesterday, and some of my husband's personal effects may be missing.'

Mr Bucket rubbed an imposing forefinger against the side of his nose for a moment. 'I see.... Well, as you know I cannot involve myself in the more pressing case in which you are sadly embroiled. But burglary is different. A burglary is a burglary, and must be looked into. I shall call round tomorrow at ten o'clock sharp – if that would be convenient?'

'Certainly! You are most kind, sir!'

'What was all that about?' Gordon asked as they entered the Back Hall and took their man to be booked in by Sergeant Raddle. 'Not just the lady, but the boy's message....'

'That,' replied Mr Bucket, 'was about something fishy. That's what *that* was all about.'

V

THERE WAS DISQUIETUDE in Northumberland Gardens. Commotion reigned, and ominous forces lurked. The tumult blighted the peace of that green oasis, which lay surrounded by the tall buildings and busy carriageways of the nation's – nay the *world's* – capital city.

More accurately, the disquietude and the tumult was in the head of Sir Marriot Ogle-Tarbolton, joint commissioner of the Metropolitan Police. Northumberland Gardens herself was still; still and white – for her verdancy was hidden by the frosty embrace of February. But her equanimity was unaffected by the disorder inside the head of the head of the detective department, gazing upon her through care-narrowed eyes, through the ice-crinkled window of his office. He was a short, corpulent man, gloriously and vainly bewhiskered, but with a bald dome which had numerous strands of hair carefully arranged across it, valiantly attempting to disguise its pink nakedness.

There were some who were expecting – even willing – the nascent detective force to fail. It was un-British to have police officers disguised as civilians prowling the streets, they said. It smacked of some foreign tyrannical state, they claimed. Sir Marriot Ogle-Tarbolton knew they would use any excuse as ammunition to bolster their case. The Commissioner himself believed almost fully in the concept of the detective officer ... it's just that their methods seemed to him so ... so ... *arcane*. Uniformed peelers were straightforward, predictable men, easy to deploy and control: just like the soldiers under his command when he was a colonel of the Rifle Brigade. With the detectives, it was somehow unnerving the way they seemed to obtain results like a magician producing a rabbit from a hat. How could he be sure their modes of operation were always completely principled? Might some major scandal one day emerge – news of dishonourable practices which exposed the Commissioner's lack of understanding of and control over his force? And now this latest development. Just the kind of fraught and delicate matter which, if not handled in the correct manner, could provide his enemies with the ammunition they needed.

It was not that he didn't have the highest regard for Inspector Bucket. On the contrary – a steadier fellow you could not hope to find. Neither was it a lack of policing expertise. He was experienced, efficient, highly regarded. It was just that he had ... a way of *dealing* with people, of *addressing* them, which ... well, it wasn't the kind of thing people who moved in certain circles of society were used to or were likely to take to kindly. That it got results was without a doubt. Sir Marriot Ogle-Tarbolton had seen Mr Bucket in action – how he gained the confidence of the wary, how he had them confiding in or agreeing with him without their really realizing that their position had turned face-about. It would never work on *him*, of course, and other intelligent and lofty people might be offended by the very attempt. Perhaps if Sir Marriot were to follow his original instinct after all and allocate the case to a senior, experienced uniformed officer, at least the interviewees would not be surprised at certain—

A knock came at the door. Sir Marriot dragged his gaze from the winter scene outside and tried to gather his thoughts.

'Enter.'

Mr Bucket appeared, carrying a small, rather dog-eared piece of paper. 'Good morning, Sir Marriot. January's expenses as promised,' he said, presenting the piece of paper. 'Nothing out o' the ordinary in there to bother your head over unduly, sir.'

Sir Marriot glanced at the sheet. *He* would be the judge of that. 'Hmm. Nothing out of the ordinary indeed – since the total under "Refreshments" seems to be consistently at a level which—'

'Bearing in mind, Sir Marriot ...' Mr Bucket jumped in with a raised forefinger. The Chief's left eyebrow twitched slightly. He hated being interrupted, but allowed Bucket to carry on. 'Bearing in mind that information does not come cheap, as they say.

Intelligence as precious as jewels may be obtained for the price of a dish of bloaters, a glass or two of gin, *and cetera*, sir. And that's a fact.'

'I'm sure it is, Bucket. At least it's not as large a figure as Inspector Stope's, I suppose.' Sir Marriot squiggled his initials at the bottom of the piece of paper and handed it back to Mr Bucket.

'Very generous to his sources is Mr Stope, sir. Good morning, Sir Marriot.'

Mr Bucket stuffed the sheet into his pocket and turned to go, but he was called back.

'There is a case....' The words emerged reluctantly, like an embarrassing confession.

'Ah.... With respect, Sir Marriot, I have an appointment this morning with a very respectable lady on account of a burglary which—'

'I know about that, Bucket. I've sent Gordon. There's something else I need you to look into.'

For once, Mr Bucket was taken by surprise. 'You know about the...? Mr *Gordon*...?'

'He reported in half an hour ago, Bucket. He's a very keen young man.'

'A very promising officer, that's plain enough.'

'He can look into a simply burglary – it will do him good to give him his head on a case like that.'

'An inspired decision, that's what that is, sir.'

'And I want you to devote all your energies to this *other* case....'

'Wild horses wouldn't drag me away from it, Sir Marriot, whatever it may be. On that you have my word. *However* ... Mr Gordon, as well as being a very promising detective officer, is young, tall and handsome, as you might say....'

Sir Marriot Ogle-Tarbolton raised a quizzical eyebrow.

'And Mrs Scambles is young, beautiful and distressed. And lonely....'

'From what I hear, Mrs Scambles is a most reputable lady, Bucket. I hope you are not suggesting—'

'Oh, perish the thought, Sir Marriot! But there the situation is. And Mr Gordon not being experienced in the ways of the world, as you might term it, a fatherly eye *might* be kept on the matter from time to time – even while devoting the *whole* of one's attentions to the case you are about to unveil. Having been allocated by your good self to show him the ropes, I can't help feeling a sort of responsibility towards the young gen'lman, Sir Marriot.'

The Chief clamped his teeth together and let out a resigned hiss from his bulbous nostrils. 'Yes, well. As long as the situation I am about to explain takes *absolute* priority....'

Mr Bucket prodded the air with his finger once more. 'On *that* you may depend, sir!'

Sir Marriot rose from his chair and went to the window, where he stood with his chubby hands clasped behind his back just above the swallowtails of his coat, crumpled from long hours sitting at his desk. '*Ferns*, Mr Bucket.'

'Upon my soul,' exclaimed the detective. 'Not *more* gone a-missing?'

Sir Marriot swivelled round. 'You know about the ferns?'

'I chanced upon a theft of same only recently.'

'Well, it wasn't an isolated incident. Now, Bucket, this investigation will bring you into contact with a certain kind of person with whom your duties do not normally—'

'Like Mrs Crouch, wife of Henry Dranfield Crouch, the cotton magnet?'

Sir Marriot winced at the pronunciation of the word *magnate*. This was just the kind of reason he wanted to keep Bucket away from these people. 'You know of her?'

'Like old pals, me and Mrs Spongler! T'were the loss of *her* ferns I was called to look into!'

Sir Marriot winced again. 'Well, there has been another theft like it. In fact it is the third – a report of a similar, earlier case in Chelsea has since come to light and I suspect there are others which have so far gone unreported. The thing is, Bucket, this second one concerns Lady Rhynde, the wife of the Home Secretary. The Home Secretary has personally approached me, and I have given him my word that I shall put my best man on the case.'

'Ah!' said Bucket knowingly. 'I begin to see, sir. Utmost tact and expedition to be employed! Well, don't you worry your head about *that*, Sir Marriot. I'll soon get myself on matey terms with Lady Rhynde.'

'Yes, but Bucket, that's just what—'

Mr Bucket silenced his chief with a tap of his fat forefinger to his nose. 'You can leave it all to me, Sir Marriot!' There was *possibly* the hint of a twinkle in his eye, but it could have been moistness due to the cold, and anyway, Sir Marriot was too agitated to notice it.

'Of course, Bucket, and I know I can trust you, but—'

'That's very touching, that is, sir,' said Bucket earnestly. 'All kinds of low and dishonest people say the very same thing to me during the course of my duties and I don't necessarily believe 'em. But coming from *you* – a man esteemed for his honour and integrity, an officer and a gen'lman – I *know* I can trust it, which is very uplifting for the soul if I may make so bold, sir.'

'Er, I'm glad to hear it, Bucket.' Sir Marriot Ogle-Tarbolton sighed, sinking back into his chair. He provided his inspector with some of the basic facts of the case, then sent him on his way and returned to his contemplation of Northumberland Gardens, where the disquietude and tumult had increased in intensity.

Spud's arms were aching. The much-repaired leather strap which normally went round his neck and held his tray of nuts had snapped again, and this time it had given up the ghost altogether. It had become too short to tie yet another knot in, and he had nothing to repair it with. He would find a replacement in the gutter or on a dung heap soon, but in the meantime he would just have to carry the thing in his deadened, frozen fingers. The consolation was that he didn't have far to go, for the lights of the Ten Bells were just a little way ahead, beckoning him. He pushed through the door, drew in a breath to commence his familiar cry, but was cut short. He had hit a grey wall of tobacco smoke. Spud didn't smoke himself – had never been able to afford the baccy for one thing – and the pungent miasma made him catch his breath and hindered his progress almost as if he was walking through water. But although he never got used to it, it was nothing new, and Spud soon found his voice.

'NUTS! Walnuts, Spanish nuts, hazelnuts! *Get yer nuts!*'

There must have been around twenty people inside, but at first it was as if Spud was an invisible presence, a ghost – an all too familiar and depressing sensation. It had been a slow time of late, what with the weather and all, and Spud hadn't eaten since early that morning when one of the Jews at the market where he obtained his merchandise took pity on him and gave him a couple of slices of stale bread and butter. He could always eat his remaining nuts as a last resort, but they wouldn't fill the hole and anyway, he could eat much better on the proceeds if he could but sell them all. As he meandered between tables, a man near the bar who hadn't even looked in his direction gestured with his hand and uttered some words Spud couldn't quite make out. No matter – he had made his first sale.

Close by, a recruiting sergeant was buying two young men drinks and endeavouring to persuade them to enlist in his regiment of the line, albeit in a friendly and jocular manner. One of his intended recruits noticed Spud and called him over.

'Why, here's a fine fellow who will take your shilling, Sergeant!'

This caused much mirth, and Spud knew it was on account of his being only twelve years old – and small and scraggy, even for that. He decided to go along with the fun.

'I would go for a drummer boy if only you will buy some nuts from me!'

The sergeant pulled a face. 'Me ivories is no longer equal to nuts, sonny. Last time I ate a hazel it fair broke one at the back into pieces.'

He opened up his mouth to display the evidence, but Spud couldn't make out which of the blackened stumps he was referring to. The youth who had summoned him bought a handful of mixed nuts, then Spud began to wander back towards the door. It had been a worthwhile visit after all. A couple more such sales and he'd be able to round off his night with a trip to the oyster man on Fenchurch Street. But just as he was about to leave, yet another patron of the Ten Bells summoned him. This was a big, tough-looking man with a scarred face and shaven head. The man was smiling, but something about him sent a cold tingle down Spud's spine. The man raised a great gnarled hand and pointed to a side door.

'In that there bagatelle room you're sure to find further custom, young sir.'

Spud looked at the door, shrugged and entered the room. But once inside he saw that the tables were deserted and there was not a soul there. He heard footsteps behind him, and turned sharply. The big man had followed him in – and was now closing the door. Spud felt his heart race, and he glanced round for other doors and windows.

'Easy there, young chap,' the man tried to reassure him.

'There's nobody here. You said—'

'I said you'd find custom.' He peered at Spud's tray, chinking among some coins in his pocket as he did so. Spud began to sort out some nuts, but the man stopped him and reached into the tray himself.

'Walnuts is me favourites!' He gathered a few up in his big paw, then rummaged through the remainder and picked out the biggest of the lot. He slapped the coins that he had fished from his pocket into Spud's palm without even looking to see how much there was. But Spud's practised eye could tell from a single glance how much he'd been given without the need to count it out – and it was easily double what the nuts were worth.

Holding the biggest walnut in his left fist, the big man began to squeeze, still smiling and looking Spud in the eye as he did so. His face was relaxed and there was no sign that he was straining unduly with effort – but within a couple of seconds there came a muffled CRACK. It sounded like the breaking of bones. Bits of shell and crumbs of walnut escaped from his grasp. Finally, he spoke.

'*Tom Prike!*'

Spud felt the colour draining from his face. '*I* ain't Tom Prike, mister. Tom's older than me and—' But that's not what the man meant, and the man knew he knew it.

'Tom Prike 'as made 'imself scarce but I need to find 'im. One good turn deserves another, after all!'

'Look mister, Tom's my chum....'

'But that's just it – 'e ain't in trouble! Someone just needs to talk to 'im, that's all.'

'He wouldn't tell me where he was going. Wouldn't tell anyone.'

43

'You could find out. People like you and me – we can find things out when we really need to, and *I* really need to.'

'Mister, please....'

'And because *I* really need to and I've found you, now *you* really need to. S'just the way it works.'

'He's my *chum*, though, mister!' But Spud couldn't look him in the eye, because he knew he had no choice.

'Got nothing against 'im meself – don't even know 'im. But the task was passed on to me and now I'm passing it on to you. And when you find out and tell me, it must be the truth, mind. You need to walk these streets regular to earn your crust, so you won't be hard to find.'

Spud let out a troubled breath, and his head drooped in something between a crestfallen sag and a nod of assent.

'I'll do me best.'

'I don't want yer best. I just want Tom Prike.'

Upper Grosvenor Street, Mayfair. It was an area where the atmosphere of nobility lingered in the air like smoke from expensive cigars. The very omnibuses which plied their trade along Park Lane and Oxford Street seemed to do so with greater deference; less of the mad scramble and competition for fares here than elsewhere. It was the sort of place where one might indeed expect to find a Home Secretary's residence. Mr Bucket, watery-eyed, clad in great coat, scarf, gloves and any other item of apparel he could find to ward off the cold, counted down the house numbers until he arrived at number 22. This was an area which even he was less familiar with. Peterborough House was a tall, fairly modern building: imposing but in a restrained, dignified way. After taking in the splendour for a moment and allowing himself a slight smile as he pictured his telling of the tale to Mrs Bucket that evening, he walked boldly to the colonnade, immaculately polished, deep blue front door and gave the shiny brass knocker a double rap.

A tall, funereal-looking butler with long black hair slicked down with macassar opened the door and gazed disdainfully at the caller. His lips were pursed – he was waiting for the visitor to announce himself; and he would wait there silently with pursed lips all morning if necessary. But Mr Bucket didn't speak for a moment. It's not that he was struck dumb at the thought of visiting the home of a senior member of the government, nor by the butler's jowly funereality. It was something else ... *something* about this man. For Mr Bucket felt there was something familiar about him, but he was blowed if he could put his finger on it.

He gave up and declared cheerfully, 'I am Inspector Bucket of the Detective, and your mistress is expecting me.'

The butler's expression remained unchanged. He turned and retreated into the house. Mr Bucket thought he might have heard some sort of grunt, and if he had it would almost certainly have been an invitation to follow, so he did, and closed the door behind him. The intense blueness of the morning sky was shut out and now he was in a dark hallway, decorated in muted colours, furnished with items made of dark-coloured timber. He followed the servant up the stairs to the drawing room, staring at his back as if it would reveal to him where he had come across this man before – if indeed he had. Then Mr Bucket was left alone. It was a large room, as he had imagined it would be, seeming to occupy most of the first floor. And it was opulently decorated – as he also imagined it would be – although almost every item of decor seemed to be either solely or predominantly a sort of mauve colour. It was all very impressive, but even though Mr Bucket was no authority on such matters he couldn't help thinking that Mrs Bucket had more taste and imagination where interior decoration was concerned. But it was the great table in the centre of the room which was of most interest to the detective. He soon noticed that dominating the centre there were ferns growing in pots, and beside them a sort of album: which by its bulk and general appearance he suspected also harboured a collection of what, to his mind, was nothing more than a lot of very plain green leaves. He then spotted that even a number of vases and jugs, which adorned the table, had fern designs engraved or printed upon them.

So not all had been taken. Lack of time, or were specific specimens only coveted?

He was kept waiting for a shorter time than he expected. A woman, who he was sure must be Lady Rhynde herself, swept into the drawing room with the butler at her shoulder; the latter stopped just short of entering the room, gave a slight, funereal bow to his mistress's back, then closed the door to leave them alone.

Lady Rhynde glided gracefully across the room towards Mr Bucket, wearing a pleasant smile and proffering an outstretched hand. She was petite, younger than he had pictured her, with a white yet healthily glowing complexion.

'Sir, how very good of you to come!'

'Inspector Bucket at your service, ma'am,' he replied, taking her hand.

'I am very annoyed at what has occurred but I should never have demanded the immediate attentions of such an eminent officer of the police. They are, after all, only ferns and may be replaced. But my husband insisted....'

'A theft is a theft, you know. Your ladyship's privacy has been invaded, which just won't do whether it's ferns or the family silver which has been a-lifted.'

'But *has* my privacy been invaded? That is the question, Mr Bucket.' As they talked, Lady Rhynde directed him to another part of the room where they settled into a pair of mauve and cream armchairs with soaring backs leading to a sort of Norman arch, like thrones from a children's nursery tale. She lowered her voice. 'One hears that many of these crimes are committed by one's own servants. I have no reason to suspect any of them – but no doors or windows have been broken, and no intruder seen.'

'Your ladyship is correct,' Mr Bucket agreed. 'Just as likely is that someone on your staff either allowed entry to an outsider, or passed on a key so that a copy might be made. That's the way many of 'em operate that is, ma'am.'

'But if that is the case, I can't think which of them it might have been. I consider myself a good judge of people, Mr Bucket, and a woman in my position – more particularly my husband's position – must choose her employees with the utmost care. I like to think that I am on friendly terms with all of them, and ordinarily I would stand by each and every one if any accusations were made against them.'

'The butler, ma'am?'

'Chuddersby?'

Mr Bucket cocked his head to one side. '*Chuddersby* … ' he muttered, almost to himself, before returning his attentions to Lady Rhynde. 'Yes, him. Would you say you are on friendly terms with him? Only – begging pardon, m'lady – but he don't exactly seem the friendly sort to me.'

Lady Rhynde smiled. 'Oh, Chuddersby is just … Chuddersby! I have no more reason to suspect him than anyone else. And he came to me on an impeccable recommendation and with the best of references from Baroness Sowerby.'

'Sowerby? A relation of the Home Secretary?'

'Cousin of the Earl of Runnymede actually.'

'I see. And there has been no suspicious activity of late? Nothing out of the ordinary has occurred?'

Lady Rhynde pondered this for a moment. 'Nothing.'

'And about these ferns....'

'There was the gipsy woman, but—'

'*Ah*!' Mr Bucket's heavy forefinger was raised like a flag.

'But Mr Bucket, she has called here before without anything untoward happening. She mends chairs – I have seen her at work: a very dextrous lady, and of a very kindly disposition.'

Mr Bucket's flag was yet to be lowered. 'Kindly in appearance *and* dextrous. All the hallmarks, your ladyship, all the hallmarks.'

Lady Rhynde shrugged. 'Of course it is possible, but I doubt that she would have had very much opportunity to—'

'*Not very much opportunity* is all that's required, I can assure your ladyship! *Not very much opportunity* is *ample* opportunity for those skilled in such matters. Now, the woman in question may very well be innocent of any wrongdoing and I do not intend to get all heavy-handed in the matter, rest assured, ma'am. That is not my method. However, in the absence of any other suspects, perhaps I might take some particulars. I take it that this is one of her regular haunts, so to speak, and that she might be found in this vicinity from time to time?'

'I believe so. She is a very little person, rather hunched over, with dark hair half-turned grey. She habitually wears a scarlet shawl and has very noticeable, large brass earrings. Oh, and she has very low, dark, heavy eyebrows.'

Mr Bucket gazed at his interviewee with open admiration. 'Excellent, ma'am. There is a great demand for folks with abilities such as yours in the Detective Service should ever you be that way inclined.'

'I doubt very much whether they would be willing to recruit a lady, Mr Bucket!'

'That would depend upon the lady's *connections*....'

Lady Rhynde laughed lightly. She provided him with such information as she could regarding the ferns, Mr Bucket politely declined the offer of a pot of coffee and soon the consultation was over – but for one final question, which occurred to him just as they were about to part company.

'The butler – Chuddersby – your ladyship.'

'Yes?'

'How long has he been with you?'

'Not a long time. My previous one eloped with one of my maids – about two months ago.'

After leaving, Mr Bucket immediately sought out the policeman whose beat this was and ascertained from him that he was aware of the gipsy chair-mender in question, and an arrangement was made for the detective to return at an appropriate time so that he could speak to her.

He was making his way back to Great Scotland Yard when, walking along Piccadilly, he passed Duke Street – and then he had it. *Duke ... Juke* – Jukes! *That* was the answer to the conundrum. Alfred Jukes, not Chuddersby, was the real name of Lady Rhynde's butler, and Mr Bucket knew it because he had collared Alfred Jukes some years ago for receiving stolen goods in his dolly shop. Eighteen-month sentence, if Mr Bucket remembered it right. Maybe Jukes only wanted to conceal his criminal past to get an honest job. Or maybe he had something else to hide....

VI

GORDON WAS AS surprised as he guessed some of his colleagues were at his being invited to undertake an investigation unsupervised so soon in his career. He had been a member of the Detective Force for less than a week; and further, as Sergeant Blacksnape had already pointedly alluded to, he had no previous experience in police work in the way that all the other detective officers, without exception, had. Something about the Commissioner's manner had given Gordon cause to wonder whether there was an ulterior motive for him being handed this case. Was it yet another 'family favour', or was there something else, something he was as yet unaware of? Nonetheless, here he was on his way to Russell Square to pursue a case of burglary. To tell the truth, he wasn't heading *directly* to Russell Square, for another matter had been on his mind since the previous day. It wasn't so much a conscious decision: his feet seemed almost to guide him on a very minor detour in the direction of Coventry Street. The sky was like a sheet of the blue Arctic ice Gordon had read about in the tales of hardy explorers like Franklin and Parry, save for plumes of smoke rising from every chimney far as the eye could see, smudges of dirty black against the pristine heavens. It was bitterly, bitterly cold once more – another factor which had brought him to the area he now found himself in. And there he saw them: in exactly the same spot, on a packing case at the end of the same alley where he had first encountered them with Mr Bucket the day before. As far as he knew they were to be found there every day of their short lives, come snow, come rain, come shine. As before, Annie the elder one of the two bare-headed, bare-footed girls, was calling out to passers-by boldly and stoically, while her sister Elsie sat beside her cross-legged on the box. But this time Elsie seemed in an even sadder state than she had the first time Gordon had seen her. There was a ghost-like look about her; her eyes gazed vacantly at the boot-print patterns in the frost on the pavement, never looking up even when her sister sold a bunch of flowers to a passing gentleman. Yet she was not shivering as she had been before; Gordon did not know whether this was a good sign or bad ....

He walked over to them.

'Buy some lovely lavenders fer yer sweetheart, Guv?' cried Annie as raucously as any brawny market trader.

Gordon removed a glove and dipped a hand into his pocket. 'Do you not remember me, Annie?'

She scowled at his features with suspicion and a hardness in her eyes, which saddened Gordon almost more than did the conditions which seemed to be their lot in life. 'I ain't done nuthin'.'

Gordon adopted what he hoped would be a reassuring smile and crouched down before her, giving her most of the small coins he had with him. 'I know that, child. I'm Mr Gordon and I was here yesterday with Mr Bucket – he bought some flowers too.' He was going to explain more, but the mention of Mr Bucket caused her face to immediately brighten.

'Oh, yeah. Remember you now, aw'right, mister.'

Gordon suspected she didn't remember him at all. 'I shall take two bunches, if you please, Annie. I don't currently have a sweetheart, though. Perhaps the flowers will bring me luck in that direction!'

'Ah, you'll be aw'right, mister. Seen a lot more uglier mushes than yours abaht the place.'

'Oh ... well, thank you, Annie. And how is little Elsie?' He turned his gaze to the diminutive slumped figure, which still had neither moved nor acknowledged even being aware of his presence.

'She don't care for the cold – do yer, Elsie?'

The little mite looked up at her sister, glanced briefly at Gordon, croaked some unintelligible reply, then cast her eyes downwards again and attempted to pull her threadbare shawl tighter around her frail body.

'Do you live near here, Annie?' he asked. 'What of your parents – do they have employment?'

She adopted her suspicious air again. 'Don' live far off.'

'There's nothing to worry about, child. I just wanted to … well, it's nothing to do with police work, rest assured.'

'Me 'n Elsie live in Golding Court. Ma says Pa were a so'jer, but we don' know nothin' abaht 'im, mister.'

'Does she have a job?'

'A bit o' needlework when she can get it. But 'er 'ands is dodged up now, and it don't come as easy to 'er as it used to.'

Gordon straightened up. 'Well …. It is excessively cold of late, but they say it is to change and get warmer and wetter very soon. Anyhow, take care. And take care of your sister!' It all sounded so horribly, pathetically inadequate, but he could find no other words. He hesitated before carrying on his way; he wanted to do more – but at least he had given them precious money. Other than taking them home with him, what more could he do? Gordon walked on. A second later he heard Annie's voice. He thought at first that she was resuming her sales patter, but she was calling his name. He stopped and looked back. She was slipping the money he had given her into her pocket, and she smiled for the first time. It was as if a light had illuminated her features from within, and Gordon saw that she was far prettier than he had appreciated.

'Thanks, mister,' she grinned. And this time he knew she meant it. 'And I wuz joshin'. Ye'r proper 'andsome really, Mr Gordon.'

'I shall see you again. Take care.'

Thanks no doubt to his novice's over-enthusiasm, and despite his brief detour, Gordon arrived at the Scambles' house in Russell Square a good fifteen minutes earlier than the time appointed by Mr Bucket. He walked past the front door, wrestling with the idea of taking a turn or two around the square to pass the time. But the cold was so pervasive and dispiriting that his resolve lasted only a second, and he turned about and approached the house. Upon knocking, Gordon was surprised to be almost instantly greeted by Mrs Scambles herself. An image of her counting down the minutes and perhaps even impatiently peeping out of the window sprang to mind, and he was glad he had chosen not to circumnavigate the square shivering and sniffling for a quarter of an hour while she perhaps looked on.

'Oh – no Mr Bucket?' she queried – yet smiling agreeably and showing no sign of disappointment.

'Mr Bucket has been assigned to an important matter by our senior officer. I was with him yesterday when you—'

'No need to explain – I remember you very well, sir!'

Now, Gordon had stared steadfastly into the eyes of a Chinaman rushing at him with a thrusting bayonet, intent on taking his life; but Mrs Scambles looked at him with her extraordinary blue eyes – looked *into* him, more like – in such a direct and striking manner that he was quite overpowered and had to avert his gaze. He felt quite sure it was all perfectly innocent and merely her natural, open way; and in what was, he was also sure, an effort to put him at his ease, she took his arm and ushered him indoors.

'Come, sir. Do not linger in the cold.'

She led Gordon into her drawing room and summoned a maid, ordering coffee for them both. There was a good fire crackling in the hearth, and the warmth of the room felt like a soothing embrace after the freezing air outside.

'I did not have the opportunity to introduce myself properly yesterday.' She held out her hand – surprisingly plump and child-like for such a relatively tall woman – and gave Gordon's a little squeeze when they shook. 'Eleanora Scambles, wife of Doctor Jonathan Webster Scambles who, I am sure you know, is, owing to a most unfortunate error, at present incarcerated and awaiting trial for murder.'

Still clutching his cold hand in her own warm and soft one and giving it an extra press, she added, 'I hope that doesn't sound like a discourteous attack on yourself or Mr Bucket. It is, I'm sure, merely a terrible but completely understandable mistake.'

Again, he wilted before her gaze and took a sudden interest in a sewing table on his right. 'No offence taken, I assure you, Mrs Scambles. My name is James Alexander Gordon, and I am a sergeant of the detective force.'

'Would you like me to have your coat taken by the maid, Mr Gordon? It is perfectly warm in here.'

'Thankfully so!'

Gordon had expected her to await the maid's return with the

coffee, but he was in the act of removing the coat himself when she moved swiftly to help him. She took the garment, which was rapidly becoming damp now that the frost upon it was melting, and in a quick and subtle movement smoothed and straightened his stock, which had partially come adrift from his waistcoat. The maid arrived with the drinks as this was happening, and he took an involuntary step back from Mrs Scambles and cleared his throat. But neither the maid nor her mistress seemed to make anything of the situation or register any reaction in their faces, and Gordon reproached himself for interpreting what he felt sure was merely a caring and friendly gesture in such a cynical way.

She got him to sit on a chintz-covered sofa, and such was his state of mind that for a moment Gordon thought Mrs Scambles was going to sit beside him, but she drew up an ornate, wooden-backed chair and placed it opposite him. 'Mr Gordon, on the day I first told Mr Bucket about my poor husband's arrest, I *thought* – I would put it no stronger than having *sensed* – that I was being followed on my way home. I did once stop and turn round, and I caught a glimpse of a man slipping into a shop. Of course, it may have been his intended destination, but....'

'Did you get a look at him? I mean to say, could you describe anything at all about him?'

She shook her head. 'It happened too quickly. He may have been taller than average, but I couldn't guarantee even that as a fact. But then the following day I fancy I saw a suspicious fellow lurking about the Square. I was writing letters, and my desk is by the window for the light. I noticed him glance briefly up at the house as he walked by and thought no more of it. But some minutes later I saw him doing the same thing again – he had clearly walked all the way round the Square at least once.'

Gordon reddened slightly, remembering that he had almost done the very same thing. 'It is interesting, but there might obviously be an innocent explanation. I am new to London myself and often seem to wander in circles while getting my bearings! But presumably you did get a good look at *this* man. Might it have been the same one?'

'Even though I only managed a fleeting glimpse of the first man,

I sense they were not one and the same. The person who passed the house seemed shorter and perhaps – though it's impossible to be certain – more shabbily dressed. He was certainly not a gentleman, but more like a labourer of some kind. His head was shaven and his nose quite flattened to his face; his coat was black and possibly tied at the waist with dark cord rather than fastened with a belt. I really should be able to say more – you must think me a silly, empty-headed thing ....' Her remorseful sapphire eyes gazed up at Gordon like those of a child expecting to be scolded, and he hastened to reassure her.

'Not at all, madam. At the time, these things may not seem important. It is only afterward. Do not blame yourself.'

Gordon was not sure whence, during his mere days as a detective officer, he had dug up that pearl of investigative wisdom, but it had the desired effect. Her face brightened and she leaned forward and touched him lightly on the knee. 'You are so understanding, Mr Gordon!'

The muscles beneath her touch tensed involuntarily and he rose to his feet – perhaps a little too quickly, for he thought he detected a slight smile fleetingly play upon her classically full and shapely lips. 'May I see the place from where the items were taken?'

'Of course. As far as I can tell, only my husband's study was disturbed. This way, Mr Gordon.'

Dr Scambles' study was much colder than the parlour, having no fireplace of its own – not to mention having been unoccupied for some days due to the enforced absence of its owner. There was ice on the insides of the windowpanes, and Gordon could see his own breath as soon as he entered the room. It was towards the rear of the house, but as far as he could tell from the route they had taken it could only be accessed from either the front hallway or from a door leading in from the garden at the back. Then, his mind went blank. What other things did detectives look for in such circum-stances?

'The only area which was disturbed was his writing area, Mr Gordon,' said Mrs Scambles gesturing to a plain, sturdy mahogany desk. To his eye everything seemed to be in order. There were several quill pens, a pen-knife and ink pot, a pile of papers neatly stacked in one corner, a couple of small ornaments in the other and various other items one would normally associate with such a gentleman's working area.

'Has the maid put everything back in its place since the incident?'

'That's the problem, Mr Gordon. There has barely been an "incident" as such. We *think* a silver snuffbox may be missing, but no one is sure and what you see is more or less what we found.'

'Then ....'

'But Polly has been with us since we married and moved into this house. My husband is *very* particular about where everything on his desk is placed, almost to the point of ... well, if anything is ever found out of place....'

She seemed about to expand on this subject, but contented herself with repeating, '*Very* particular. And Polly has come to know exactly how everything must be after she has tidied and dusted. On the day in question – the morning after I saw the man loitering in the Square and looking at our house – Polly reported to me that something was amiss. Items on my husband's desk were not in their usual place. All was very *tidy* – but she knew that things had been moved. She also believed that something was missing.'

'The snuffbox?'

She sighed. 'No. My husband would never normally leave it in here, but on the day he was arrested he feels he may have momentarily placed it on his chair before leaving the house – but equally he thinks it could be at his surgery. Polly herself is sure that there was *something* on the desk – some other item which wouldn't normally be there, but which my husband had left out for a particular reason before his arrest – and *that* had gone. Try as she might, she cannot remember what it was. I'm afraid she is not an intelligent girl, Mr Gordon.'

Gordon stared at the desk for a moment as if it might offer up some sort of clue. 'Have you asked your husband? I take it you have been visiting him?'

'Every day, Mr Gordon. But he cannot recall leaving anything out of the ordinary on his desk. As you can imagine, after everything that has happened to him his mind has not been as composed as it might normally be.'

'I quite understand, madam. And no other servants might have been in here and moved things?'

'Only Polly and myself are allowed in here. I have questioned everyone closely, and all swear they have never entered the room.'

'Do you think it would do any good if I were to discuss this with your husband? See if I can jog his memory?'

Her lustrous eyes clouded with misgiving. 'My husband's moods can be … *unpredictable*, Mr Gordon. His mind is preoccupied with his present unfortunate situation, and he believes that this particular matter is of no importance whatsoever.'

'Sadly, I can think of no other course of action – even assuming my superiors agreed that I might be permitted to see him. But I can assure you that, should I visit your husband, I would treat the matter with the utmost caution and discretion.'

'I know you would,' she smiled, the brightness returning to her face in that mercurial, child-like way of hers. 'You were an officer of the army, Mr Gordon?'

This observation momentarily caught him off balance. 'Yes, but who—'

'No one informed me, sir. It's just that you have a certain way of deporting yourself that I have seen only in officers of the highest and most refined calibre.'

She took a step closer to him and he stood transfixed by her gaze, when suddenly, a most artificial-sounding cough from behind the slightly open door of the study broke the silence.

Mrs Scambles grinned at Gordon as if they had just shared a private joke. 'What is it, Polly?'

The door opened fully and the maid stepped across the threshold. 'Beggin' your pardon, ma'am, but there's this gen'lman to see you.' She held out a calling card.

Mrs Scambles took the card and studied it. 'It is not a name I recognize…. Polly, perhaps you will speak to this policeman about my husband's study while I talk to my visitor? He is from the Detective Department, and you must answer all his questions honestly. I shan't be many minutes, Mr Gordon.'

Polly looked to be in her early twenties, with a pale, hangdog face. As soon as Mrs Scambles had mentioned the word 'police' her complexion had turned a kind of grey colour and she seemed to almost shrink bodily, as if attempting to disappear within herself. Gordon questioned her briefly, without any hope of gaining useful intelligence. Not only was he sure that she would have already imparted any helpful knowledge to her mistress, but she was so utterly intimidated by his status as a detective officer as to become almost verbally incapable. Impressed as he was by this demonstration of the power of his new position in society, it was of no practical use here and so he quickly dismissed her. He decided to make his way to the hallway and wait for Mrs Scambles to emerge from her meeting.

It had clearly been a very brief interview, since the door opened and a man emerged almost as soon as Gordon turned the corner into the hall. He was tall – Gordon was a little over six feet and before he replaced his hat he could see that the visitor would have been at least a couple of inches taller, with rather long, greasy-looking hair. Turning immediately away from him in the direction of the front door, he did not see the detective but strode purposefully towards it and let himself out. Something seemed odd about this little scene. Gordon would have expected either Mrs Scambles or a servant to have shown him out. And there was something else; it wasn't something he could put into words, just an uneasy feeling – hopefully, he thought, borne out of his new-found detective's way of thinking and viewing things. When Mrs Scambles didn't emerge from the drawing room, Gordon tapped lightly on the door; on receiving no response, his misgivings were heightened further, and he gently pushed it open and went in. She was standing with her back to him, facing the fire, her arms hugging her waist. Gordon could hear no sound, but her shoulders were gently convulsing and he quickly realized that she was crying. He approached her hesitantly.

'Mrs Scambles?'

She didn't turn, but through her quiet, half-suppressed sobbing, said simply, '*That man....*'

Overcoming his desire to question her further, Gordon hurried to the window. He was just in time to see the tall, dark figure with the top hat about to depart Russell Square on the far side and he was torn between trying to catch up with him and not wishing to leave Mrs Scambles in her current state of distress. Since he had no idea as yet what, if anything, he might be guilty of, Gordon reluctantly watched the man disappear from view.

'Mrs Scambles – what has occurred?'

She took a deep breath and straightened up, turning to him so that he could see her moist eyes. She was trembling slightly. 'He … he said that if I continued to ask questions about the murder of Edward Mizzentoft… *I should soon be found floating in the Thames.*'

'Edward Mizzentoft?'

'The businessman whom my husband is supposed to have killed.'

Gordon now cursed himself for not having pursued this scoundrel. 'Did he say anything else?'

'Only to point out that he and those for whom he was acting obviously knew where I lived – they also know the places I frequent, and nearly everything about me. They can apprehend me at any time it suits them. *And silence me.*'

Gordon expected her composure to crumble at this revelation, but to her great credit she looked him in the eye and related the information in a tone almost of defiance. He quickly decided what he needed to do.

He asked for the card the man had given her. 'I will go immediately in the direction this monstrous villain took and see if I can catch sight of him. In the meantime, admit no visitors and instruct your servants to answer the door to no one. If there is a firearm or any other weapon in the house I suggest that it is put into the possession of any capable male member of your staff and kept with him at all times. I assure you I will return once I have consulted Mr Bucket.'

Within moments Gordon was out of the house and hurrying westwards across Russell Square. It was just possible that if the man had stopped somewhere to meet an accomplice, or for any other reason, he might spot him. He quickly reached Tottenham Court Road, and there any optimism he had quickly evaporated. Every other gentleman on this crowded street wore a long black coat and a tall hat – and Gordon had not even seen his man's face. Feeling somewhat less of a detective than he had just a few minutes earlier, his pace slowed to a moody and dejected amble, and he headed for Great Scotland Yard.

VII

Why is she carrying an umbrella? Why?

The question was on the minds of numerous passengers on the crowded King's Cross omnibus as it rattled its way towards its Euston Square terminus. The only clouds to sully the pristine February sky these last few days had been inconsequential wisps of white cirrus. It had been freezing, icy, bright – and consistently dry.

And she was carrying an umbrella.

And it was carried athwart her lap. And the pointed end of the handle was sticking into the admittedly rotund belly of the young woman sitting on her left. Every time the omnibus rumbled over a bump in the road or turned a corner, it prodded fiercely and seemed ready to disembowel her. But she was timid, and pretended not to have noticed.

And the sharp end of the umbrella was poking into the open copy of the *Morning Herald* held by a stern-looking gent with a fiery red beard. All eyes in the opposite seats were drawn to this scene, since it was patently only a matter of time before the sharp point broke through. The fiery-bearded man was not timid, and repeatedly turned his head and glared at the woman. He felt that the fiercer his stare became, and the more he snorted and the expressed air agitated his truculent-looking whiskers, the more, surely, she must take notice. But he was above all a gentleman, and said nothing.

And the umbrella stayed in her lap. Until, that is, the sharp right-turn near the King's Cross railway terminal, when the point finally breached the gentleman's defences, which had been ever-thinning with each turn of the page. The tip of the instrument thrust itself through a major speech by the prime minister in Parliament on the Chartist Petition.

'*Madam!*' His red beard positively bristled with indignation. He yanked his paper from the tip of the weapon, causing the young woman's arm to jerk slightly, at which she threw up her arms like the leading lady in a second-rate stage melodrama.

'*Aaaagh! Murder! Police!*'

She then commenced to poke savagely at him with the self-same umbrella point. Each time she pulled back for another thrust, the handle jabbed deeply into the belly of the timid fat woman sitting on the other side, who continued to refuse to acknowledge that anything untoward was even taking place – or that she was accumulating a series of bruises and experiencing a great deal of undignified abdominal wobbling. She gazed fixedly out of the opposite window. A general commotion now ensued. People at the front of the omnibus, who had no knowledge of the real cause of the fracas and naturally assumed that a defenceless lady was being assaulted, rose to express their outrage, ready to intervene if necessary. Those who knew the real cause jumped up and volubly prepared to mount a defence, and the conductor tried to break through the scrummage and make his voice of reason heard above the babble. It seemed that only three persons remained unmoved by the drama: the rotund lady on the right of the umbrella-wielder, still refusing to accept the reality of the scenes being played out around her, and two men sitting opposite.

At the mention of the word 'police' by the umbrella carrier, Sergeant Gordon twitched slightly, but Mr Bucket placed a calming hand on his colleague's arm. Before any of the passengers could come to blows, the voice of the conductor finally cut through the babble of accusation and counter-accusation: '*Eus-Ware!*' he cried. '*Eus-Ware – aw change!*' This acted like a bucket of cold water on the rumpus, and aside from a few residual mutterings and the rustle of the *Morning Herald* as the bearded man showed the wounded condition of his paper to all who would look, people headed for the exit.

Mr Gordon had learned to interpret the arcane utterances of the conductor during the course of the journey. Early on, he had interpreted the rendition of 'Oxford Street!' as '*Oswestry*' and had feared they had accidentally boarded some sort of long-distance stage coach. But the cry of '*Toh-Corode!*' had happened to come just as they were opposite a street sign for Tottenham Court Road, and this proved to be Sergeant Gordon's Rosetta Stone. Thus, on hearing '*Eus-Ware!*' he knew that the Euston Square terminus was almost upon them. With each small victory like this, Mr Gordon felt himself more and more a fully paid-up Londoner.

Mr Bucket preferred walking wherever possible, and the omnibus to cabs for longer journeys. Not only, he informed his colleague, was it cheaper, but it was where one got to *meet* people, got to *observe* people.

An icy blast of air assailed them as soon as they left the relative shelter of the omnibus and struck out in the direction of King's Cross, before turning south. When it came into view, the Coldbath Fields House of Correction seemed to live up to its name. A biting wind swept across the land into their faces and made their eyes water as they gazed upon the bleak, plain-built edifice standing in swampland and enclosed by high, sheer walls. Gordon was shuddering at the thought of incarceration in that desolate fortress – the conditions inside of which he had already heard stories – when the sound of his companion's voice and its unexpectedly stentorian tone made him start.

'*As he went through Coldbath Fields, he saw a solitary cell. And the Devil was pleased, for it gave him a hint for improving his prisons in hell.*'

'Very impressive, Mr Bucket. Did you just make that up?'

Mr Bucket laughed. 'Not I, Mr Gordon. Some versifying chap whose name escapes me.'

'I see. Do you think a gentleman like Dr Scambles would be kept among the common prisoners?'

'A man who has money can obtain certain small privileges … and as yet the good doctor has not been found guilty of anything by twelve good men and true, so I should imagine he is being treated tolerable well.'

'Oh, and what about the ferns? You were following up a lead, as I recall.'

'The delightful Lady Rhynde mentioned a gipsy woman, a chair-mender who frequents the district. I tracked her down; she is a merry old bird, much liked by all and is definitely not our thief. No, I see this as an inside job one way or another. But for now, here we are at the Prison of Hell, Mr Gordon.'

They announced themselves at the great gateway and were soon admitted. Gordon shuddered again as the heavy door slammed and reverberated behind them with an air of finality. In his imagination he had been mistakenly accused of some heinous crime, removed from his cosy, comfortable life among people of the same class and sent to this 'Devil's prison' to live out the rest of his life among cut-throats and villains. No one believed in his innocence, and there was no way of proving it. The eventual fate, perhaps, of Dr Scambles.

'This way, gents,' mumbled the elderly officer who had been detailed to take them to see the prisoner. They walked across a courtyard, deserted but for a bedraggled prisoner being escorted across it by two burly guards, passed through a doorway and entered a second, larger yard. This time the prospect was completely different. The flagstones of the yard rang to the footsteps of groups of hunched prisoners wearing drab uniforms with numbers pinned to their backs, walking in circles under the bored gaze of a number of warders. Curiouser still, above this scene was an enormous tread-mill which ran along the whole of the far wall of the yard and was accessed by some steps leading up to a platform about ten feet above ground level. In some ways it resembled a rudimentary grandstand. The machine was kept in motion by around a dozen men in sepa-rate, individual stalls; they had their backs to the yard and trod wearily but continuously to keep the gigantic wheel revolving. But Dr Scambles was evidently not here because they moved on to the next area. Now they were in a vast, cold, dank room where row after row of men wearing the same drab uniforms and soft caps were seated on the floor like Mahometans at prayer, watched over by prowling officers. The men appeared to be manipulating pieces of old rope, and a musty smell of tar pervaded the arena. Everything was done in silence, with only the odd cough or shuffle impinging on the cathedral-like quiet of the place.

'Oakum picking, sirs,' mumbled the guard. He left Bucket and Gordon just inside the doorway and spoke to a man standing on a platform overlooking the whole process.

This man barked out, *'Scambles! Prisoner R218 Scambles to report to the interview room immediately.'*

A couple of minutes later, the detectives were in a cold little room with whitewashed walls, sitting on uncomfortably hard chairs and staring across a small trestle table at Dr Jonathan Webster Scambles. A guard had been posted outside the door, but otherwise they had been left to speak in private. Dr Scambles was a thin, sinewy man; he had prominent veins at his temples, naturally gaunt cheeks and cold, yet piercing grey eyes behind small circular-framed spectacles. Even seated, it was clear that he was a tall man, and despite his lack of bulk there was an air of wiry strength about him. The detectives reached across the desk to shake his hand, which felt cold to the touch. Perhaps it was merely due to the coldness of the place.

'I am Inspector Bucket of the Detective, and this is my colleague Sergeant James Alexander Gordon, of that ilk. I trust you are being treated well?'

Dr Scambles' lips took on something resembling a narrow, slightly crooked smile. But it might equally have been a sneer. 'I am still alive.'

'As I am sure you know, this is but a temporary measure until the trial.'

'Ah, yes. I will then have somewhere more comfortable to look forward to, such as the end of a noose if Scotland Yard gets its way.'

'Scotland Yard is only interested in the evidence and where it leads, sir.'

'And you are here because you have new evidence regarding my case?' Dr Scambles eyed them coolly through the thick lenses of his spectacles. He was not excited, he did not plead. He might even be interviewing them rather than the other way round.

'As a matter of fact, my dear fellow, we have not come about the matter to which you refer at all,' Mr Bucket revealed. Dr Scambles held his steady gaze upon the detective in a way which Gordon had not seen a man do before. No trace of a reaction could be ascertained in the doctor's countenance except perhaps, a certain almost imperceptible tightening of the thin lips. He did not ask Mr Bucket to enlarge upon his surprising statement. After a pause, the detective took it upon himself to explain.

'My sergeant was recently called upon by Mrs Scambles to look into a burglary at your residence....'

Mr Bucket paused, perhaps again awaiting some sort of reaction, for Gordon had passed on Mrs Scambles' warning that this was a matter only likely to irritate her husband. But again, none was forthcoming; so again, Mr Bucket continued.

'We are led to believe that one, possibly two items were taken from your study.'

Mr Bucket fixed Dr Scambles calmly with his dark, searching eyes. Dr Scambles fixed Mr Bucket with his stony, pale ones. Gordon watched with fascination.

Mr Bucket persisted patiently. 'What might it have been, eh, Dr Scambles? Of particular interest to me is that something is possibly missing from your desk. I know you've said you don't recall, but I ask you – now that you've had further leisure, as one might say, to contemplate it – to really search into your memory. You see, it is my opinion that—'

The eruption came violently and without warning.

Scambles leapt to his feet with such force that the table flew upwards and spun in mid-air with its legs arcing and slashing towards the faces of the detectives, who both instinctively pushed back in their chairs with raised arms shielding their faces.

'I AM ROTTING IN HERE WITH VILLAINS FOR A *MURDER I DIDN'T COMMIT.* I DON'T GIVE A DAMN ABOUT SOME TRINKET TAKEN FROM MY WRITING DESK!'

Spittle flew from Dr Scambles' lips; his normally pallid face had turned scarlet. Even his eyes seemed to glow red like those of a fairy tale demon, and the veins at his temples bulged. The table clattered to the floor at his feet and he kicked it out of the way and advanced towards the detectives. The officers sprang to their feet, ready to meet his advance. Then the door flew open, and the guard rushed in. More running footsteps could be heard outside, but Mr Bucket raised his hand.

'We don't require any assistance, my good man.' The guard halted, and Dr Scambles also paused, as if meeting some invisible force emanating from the detective's outstretched palm. But his face remained a mask of barely human fury and enmity, and his fists remained clenched.

'The prisoner,' explained Mr Bucket, 'had a minor accident in rising somewhat abruptly, but all is well now – ain't that so, Dr Scambles?' His arms were relaxed and held loosely by his sides while he smiled affably at Scambles, who remained looming a good six inches over him, well within striking range. Then the detective calmly bent down, righted the table and carefully arranged it in its former position. 'Dr Scambles has expressed his frustration at his current unfortunate situation – but *he* is now prepared to regain his seat and discuss things like the proper gen'lman he is – that's what *he* intends to do.' Mr Bucket smiled and looked benignly upon the physician. After a few seconds, intellect regained control over instinct; the redness drained from Scambles' face and the veins subsided; the fists unclenched, and he sank into his chair. Mr Bucket's knowing glance towards the guard was enough to send him back out of the room.

'I haven't come about the murder and I know that's galling. Would be for me. Another detective officer is handling that case – a very capable officer, a very experienced officer.' Dr Scambles' lips parted, but Mr Bucket raised his stout forefinger and silenced him. 'I don't know a great amount about the medical field, sir. My cousin's boy is studying in that very profession, but Mrs Bucket and myself don't have a lot to do with 'im – bit of bad blood going back so far no one can quite remember what started it, but there it is. But what I *do* suspect, Dr Scambles, is that if you were treating a patient and another doctor tried to stick his oar in with a different opinion on the cause and treatment of the illness, well, it wouldn't sit easy with you, would it now?'

'It is not the same. Not the same at all.'

'Ah but pretty close, I say. And I say something else. I might not be able to interfere with my colleague's investigation – *but I do believe that whatever was taken from your desk might appertain to said case.* What do you say to that, now, Dr Scambles? *That* would give me cause to combine my brains with the very capable ones of Inspector William Stope to see what we could come up with!'

'I still don't see how the two matters can be related … ' said the doctor – but now he seemed more reflective, as if he had been given a lifeline.

'Well I ain't *exactly* sure that *I* do as yet, Doctor. But perhaps in that respect medicine and detective work aren't so far apart. We spots a symptom that don't seem quite right, and even though we don't always know where it might lead or whether it might be a red herring, we feel obliged to look into it, see what comes up. Ain't that close to the mark?'

With some reluctance, Scambles was obliged to nod his head.

'There, then,' said Mr Bucket, rising to his feet and holding his hand out across the table. 'All is not lost! There are still avenues, Doctor. *Avenues*!'

Cursory handshakes were exchanged, and the detectives left the room, walking past the somewhat bemused faces of the prison officers gathered tensely and expectantly outside.

Mr Bucket buttoned up his coat, ready to face the frozen outdoors. 'Never known such cold as of late,' he announced to no one in particular. 'But they do say the weather's about to turn.'

VIII

I T BEING A Sunday and with no cabs available, Gordon called upon his friend Lieutenant-Colonel Daird at the Horseguards just across the road from Great Scotland Yard for the loan of his Brougham. This suited his purposes well, since a hansom may not have been capable of carrying the volume of personal belongings he suspected would be coming on this particular journey – for he was to escort Mrs Eleanora Scambles to the home of Mrs Bucket's sister; a temporary measure for her own personal safety, which had been agreed upon by all concerned. Mrs Bucket's sister normally took in a lodger, but as luck would have it the room was currently vacant, and while it might not be the kind of accommodation Mrs Scambles was accustomed to, her security was presently the overriding concern. The housekeeper's husband also happened to be a policeman – a constable of the Marylebone Division – which was an added bonus.

Daird's coachman guided the vehicle along Whitehall, and as it trundled sedately through Trafalgar Square Gordon looked out at the little knots of people promenading in their Sunday best attire, circumnavigating the Square like proud skaters circling a frozen pond. He saw others walking to church in family groups, servants in tow, and felt a tiny pang of guilt. Not because he wasn't going to church, but because he had no such belief in the first place; no faith whatsoever, in fact. His guilt was born out of this being something of a dark secret. It didn't do to swim against the tide, either in society or one's profession, and the easiest, albeit the cowardly option was to simply nod sagely when the Lord's name was evoked to save mortals from a precarious situation, and nod sagely again when He did no such thing and the tragedy was put down to the

mystery of His ways, as when his beloved elder sister and only confi-
dante had died from diphtheria at the age of twelve.

The coach scrunched into Russell Square, where a frost-encrusted
Charles James Fox gazed down upon Gordon from his plinth like an
emaciated polar bear, then after a few more yards it pulled up outside
the home of Eleanora Scambles. A footman opened the door, and it
was suggested that the coachman come inside and warm himself
below stairs while Gordon himself awaited the lady of the house in
the drawing room – she was still finalizing her preparations for the
journey.

He had been looking out across the Square, enjoying the heat
from the well-stoked fire for a few minutes, when the door opened
and Mrs Scambles swept in and greeted him like an old friend.

'Mr Gordon!' She held her hand out, Gordon assumed for him
to shake, but as he attempted to do so she turned the back of her
hand upwards and raised it towards his face for him to kiss. Not
wishing to seem coldly formal, he hesitantly touched her hand with
his lips.

'Another cold day, Mrs Scambles,' he ventured awkwardly.

'So I can tell, sir,' she replied. She had yet to release his hand, and
made a great show of patting and rubbing it to generate some
warmth. 'And not only a very cold day!'

She beamed at Gordon expectantly as if he should know what she
meant. 'I'm really not sure I—''

With a furtive grin Mrs Scambles turned to a bulging carpet bag
on the nearby sofa, part of an assembled collection of luggage he
assumed was to accompany her to Pimlico, and delved inside it with
her back to him. When she turned back she was holding out a small
blue box, slightly larger than those for finger rings. 'What day is it,
Mr Gordon?' she asked with a twinkle in her beaming blue eyes.

He shrugged. 'Sunday ....'

'In what month?' she giggled.

'The month is February, Mrs Scambles, but I'm sure I don't
know—'

'Sunday, February *the*...?'

'It is February the ... *ah* ... er, I—'

'Not only is it the day we honour the worthy Saint Valentine, but it is a *leap* year, when, as I'm sure you are aware, it is the *lady's* obligation to profess her love to the gentleman!'

'Mrs Scambles—'

'Normally my husband would make the first female caller to the house his valentine for the day. Harmless fun, Mr Gordon! Now that it is a leap year, however, I determined that the first male caller should be *my* valentine – and here you are!'

She held out the box again, and Gordon had no choice but to take it. Inside was a very expensive double tie pin, with blue enamel scrolling and rose-cut diamonds.

'Mrs Scambles, this is too much!'

'Nonsense! The least you can do is kiss me, according to custom!'

She turned her cheek towards him, pouting in mock disappointment at his less than enthusiastic reaction to the gift. Gordon leaned forward and pecked the smooth skin of her face with its natural blush. As he did so he could not help but notice the most subtly exquisite perfume he had ever smelt on a lady, and the delicate white curve of her exposed, slender neck. When his lips touched her cheek, he heard her let out a little sigh of bliss.

'For a tall, strong-looking army man you have a very gentle touch, Mr Gordon,' she said in a hushed tone.

A thousand thoughts coursed through his mind, and he was certainly no longer troubled by a coldness in any part of his anatomy. 'A very happy Valentine's Day, Mrs Scambles. And,' he added hastily before there could be any further developments, 'how have you been? No further visits? No suspicious activity?'

She held him captive in her radiant gaze for a second longer, and when she chose to release him it was as if a candle had been extinguished. Her face darkened and her brow furrowed. 'I keep fancying that I hear noises, Mr Gordon, particularly at night. I wish I had some capable person close at hand so that I might rest easy.' She dramatically clutched both his hands in hers. 'Someone strong and courageous whose protection I might call upon in my time of need....'

He gently but firmly untangled their hands. 'Why, here you have your servants, and where you are going you shall have Mrs Bucket's sister – and her husband is himself a policeman.'

She half-turned away and pressed the back of her hand to her forehead in theatrical fashion. 'This whole business has been such a very great strain on my nerves, Mr Gordon.'

'I'm sure it has, Mrs Scambles.'

'I don't know how much longer I can withstand the torment I feel. It seems ... it seems that my very life-force has been gradually sucked from me....' Her voice first became a whimper, then trailed off completely. She took one step in Gordon's direction, then swooned directly into his arms. He found himself holding her up with his arms wrapped around her narrow waist and what he discovered to be her surprisingly full bosom pressed against his chest.

'Come, Mrs Scambles. Have strength!'

Gordon hauled her towards the sofa and laid her upon it, whereupon she opened her eyes and reached up and grasped his arms, pulling him closer. 'Oh, Mr Gordon. I do not know how long I can bear to live with the anxiety of what has happened to my husband. I would do anything for someone who could somehow intervene, somehow secure his release....' She looked him directly in the eye. '*Anything!*'

IX

WHERE WAS TOM Prike?

This was the question being asked in the rookeries of the East End. It was being asked by Mr Bucket, as he prowled the brooding alleys and rude lodging houses of Whitechapel. It was being asked by those whom he had sent abroad, and those were legion since Mr Bucket sensed that this would not be an easily accomplished quest. Bob Moaks said Tom had taken the train to Portsmouth two days since. Rawbone Sal knew for a fact that he was seen coming out of the beershop in St Giles not an hour ago. Stumpy had heard that Tom was back with his girl, who lodged near Cable Street in Shadwell. Mary Ann Jemps hated to break it to Mr Bucket, but Tom Prike had had his head smashed in by an iron bar during a drunken argument with a soldier, and his body had been dragged out of the Thames that very morning.

But Mr Bucket believed he had the scent of Tom Prike, and felt confident that however elusive the lad might be he was not very far away. His nose and his feet led him along the Commercial Road, where a brief conversation with two different constables walking their beats turned up no useful information. A third policeman was not to be found where Mr Bucket might have expected, but a little ferreting found him smoking his pipe in a doorway down an unnamed yard off Hanbury Street.

'Nice little spot for a break, Constable. All sheltered from this cold wind that's a-getting up.'

The policeman whipped the pipe from his mouth and held it behind his back. Mr Bucket couldn't see his face, just the dark shape of a thick-set man in the shadows. 'And 'oo in all the world might you be? And what business is it of yours?' The voice was low and gruff.

'I might be Inspector Bucket, A Division. Or then again I might be Jenny Lind. What do *you* think, eh?'

There was a sudden shuffling of feet, straightening of uniform and tapping of pipe against wall. The constable stepped forward into what little light was afforded from the gas lamps. 'Heard a noise ... all seems well. Got to look into these things....'

'Very commendable, Constable. Know of a lad name of Tom Prike?'

'Do indeed, sir. Know 'is pa anorl – nasty piece o' work. Knocks 'is missus abaht somethin' 'orrible – and I dare say the lad too. I mean, we are all inclined to do such things when in drink – but 'e does it stone cold sober!'

'And have you seen him about the place – Tom, that is?'

The constable thought for a moment. 'You normally see 'im 'ere, there and everywhere, but 'e's bin very quiet of late, 'as young Tom. But now I come to think of it I reckon I did see someone lookin' very like 'im lurkin' abaht the back of Paddy's Goose as I was makin' me way to start me beat.'

'Which would have been how long ago?'

'Hour and 'alf, give or takes a minute.'

'That'll do for me, Constable, that will do for me. Tell Sergeant Allen that Inspector Bucket asked after him. And tell him Inspector Bucket was most impressed with his constable's assistance and powers of observation.'

'Righto, Guv!'

Mr Bucket turned up his collar and lapels the better to protect his neck and face against the bitter wind. He left the yard, headed down Hanbury Street and within a few minutes was entering the White Swan, known to all and sundry as Paddy's Goose. Paddy's Goose was owned by one Patrick Flaherty. It was patronized largely by sailors and inhabited by a certain class of lady to whom sailors were drawn when in port. The sound of a piano, singing and laughing voices could be heard from behind a door to Mr Bucket's right. A slim but big-boned man lounged against the frame of the door, and upon spotting Mr Bucket, eyed him up and down in a blatant and surly manner. Mr Bucket nodded and smiled.

'Where might I find the owner of this establishment?'

'Not in.'

'I didn't ask whether he was in or not.'

'You wanna watch your cheek.'

'And *you* want to get a more civil tongue inside that bloomin' head of yours.'

Without warning the man used the wall against which he was leaning as a sort of springboard, propelling himself at Mr Bucket – but the detective anticipated him and was already thrusting forward himself, raising his forearm to the thug's throat and using his momentum and greater weight to jam his would-be assailant against the wall. Just then, a door at the end of the hallway opened and another man emerged. He was larger and more athletically built than the first, and more smartly dressed.

'Hook it!' Mr Bucket ordered. 'Me and pally here are having a little chat and we require a little privacy – don't we, my friend?'

The man was pinned so firmly by the throat that it was all he could do to breathe, let alone speak. The interloper glared at Mr Bucket and moved a step closer – but it was a hesitant step, and when Mr Bucket repeated his order to 'hook it' in a firmer voice, there was something about this visitor's tone and presence which caused him to capitulate and retreat back through the door whence he came.

Mr Bucket turned back to his captive. 'Tom Prike – where might I find him?'

The man was about to speak when Mr Bucket, instead of relaxing the arm against his throat, pressed it harder.

'*How ... urgh! How can I answer ... with you choking me so?*'

'If I thought you was about to give me an *honest* answer I would ease up like a shot, I would. But *am* I going to get an honest answer – straight off, like?'

The man nodded enthusiastically, and Mr Bucket let him go altogether, letting his hands drop and backing off a little. '*You're* a very sensible man – that's what *you* are. Some might have attempted to draw the whole matter out and waste everyone's time, and that gets very tedious. And since they'd have told the truth in the end anyway, *your* way is by far the wisest for all concerned.'

'Tom's layin' low fer a bit....'

'Someone out to get him, eh?' The man nodded, and Mr Bucket quickly added, 'Well, it ain't me, and I can promise you that as one man to another. I just want a word – might even be able to help him.'

'You're a peeler?'

'My word, you really are sharp as a pin,' Mr Bucket beamed, patting his man on the shoulder. 'We could do with more men like *you* on the force. Too many numskulls. Need more bright fellows like yourself. Is he here somewhere?'

The man nodded in the direction of the stairs.

'Which room?'

The man leaned closer, whispering, *'First landing, second on the right.'*

Mr Bucket winked conspiratorially at his man, then proceeded up the stairs slowly and with surprising grace and stealth for a rather portly figure. He heard all sorts of noises coming from the rooms on this corridor: some hinting at gaiety, some inebriation and some conjuring up other images altogether. He paused at the second door, listening and contemplating, then something – call it instinct, call it second-sight – whatever it was, it caused the detective to suddenly abandon all thought of covertness and burst into the room, sending the door flying back and crashing into the wall. And it was as he thought. The room was empty; the window was open and an icy draught passed around him and seemingly right through him. It seemed impossible, but Tom Prike had somehow been tipped off. Mr Bucket sighed, adjusted his hat and returned down the stairs, out through the hallway and into the cold night air. He did not, though, turn right out of the building to head back the way he had come. He went left, and glimpsed down an alley running along the side of the building, which appeared to lead past the rear of Paddy's Goose. He ventured this way: his footsteps were regular and unhesitant, not furtive and searching. And he whistled. He issued forth a very fine rendition of *Rule Britannia* into the cold night air. Then, as he walked past an untidy collection of dustbins and empty packing cases outside the back door of Paddy's Goose, Mr Bucket, without warning, swiftly raised his stick and whacked it down upon the nearest bin, causing a resounding *clang* to reverberate around the alley. At the same instant, he cried, 'Why, *there* y'are!' in no particular direction, and stopped dead, waiting and watching. There came a panicked commotion from the back of the pile of packing cases, and from inside one of them emerged a scraggy youth who commenced to run.

'*Tom – it's me!*'

The lad stopped and let out a strange little noise under his breath. 'Gawd, Mr Bucket. Yer *shun't* 'ave.' There was dread and despair in his voice. '*Yer really* shun't 'ave....'

'Now, Tom ... no one can see us here. I got a strange message from you, I did. What's it all about, matey?'

'I can't, Mr Bucket ... not this time – *please!*'

'Look'ee here, Tom – no one will ever know what you've told me. You know that, don't you?'

'But it's different this time....'

'You said, "Let the doctor take the rap" – that's the little tale I got told to me. What's it all about, eh Tom?'

'I saw somethin', Mr B. Somethin' what shocked me – and I've seen some things....'

'Yes? And what was it you saw, lad?'

'It ain't so much *what* I saw as *who*. I mean, I'd heard rumours, but—'

'The *who* and the *what* in equal measure make my day, no end,' probed Mr Bucket patiently.

'I started asking around, asking questions – that was my downfall, Mr B. Shoulda let it be. I heard tell of a man calls himself Chuddersby, and that trail led to another known as the General. Both very bad men, Mr Bucket. Very bad.'

'But that's not all, is it Tom? There's another link in the chain.'

'Would you ask me to cut me own throat? That doctor's a wrong 'un, Mr B. I did learn that. Don't matter whether 'e did it or not – just let 'im 'ang and it'll be the easier for all of us.'

'Now Tom, you know I don't operate along those lines.'

There was a short silence from the boy. It was a thoughtful silence. A tortured silence. Mr Bucket had been very good to him over the years ....

'Find the General. Probably lordin' it in a beershop on Earl Street,

Seven Dials. It starts with the General and goes up from there – but I *begs* yer not to mention me name, Mr B.'

'Tom ... ' began Mr Bucket. But Tom Prike's footsteps were already receding into the darkness.

There was another figure. He lurked unseen in the shadows at the end of the alley – far enough away to remain unsuspected, unseen; but close enough, we may be sure, to have caught some, if not all, of what had just be said.

Gordon had left Mrs Scambles in the very capable hands of Mrs Bucket's sister and was making his way home by a circuitous route, which allowed him, even in the dark, to admire the gradual rise of the numerous tall and majestic buildings along Coventry Street. The weather was turning. Heavy grey clouds were blowing in from the west and massing over London as it slept. Icicles hanging from gutters and window ledges were dripping; the silvery sheen covering roofs and streets was fading to black. Gordon was in a mellow, intro-spective mood as he sauntered along the streets of the metropolis – but it was not to last.

It was their feet that he spotted first – dirty, and calloused, covered in sores. Then the bony ankles, the string-like calves. And he knew immediately. He had seen it before on the battlefield in the grey early light of the morning after. The feet were neither white with cold nor mottled red with rheumatics, but a sort of waxy blue-grey. Just like the morning after the battle. Yet there had been no combat here other than that between two frail girls and the world; two children against the system, against nature. Gordon was surprised by the sudden catch in his throat, as if it were in the grip of the bony hand of a spectre as he crouched over the bundle of rags just inside the alley. They were conveniently out of sight and it occurred to him that it suited London nicely that they should die in the shadows, barely visible from the grand shopping thoroughfare.

Gordon reached down to pull back the shawls that had become their shrouds – but the threadbare fabric was still frost-stiffened and stiff, adhering to their scant clothing, to the exposed flesh of their arms, their faces. Gently, he peeled it away to reveal the rigid bodies of Elsie and Annie. They were huddled together in a final sisterly embrace. Annie's eyes were closed; she could have been sleeping peacefully. Elsie, though, her right arm curled around her sister's neck and her left beneath her body, clinging to her waist, gazed up at her older sister in fear and confusion through glassy eyes that would see no more of the cruel world which had no further use for her. At Annie's head, Gordon noticed a sorry-looking bunch of lavenders, frozen and preserved in that same final moment of existence as their owners.

He did not know what to do.

He could not carry two corpses through the streets to his home, but neither could he bring himself to leave them there. He could not just walk away like others who must have seen the same sight and at least suspected the truth of it, yet left them to be collected like rubbish by some street sweeper; or carted away by some uncaring official to an unmarked pauper's grave. He laid his hands upon their alabaster brows and stroked them gently, one after the other, then looked helplessly up and down the deserted street. He was a soldier. He had seen gruesome sights and death aplenty. But he did not know what to do.

X

'THIS HAS BEEN a mistake. A selfish, deluded mistake. I can't do this any more, Mr Bucket – I'm very sorry.'

It just came out like that. Gordon had rehearsed a lengthy, reasoned explanation, but as soon as he opened his mouth, those were the words which tumbled out.

'Go and tell the Chief.'

Gordon observed him for a moment. He felt sure Mr Bucket must be aware of his inner turmoil and he had not expected such an abrupt reply from him of all people. 'Very well ... but ... as your colleague and subordinate officer I thought it only right to make you aware that seeing what London is capable of, what London seems to care little about – those two little girls frozen in each other's arms – was only the last straw. Among other things I realize only too well how I am viewed within—'

'Go and tell the Chief,' repeated Mr Bucket flatly without looking up from the paperwork on his desk.

There was an uneasy silence between them. Gordon became aware of the thin splatter of rain on the window and how the dark, oppressive atmosphere outside seemed to reflect his mood. Was Mr Bucket angry with him? Did he feel betrayed? Did he think he was simply not worth bothering with, or was he testing him? For Gordon's part, he didn't know why he wasn't walking out of their little office and making his way to visit the Assistant Commissioner. Mr Bucket did, though.

'I'll be damned if I'm a-going to tell you you *can* continue in this line of work – because you're a man and you should know your own mind, Mr James Alexander Gordon of that ilk.'

He was still brooding over his paperwork – though Gordon now noticed that he didn't actually seem to be *doing* anything with it or to it. 'I know it's not only Sergeant Blacksnape who thinks it's unfair that I—'

'It *is* unfair, and there's no escaping it. But the opportunity arose and you took it, just like we all would've. *You* knew that all along – but you're here now and you can either walk away or prove that you *would* have got in on your own merit and ability.'

'But that's just it. For example, what I told you about Mrs Scambles' ... *approaches* wasn't quite the whole story. The fact is, I was tempted, Mr Bucket. I was most tempted, in a way that an officer of—'

'Why, Lord, you were tempted by a beautiful woman throwing herself upon you. Now ain't that a thing. Well, Mr Gordon, maybe we should *all* resign, then.'

'But then there was Annie and Elsie. I know I shall come across further such scenes, and worse. And you warned me I can't help all London's poor wretches, but now I've ended up paying for a proper burial, and God help me if I were to come across another such case, and another ....'

'I said you can't save all of 'em, *but you can do what you can for one or two.* And that's exactly what you did, don't you see, Mr Gordon? And I'm proud of you, because I've known little Annie and Elsie for ... ' Mr Bucket faltered momentarily – and, Gordon was sure, unexpectedly – the moment he uttered their names; he put a hand to his mouth and coughed unconvincingly. 'Little frog .... Always happens when the weather turns. Anyhow, like I say you *can't* save all of 'em – and you won't want to! Half of 'em's saucy little beggars who would call you "Uncle" to your face and have your watch from your pocket at the same time, while calling you all the names under the sun behind your back.'

Gordon stood before his superior's desk feeling sheepish but already rather better about things – yet at the same time still troubled deep down, and wondering whether on some level he had been duped like the victim of the three-card-trick. When a knock came at the door, he welcomed the interruption.

Inspector Stope thrust his large head into the room. 'A word?' he asked Mr Bucket.

'Why, Billy, come in, old man!'

He opened the door fully, and his bulk filled the frame. His eyes fell upon Gordon. 'This don't concern you.'

He wasn't unduly troubled. He knew it was just Mr Stope's way and he moved as if to leave, but Mr Bucket intervened.

'Come now, Billy. Mr Gordon and I don't want to be having any secrets from each other if we are to form a formidable crime fighting partnership, do we?'

'Come to think of it, it *does* concern him, anyway.' Mr Stope entered the room and walked across to lean his backside against the window ledge; his great frame caused the room to darken. Today in typical 'Flash Billy' fashion he wore a garish green waistcoat and sported a chunky ring on his little finger with a large sapphire set into it. He suddenly looked like a nervous suitor about to make his proposal speech, uncertain as to how to put whatever it was he had to say into words. 'The Scambles case.'

'Ah *that*! I'd been meaning to mention that to you, Billy, and I'm sure ashamed with myself for letting it slip.'

'I had to visit Dr Scambles' lawyer earlier, and it came out that you'd been to see his client at Coldbath. People around the office are starting to wonder ....'

Gordon fidgeted uncomfortably, but Mr Bucket maintained his genial demeanour. 'Coincidence, Billy. Now, we don't put much store by coincidence in this game, do we? But it's a fact, that's what it is. *Mrs* Scambles reported a burglary – *after* the murder, mind, nothing to do with all that business – and the Chief himself details Mr James Alexander Gordon to look into it. Not that there even seems to be much to investigate.'

'He was in debt,' Stope blurted. 'Up to his neck in debt to Edward Mizzentoft. Mizzentoft presented himself as the successful, respectable businessman, but it was a front. Or at any rate, most of his money didn't come from legitimate commerce but from shady money lending, debt collecting and the Lord knows what else. Quite how it came about that Scambles got in his bad books he refuses to say. But all the doctor's personal fortune had vanished, the bank and others were pursuing him and he had no way out – other than the course he took, according to his way of seeing things. That's the long and the short of it – together with physical evidence found placing him at the scene. It all comes together perfect. Scambles might play the cool medical man, but when roused—'

'Oh, we know,' Gordon said. 'He all but went for the pair of us in Coldbath.'

'Well, just so's you know.'

Mr Bucket rose to his feet and reached out his hand across the desk. 'We won't let this come between us, eh, Billy? And if I hear anyone a-starting any rumours in the office I'll put 'em straight, you can be sure of that.'

'Where are we going?' Gordon asked Mr Bucket as they tramped past the Admiralty and along into St James's Park. With the freezing rain and bitter wind he would have almost thought it colder than it had been when the sub-zero temperatures were upon them – but a picture of the bodies of Annie and Elsie flashed into his mind once more and he soon changed his mind about that. The rain had started to fall more steadily and Gordon had taken advantage of a kiosk of the London Umbrella Company he had come across and hired one of their devices at the very reasonable rate of fourpence for three hours. Mr Bucket declined to take advantage of such protection, and although he didn't categorically say so – merely muttering that such things hadn't been invented when he was a young policeman walking the beat – Gordon got the distinct impression that he thought there was something rather less than manly about such accoutrements. Perhaps it was just a fancy on Gordon's part, then, that a couple of times he sensed Mr Bucket glancing with a certain air of envy at his companion's sheltered, dry condition as compared to his own increasingly sodden and bedraggled one.

'We, Mr James Alexander Gordon of that ilk, are going to descend upon the residence of Henrietta, Baroness Sowerby of Belgrave Place. Related to our hero the Iron Duke himself, they say. In fact, I may well let you do the talking on this occasion. You're more used to dealing with folk like that – I might commit all sorts of forks passes in such company, I might.'

'Surely not, sir. I take it this is the business about ferns?'

'Correct.'

'Is this really a job for the detective department?'

'The job itself might not be – but the folk involved puts things in a different light as far as our superiors and betters are concerned. Neither party wants lowly constables being seen knocking on their doors and trampling through their houses with their muddy boots. Mind you … ' Mr Bucket trailed off, glancing down at the state of his own footwear.

'These plants must be worth quite a bit to cause such a spate of thefts.'

'Some of 'em can cost a great deal, as I have fervently discussed with Mrs Bucket only too often. Money might not be at the bottom of it, though.'

'What do you mean?' Gordon asked. But just then, a most curious incident occurred. A woman came hurrying towards them. Mr Bucket spotted her and addressed her in a friendly tone, yet with barely a pause in her step she merely pressed something into his hand and continued on her way. Mr Bucket stopped in his tracks and watched her go, stroking his chin.

'Well, well. What's got into Emeline?'

'Who is she?'

'She's the wife of Mick the Whippet, one of my snouts. I use the term "wife" in the loosest of senses.'

Mr Bucket looked at what had been presented to him in so furtive a manner. It was a roughly torn piece of newspaper, which he opened out to reveal a message scrawled across it in thick, crudely formed handwriting. He then passed it to Gordon:

TOM PRIKE DANGER
7 DILS

'Seven Dils?'

'Seven Dials, a district just up a way from Charing Cross.' He stared at the scrap of paper as if hoping it might reveal something more.

'Should we go?'

'Got an appointment. These aren't the sort of folks you stand up….' But he seemed preoccupied as they carried on their way. 'Tom Prike's crafty, he is. Knows how to take care of himself. But we'll go there directly, though.'

'Is all this something to do with the Scambles case?' Gordon asked.

Mr Bucket tapped his nose in that familiar fashion. 'We'll make a detective of you yet, Mr James Alexander Gordon.'

'Inspector Stope mentioned Dr Scambles being in debt to Mizzentoft. Having witnessed the doctor's outburst, I could easily imagine him losing his self-control if confronted by someone who was, shall we say, being *persistent* about the repayment of money.'

'What about *Mrs* Scambles?'

'Mrs Scambles? I confess I was discomfited by her … forwardness, but *murder*? Besides, is there anything to implicate her?'

'Where the husband is implicated, suspicion must always fall upon the wife. Or vicey versy. Why was he in debt – was it to do with her?'

'But still – a woman committing the bloody murder of a man?'

'Not unknown, though they usually resort to poison. But enough of this. Some policemen may jump to obvious conclusions and some may cut corners, but not Billy Stope. We may not be able to help ourselves in taking an interest – particularly in view of Mrs Scambles now being on our hands, so to speak. But the murder itself is still not our business, however much peripheral matters might cause us to stray in that direction.'

Mr Bucket still had a slightly distracted air about him as he said this, and Gordon wasn't entirely convinced that even he still truly adhered to this view.

They had arrived at number 5, Belgrave Place, Baroness Sowerby's stately residence with its impeccably whitewashed frontage complete with first-floor balcony. The interview was to take place in a surprisingly capacious and well-furnished solarium at the rear of the house where the owner awaited them. Baroness Sowerby was a tiny, bird-like woman with silver hair drawn so tightly back that it appeared to tighten the skin of her face. She spoke in short, sharp sentences, all the while holding a lorgnette, which she raised to gaze through at them every now and then as if to remind herself what they looked like.

'It was a maidenhair spleenwort. The total value of all these,' she gestured to the bewildering collection of plants which surrounded the detectives on shelves, on tables, on windowsills, 'is two hundred and fifty pounds. That one specimen alone was worth that and more. It was collected for me personally by an explorer friend of my husband.'

'I take it there were no signs of a break-in?' Mr Bucket inquired.

'Oh, but there were, Inspector.'

'What occurred, my lady?'

'Someone forced their way into this very room.'

Gordon got up and went to inspect the door leading to the garden. 'The lock seems to be intact, my lady.'

'I've had it repaired, naturally.'

'Ah. It's just that the lock and doorknob look almost original.'

'I insisted that the new knob was identical to the old. And it has been repainted, of course.' She held her spectacle up to get a better look at him. 'Do you doubt me?'

Gordon's heart lurched, aghast at the thought of upsetting someone so influential at such a delicate stage of his fledgling career. 'Not at all, my lady. The craftsman has made such a fine job of it that it's hard to tell there has been any repair. He is to be complimented!'

'And when did this distressing incident take place?' asked Mr Bucket.

'Two days ago.'

'During the night?'

'It must have been, because I hosted a meeting of the Society here in the afternoon and the ladies were admiring the fern. I am an early riser and the first thing I always do is come in here – and the following morning is when I discovered the theft.'

'The "Society"?' Mr Bucket queried.

'The National Truss Society for the Relief of the Ruptured Poor. I am its chairwoman.'

'I see.' Mr Bucket's reply was quite casual, but his forefinger moved to the side of his nose – usually, Gordon had come to notice, a sign that his profound and inscrutable mind was hard at work. He rose to his feet. 'Thank you for your time, my lady.'

'Is that all?' she asked brusquely.

'I don't need to take up any more of your ladyship's time. We have a very strong suspect in this case, and I do believe it to be only a matter of time before we swoop.'

*

'A *very strong suspect*?' Gordon queried after they had left Baroness Sowerby's house and were making their way past the Queen's Palace. 'You didn't mention this before.'

'That, Mr James Alexander Gordon, is because we didn't have one before.'

He was clearly in one of his enigmatic moods so Gordon didn't trouble himself to press him. 'Well, Baroness Sowerby's story didn't satisfy me. For one thing, I do not believe her solarium to have been broken into. I swear the lock was the original one – and anyhow there would have been a smell of paint had it been replaced and repainted only two days ago. I should have liked to have stayed longer and looked into it more thoroughly.'

'Commendably perceptive. But I doubt whether we should have a-gleaned any more by staying longer, and presently I'm more concerned about young Tom Prike and the message we received.'

If it had been anyone else, Gordon should have been irritated at the thought of pertinent intelligence being withheld from him – but Mr Bucket had his methods, and at least for the time being, he was happy to go along with it and let the enigmatic detective guide him in his own way. The walk to Seven Dials was not a long one, which was just as well since the sky was a brooding dark presence that felt almost low enough to reach up and touch, and the rain fell as heavily as ever. Even though it was mid-afternoon, darkness was already coming on, and as they approached this notorious place from St Martin's Lane it took on the appearance of one of the entrances to hell itself. They entered a space around which several roads converged – presumably seven, though Gordon didn't count them – like the hub of a wheel. Tall corner buildings watched over the circle they formed like the mysterious standing stones of the Druids, as if guarding the entrances to the streets at their backs and the narrow alleys and passageways that ran off them. A disreputable assortment of characters inhabited this stage-like area, and, perhaps partly due to the darkly portentous weather, of all the unsavoury places Gordon had so far come across during his short time in London, this had the most menacing aspect. He had a constant feeling of being observed, of being measured up, of his presence being resented.

Mr Bucket was, as usual, unperturbed. 'Gets its name from a great big sun dial that used to stand in the middle, this place does. It had six dials on it.'

He was about to query whether he really meant six, not seven dials, but thought better of it. *London.*

'Now, Mr Gordon. The place where we are a-going ain't like any place you've been to afore. I can tell you are a man who has taken care of himself and I dare say you boxed a bit in the army, but make no mistake that the men in the place we are about to visit are of the most dangerous type: vicious, heartless fellows who have fought for money – and sometimes even for their lives. A strong and fit man like you could out-box them and out-think them, avoid one of their blows and land two of your own. But do you know what would happen? They would laugh in your face and come back for more. You could break their noses, split their lips and knock their teeth out yet they'd keep coming back at you till it quite broke your heart, Mr Gordon. I've seen it happen. I still say the two of us might settle with two or three of them – but they'll know who we are and what we are, and if two or three rise up, then four or five, six or seven are liable to do so.'

Gordon wasn't exactly afraid as Mr Bucket led them into the shabby beershop on Earl Street, which might at a glance have easily been taken for an abandoned, derelict property, but he was certainly on his guard to say the least. It was as if they had intruded upon a private party. The smell of beer, tobacco and unwashed bodies hit him immediately, and while the room didn't exactly fall silent upon their arrival there was a slight but noticeable diminution in the general hubbub. Harsh bursts of laughter from gap-toothed mouths set in unshaven faces faded momentarily. Numerous heads turned their way then came closer together, no doubt to discuss who they might be and what their appearance might mean. The only patrons who remained oblivious to their intrusion were a group of men arranged round a circular table, engrossed in a game of cards. Piles of coins on the table explained their lack of interest in Gordon and Bucket. For men such as these, the stakes must have been high.

They went to the bar – actually nothing more than a heavy wooden table with two casks upon it and some bottles on shelves behind, and were served beers by a sullen landlord who betrayed no sign of recognizing Mr Bucket yet certainly appeared to be aware that this visit was not an entirely social one. Gordon noticed that Mr Bucket's ever watchful eyes rarely strayed from the card players. There were few chairs in the dingy little room so they stood by the table, and Gordon sipped his cloudy, flat ale self-consciously while wondering what Mr Bucket's next move might be.

Although he tried not to stare too obviously, it soon became apparent that there was a certain tension at the card table, as if a winner-takes-all game was building towards its climax. While Gordon was looking round the room he heard a hand of cards being slapped down hard, followed by a very vocal release of pressure: groans, gasps, laughter, curses. He assumed this was an end to that particular diversion and was distracted by the sight of a crooked little old woman who had arrived with three empty bottles of her own, which she demanded the landlord fill for her to take away. But then a steady yet clear and forceful voice caused a sudden hush to fall over the room.

'General, I do believe all was not as it seemed during that hand.'

Gordon turned to look, and in the same instant Mr Bucket subtly touched his sleeve, whispering, '*The big pugilistic-looking fellow has just won the whole pot, but by underhand means – and the soldierly-looking fellow knows it. And it's going to turn very ugly unless I'm very much mistaken, Mr Gordon of that ilk.*'

Gordon felt a surge of anticipation, and his whole body tensed. There were six men altogether at the table and they all looked to be of the rough type described earlier by his chief; at least two of them had already reached slyly into their jackets, as if preparing to arm themselves. The burly, shaven-headed man who had been called the 'General' was glaring at his accuser with such burning intensity that it seemed only a matter of time before some sort of violent encounter would take place. With his flattened, misshapen nose, massive fists and fairly recent scar across his right cheekbone, the General certainly did seem, as Mr Bucket suggested, to have had a pugilistic background. His accuser was a broad-chested, straight-backed man with a tanned face – every inch the soldier, as Mr Bucket had noted. He puffed coolly on his pipe and his demeanour was far calmer, yet his eyes attested to the steely resolve of a man who was not prepared to back down. Gordon began to move forward, thinking this was a situation better nipped in the bud; but Mr Bucket, whose eyes flitted keenly from one individual to another at the table, swiftly moved his cane across his assistant's legs as a sign for him to wait.

'All was not as it seemed?' hissed the General in a cockney accent strongly laced with Irish. 'All was not as it seemed? It seemed to *me* like I beat yer fair 'n square. What's not right about that, mister?'

'I don't want to embarrass nor cause no sort of a fuss. All I ask is that you give me back my stake and we'll say no more about it.'

The General's face visibly reddened, making the old scars around his eyes and forehead turn white, the fresher one on his cheek seem as if it might burst open anew and his bloodshot eyes bulged a little wider. 'Don't want to cause a fuss, is it? 'E accuses me of cheatin', but *'e don't want to cause no fuss – oh, no!*'

'You passed something to your mate there. Looked like a card. And he passed something to you – also looked like a card.'

The General sprang to his feet, sending his chair clattering backwards across the stone floor. The men either side of him rose too. One whipped out a life-preserver; the other's hand remained in his jacket pocket, readied on whatever weapon he had concealed. The military man's strong, weathered hands remained spread out on the table before him, his steadfast but composed gaze fixed on the General – who seemed to have exhausted whatever limited vocabulary he possessed. He stood with legs apart like an angry bull, chest heaving, the ugly veins about his temples throbbing, then suddenly he swiped the table aside as though it were a child's toy. It somersaulted noisily across the room and opened up a clear space between the adversaries. The General moved forward, ripping off his jacket as he did so, and Gordon caught a movement of the arm from the man on his left, and a glint of steel. He had produced a knife with a thin, gleaming blade about eight inches in length. Now Mr Bucket made his move. He crossed the floor with surprising speed and poise, and the General and his men were so intent upon their accuser that Bucket had knocked the knife out of the hand of its owner with his stick before they were even aware of his presence among them. The detective surged past the would-be knife-man and advanced on the General, but the incensed knife-man was coming up behind him so Gordon sprang towards him and yanked him back by the collar. At the same time, the General took a mighty swing at Mr Bucket. He tried to duck but it still caught the side of his head, staggering him and sending his hat flying; but he stayed on his feet. The General closed again, swinging his ham-like fist. They clashed, and somehow – it happened too fast for Gordon to perceive yet he felt sure it was no mere chance – in the tangle the General was half-spun round and Mr Bucket was now behind his man with his stick across the hefty fellow's throat in a tight grip. The man with the life-preserver moved to intervene, and while Gordon struggled to keep hold of the knife-man, who luckily was of a short and wiry stature, the man who had accused the General launched himself into the melee and dealt this new assailant an impressive blow, sending him spinning across the room till he thudded into the wall. But this was the General's territory, and people who had previously been lounging with their drinks and pipes had left their seats and now began to converge in a most menacing way. Bottles were grasped; hands went into pockets. Gordon felt they had acquitted themselves well thus far, but they were in the centre of the room, cut off from the exits, and surrounded by strapping, villainous-looking men. As an officer of the Cameronians he had always been aware that one day when all was lost he might have to go down fighting to the last like a true British redcoat, but he never expected it to happen in a London beerhouse. The knife-man would be too much of an encumbrance to him in the coming battle, so he lightened the scrawny man's contact with the ground by thrusting his hand under his crotch, lifting him onto his tiptoes, then propelling him in the back with the other hand as forcefully as he could. He careered into some of the advancing supporters of the General, yelping and clutching his nether regions, but Gordon knew this was only a temporary respite. Mr Bucket was struggling to restrain the thrashing prize-fighter, pulling his cane so hard against the man's throat that his face was turning a ghastly purple; but a broken, jagged beer bottle thrown from behind Gordon narrowly missed Mr Bucket's head and smashed against the wall, and two more thugs were coming up behind the inspector now, one on either side. The sheer weight of numbers would soon, Gordon knew, be their downfall. But then Mr Bucket's voice cut through the mayhem, loud and authoritative.

'I'm Inspector Bucket of the Detective, I am, and I can promise you gen'lmen it won't do no good to go smashing up that poor landlord's establishment just because of a falling out over baccarat.'

His commanding tone at least had the effect of bringing about a pause in the disturbance. He released his grip on the General, who staggered forward, gasping and wiping his spittle-covered chin with his sleeve.

'Now,' Mr Bucket continued. 'I take it that this being your regular lay and all, you wouldn't want it to become the object of regular and thorough scrutiny by the local peelers, now, would you, General?'

The big brute glanced towards the ashen-faced landlord. 'I ain't done nothin'. Why yer come after me?'

'I ain't come after you, least not in that way, General. We have a common acquaintance whose whereabouts I want to inquire after.'

'I ain't no grass, either.'

'And our common acquaintance ain't done nothing wrong. In fact it's his own safety that's my concern.'

Gordon sensed a lessening of the pent-up tension in the room.

'Let's settle this little matter peaceably, like. Now, this man here who's upset you so also happens to be known to me – good evening to ye, by the way, Mr George!'

'Nice to see you again, Mr Bucket,' nodded the said old soldier.

'*You're* a sensible man, General; a man who knows the workings of the world, that's what *you* are. What say you give Mr George here his stake back and we'll say no more about it? You still end up the winner by a long chalk the way I see it – ain't that so?'

Mr George's face clouded over, but Gordon knew it was the only realistic way of them getting out of this place intact, and was glad when both he and the General finally gave unenthusiastic nods.

'Now, General, it's Tom Prike I came to ask about. Young lad from St Giles way. Like I say, he ain't in trouble, on that you have my word as a man.'

The General shot a quick look towards one of his accomplices, then shook his head. 'Don't know no Tom Prike, sir. Not at all.'

Bucket looked round the room. 'Anyone? It would be a great favour to me – and one good turn deserves another, as they say.'

There was some low muttering and shaking of heads – Gordon and Bucket's only reward for placing themselves in such a perilous position. Mr Bucket collected his hat and righted the table, then scooped up the coins from the floor and handed them to the General, upon which they shook hands. The circle of bodies then parted as the detectives and their new acquaintance made their way to the exit.

'I'm not at all sure he was telling the truth,' Gordon informed Mr Bucket as they strolled through the darkness of Little Earl Street.

'You're catching on, Mr Gordon. I swear I shall find out in good time. And I have a suspicion that when I do, the answer shall prove to be an important step towards solving the puzzle.'

'Which particular puzzle are you—'

They were interrupted by a voice. *'Mr Bucket!'*

It was Mr George, who had so bravely and calmly stood up to the General. Mr Bucket held out his hand.

'How goes the shooting gallery? What of Phil Squod? Still a-sidling about the place, is he?'

Mr George lowered his head and took a moment before replying. 'The muffled drums have beat for Phil, Mr Bucket. Took bad with his chest last winter. Never the healthiest of men. Didn't have the constitution to fight it off.'

Mr George delivered the news in a steady, impassive voice, but Gordon thought he noticed a watery film cross his eyes momentarily.

'That's sad news, George. Sad news indeed. Mr George here and his assistant Phil went all the way back to the army days, Mr Gordon.'

'I thought you might like to know I got a new lad in to help out, though, Mr Bucket. Name of *Tom Prike*.'

Mr Bucket grinned and tapped the side of his nose. '*Ah!* One step ahead of me, eh? Might he be lying low at your establishment?'

'He was, sir. Then he started to behave rather queer just lately and I asked him if he was in some sort of trouble, but he wouldn't tell me. He stopped going out, and I even let him sleep at the gallery. Told him I could protect him if only he would tell me what ailed him.'

'No better man for *that* sort of work, Mr Gordon of that ilk,' Mr Bucket informed Gordon.

'But something or someone had got to him very bad, and he just clammed up. Yesterday, I was away from the gallery for an hour and when I got back he'd gone. I asked around, and a friend of a friend mentioned Seven Dials – and the General's name cropped up. I wasn't here for a game of cards, Mr Bucket, but to find out what has become of him. And I have an idea about who to see next – but he won't talk in your presence, begging your pardon, Mr Bucket. Let me talk to him, then if your business might bring you in the vicinity of the shooting gallery tomorrow I might just have something for you.'

Mr Bucket nodded and briefly touched the rim of his tall hat. Then they turned and made their way back to Scotland Yard.

XI

THE YELLOW BEAMS of two bull's eye lamps converged to illuminate the small, splintered wooden panel in the rear door of Brisket, Baxter and Edge, solicitors, attorneys at law and public notaries of Gray's Inn. The pieces of fractured wood had been crudely pressed back together and the door was closed. A less alert eye might easily have missed the signs of this break-in, particularly since this was the rear entrance. But they did not escape the attentions of this detective and his constable.

The inspector managed to gently push the unsteady door open without making a sound and the two men crept inside, using their bull's eyes to make sure they didn't stumble against anything in the darkness and give themselves away to whoever was inside. There was a bump, followed by the sound of shuffling footsteps. The two men froze, and the detective pointed to the floor above; the constable nodded. They crept towards the stairway and begin to ascend, slowly and cautiously. But when they were almost at the top they were given away by a creaking tread. There was a sudden panicked commotion from above, and even before the policemen could reach the landing, two men came hurtling into the light from their lanterns.

'STOP! POLICE!' cried the constable.

The leading man was charging towards the detective as if to force his way past and down the stairs, when he seemed to think better of it and skidded to a halt. One of his feet slipped off the edge of the top stair and overbalanced him, his midriff thudding into the head of the plain-clothes man, who was stooping to lay down his lantern to free both of his hands. The criminal started to say something but the detective straightened up, grabbed the man by the lapels and with a sudden, powerful twisting motion launched the criminal headlong down the stairs. He was swallowed by the darkness, but there came a sickening series of cracks and thuds, then silence. The constable gazed at the detective in what looked like disbelief – though it might have been something stronger – and when the bigger man moved towards the second burglar the uniformed officer deftly dodged past him and grasped the crook by the arm.

'There's no use in running. You are my prisoner and I intend to take you to Bow Street.'

The prisoner peered in the glow from the bull's eyes past the constable. 'That you, Mr Stope?'

'Squibby!' declared Inspector Stope. 'I *knew* it was only a matter of time!'

'Mr Stope, these partic'lar lawyers is bigger crooks than I am – you must know that. We wuz only settlin' a score.'

'Looks like burglary plain and simple to me, Squibby.'

Squibby pulled a roll of bank notes from a leather satchel slung over his shoulder. 'It'll be Van Deiman's Land for me Mr Stope – and after all I've done for you,' he pleaded. 'I'll keep ten per cent – the rest is yours. And that's a lot, Mr Stope.'

When the answer didn't come as quickly as he expected, the constable swung his bull's eye in his superior's direction. Stope's heavy, overhanging brow cast a dark shadow over his eyes.

'You know I can't do such a thing, Squibby. We must take you in.'

'But Mr Stope—'

'You deaf, Squibby?'

'I got something else.'

'Squibby—'

'A name in a murder case.'

Stope's aggressive stance relaxed somewhat; he folded his arms across his broad chest.

'Is that so?'

'A name you don't know about.'

'Well, then, if this name leads to a conviction, I'll talk to my boss and we'll see if we can do anything for you.'

'I need more than that, Mr Stope. Beggin' yer pardon, but it don't sound very definite.'

'It ain't,' said Stope, taking a step closer to his man so that he loomed over him. 'But it seems to me you've got nothing to lose and something to gain.'

'Well, see, I was thinkin' *you* might have somethin' to lose, Mr Stope ....'

The big detective suddenly gripped the crook's jaw in one of his bear-like hands. 'I do hope your pal's all right, Squibby. I mean, he ain't made a sound since he landed – and it's a long way down.'

Squibby seemed to visibly shrink in Stope's shadow. 'Beaufort Scuttle. The brother of the wife of Edward Mizzentoft.'

Inspector Stope pushed Squibby roughly away in disgust. '*Mizzentoft?* Seems to me like the world and his wife can't stop trying to find new suspects for a murder that's already solved! And anyway, Mrs Mizzentoft's maiden name was Saddler not Scuttle, so you're talking out of your arse.' He turned to go. 'Constable, I'll lead the way. Bring this man to Bow Street and I'll—'

'Saddler was the name of *one* of his wives, Mr Stope.'

The detective froze. 'What's all this, Squibby?'

'Mizzentoft told everybody he had another business in Sheffield. Kept going back there. But he didn't. He didn't have any businesses except his crooked money-lending lark. What he had in Sheffield was *another wife.*'

Stope picked up his lantern and held it up to Squibby's face, revealing the crook's triumphant expression.

'Who was seen lurking around Bloomsbury saying he was going to do for Mizzentoft? *The brother of this other wife!* And who vanished right after Mizzentoft was skewered? *The brother of his other wife!* Beaufort Scuttle. Was 'anging round the pubs just before the murder with this northern tough, asking questions. I don't know what you got on that doctor feller, but it makes yer think, don't it, though?'

Stope didn't say anything, but the constable was staring hard at his superior, and it was clear that the news *had* made him think very hard indeed.

XII

'I SHOULD BE obliged if you would furnish us with three coffees, Kidney my good man. My usual two sugars, none for the Seventh Earl of Drumnadrochit here ... and what about you, Wart?'

They were lounging alongside Mr Bucket's favourite coffee stall on the corner of Pall Mall and the Haymarket, just a short walk from Great Scotland Yard, after a fruitless trip to Paternoster Row in search of a husband and wife coin-forging team against whom Mr Bucket had a warrant. Wart was a young villain they had apprehended ten minutes earlier in the act of relieving a younger child of half a pound of pig's face that he had been sent out to buy by his mother.

'Yer can piss in it fer all I care, Sergeant Shitbucket,' snarled Wart, who was handcuffed to some railings a few feet away. He gave his manacles another might tug as if this time he might have mysteriously developed the strength to burst free.

'That's *Inspector* Shitbucket to you, sonny.'

Wart merely growled.

'Make that another two sugars, Mr Kidney. Needs sweetening up, does young Wart. In fact, plonk one in Mr Gordon's coffee as well – *he'll* need sweetening up when he hears what he's about after this.' Gordon noticed Mr Bucket giving Kidney a sly wink at this.

'I don't like sugar. And I thought we were going to see Lady Rhynde about the ferns?'

'*I* am a-going to pay a visit to the delightful Lady Rhynde, Mr Gordon,' commented Mr Bucket as he opened up his snuff tin and offered him a little. '*You*, however, are going to Slaughter's Coffee House.'

'What am I to do at Slaughter's?'

'You are to meet Mrs Eleanora Scambles, *that's* what you are to do.'

'To escort her home again?'

'No – it's still too risky for that, for I believe the good lady knows more than she's letting on, and that someone knows that she knows and will stop at nothing to silence her.'

'Then why am I meeting her. And why there?'

Mr Bucket handed Gordon a cup of delicious-smelling coffee in a white china cup. 'Slaughter's because it suits Mrs Scambles. Mrs Bucket's sister happens to be hosting a fund-raising event at Lambeth Ragged school, so it won't be a convenient place for discreet inquiries. I'm quite certain that nobody knows of Mrs Scambles' whereabouts so it will be quite safe for her to venture out for a short time.'

Gordon knew from experience that Mrs Scambles could be free with her affections, but other than that he failed to see what material help she might be to them. 'What sort of thing do you believe she can tell us?'

'How much she knew about her husband's debts, for one thing.'

'But her husband's debts are surely nothing to do with a simple burglary. Are we still looking at the murder he is accused of?'

Mr Bucket rubbed the side of his nose with his forefinger. 'Can't discount some strange connection. While you're there you might as well ask.'

'Mr Stope won't take too kindly if he finds out.'

'If it helps solve the case he'll be a-glad of it, you mark my words.'

But this was something that had been nagging at Gordon's conscience, both personally and professionally, and he could keep it to himself any longer. 'Mr Bucket … do you suspect Inspector Stope of having missed something, of having arrested the wrong man? Perhaps even of incompetence?'

'Incompetence? Billy? *Never!* But sometimes in this game you can get so close to a case that you can no longer see the wood for the trees, so to speak, Mr Gordon. Then again, it might just be me and my naturally suspicious mind, as Mrs Bucket is prone to describe it. Or perhaps I'm just jealous that he's got a murder when I've got ferns and I'm a-looking for problems where there ain't none. Now get that coffee down your neck and away with you. We shall rendezvous again at Mr George's shooting gallery.'

Slaughter's Coffee House was a place Gordon had visited before, a very well appointed establishment on St Martin's Lane. Mrs Scambles was already there when he arrived, sitting at a small table for two by the blazing fire. Upon seeing him she immediately rose and hurried over, beaming and greeting him like an old friend. Mrs Scambles' vivacity and beauty doubtless attracted attention wherever she went, and Gordon couldn't help but be aware of a certain boost to his pride and vanity at being greeted so by such a woman.

'Mr Gordon! What a delight! Mrs Bucket's sister is a delightful host but it is still nice to see a friendly face after being away from home for so long.'

He didn't point out that this was only the third day since she had gone to stay in Camden Town, since he was sure that to her it must have seemed longer. As Gordon suspected she would, Mrs Scambles had made sure that there were no obstructions between them where she was sitting, and managed to position the chairs in such a way at the little table that that their knees were almost touching. Once they were thus seated, her radiant smile and seemingly buoyant mood evaporated somewhat dubiously yet still convincingly in the blink of an eye, and she developed a pressing need to hold on to Gordon's arm to steady herself.

'It has been a very trying time, these past few days, James – I may call you James?'

'Er ... of course.'

'Every caller to the house, every shadow that passes the window, could be *that man* or one of his agents. Needless to say, the journey here from Mrs Bucket's sister's home was most agonizing ....' Her voice wavered and she placed a hand to her brow. 'That horrid brute could have been waiting for me around any corner.'

She grasped Gordon's arm tighter and lowered her head to his shoulder as if she no longer possessed the strength to keep it raised. He glanced round the room and coughed politely, patting her gently on the back. 'Now, now, Mrs Scambles—'

'*Eleanora*, please,' she insisted, miraculously finding the power to raise her head, at least momentarily.

'Mr Bucket is a very experienced man in these matters and he assures me that no one could possibly know of your current whereabouts, and so could not know where to be waiting for you. Have no fear on that account.'

'But why do you think someone might be after me, James? Why did that evil person invade my house and behave in such an ungentlemanly fashion towards me? Do you think he could be the *real* murderer of Edward Mizzentoft?'

'Mrs … Eleanora, I must remind you that until some solid evidence to the contrary comes to light, as far as the law is concerned your husband remains the killer and will stand trial within a very few weeks.'

She let out strangled sob and drew herself even closer, this time clutching his hand. Hers was not cold with fear as he had expected, but delightfully soft and warm. Gordon felt the heat rising within him, both of public embarrassment and of … something else. 'To think I stared into the eyes of a cold-blooded murderer in my own home – yet no one believes me! Who is a poor woman to turn to?'

He tried to shuffle apart from her a little without seeming unsympathetic, yet when she lifted her head from its resting place on his arm her large, moist blue eyes were still so close as to fill his field of vision.

'Eleanora, there is no easy way to broach this subject …. There are other people who might have an interest in your husband for reasons which could have nothing to do with the murder ….'

'Whatever do you refer to, James?'

'Were you – are you – aware that Dr Scambles was … financially embarrassed?'

She let out a tinkling little laugh. 'Don't be silly, James!'

'I'm afraid it's true. I have to tell you that we now know that he was very heavily in debt.'

'Sir, if Jonathan had owed people money I should certainly have known of it. He was a *very* successful doctor!'

'I'm sure he was. But the detective in charge of the case is equally sure that at some point your husband began to pay out very large amounts to the deceased on a regular basis. The bank has confirmed that your husband was – is – greatly overdrawn.'

Mrs Scambles' lips parted and closed more than once as this information slowly began to sink in. Her gaze passed right through Gordon, perhaps into the black abyss of her own future. Finally, she gasped. *'Overdrawn? Then it's gone. All of it.'*

'I do fear so.'

Her classically shaped lips narrowed and tightened, and the paleness of shock in her features turned into heated flush of rage before Gordon's very eyes – and this time he knew it was not an act.

The veins in her neck stood out; her bosom heaved quicker and quicker. *'Then let him hang!'*

Gordon couldn't have been more shocked had she torn off her own dress in full view of everyone in the room. 'Mrs Scambles ... Eleanora ... there might very well be some explanation for his misfortune of which we are—'

'Oh, there certainly is an explanation,' she spat, almost as if it were her husband before her and not Gordon. *'Greed!* Greed and foolishness. Yes, he is a clever man when it comes to facts and figures, anatomical diagrams and bodily organs. But he is ignorant of the ways of the world, and he is ignorant because he is cold, aloof, unable to understand what people think, what they feel.'

Gordon was stunned into silence by this abrupt revelation of a side to the woman he could never have guessed at, and he could only let her continue.

'He never loved me, James, not even at the start. He was only interested in me as a plaything, something to be kept in a box and brought out to amuse him whenever the mood took him – and that particular mood soon become more and more infrequent. I remained loyal to him because he let me entertain myself with his money, no matter how extravagant my desires. Now I know that not only did he make a fool of me in that respect, but that there will be nothing for me whether he lives or dies – so I say let him meet the fate he deserves!'

If it had been any other person, Gordon would have put this display of callousness down to the shock of all she had been through, but in Mrs Scambles' case he could tell that she was in complete control of her faculties, and no platitudinous mumblings from his lips would have had the slightest effect. Gordon didn't doubt, having met him, that all she said about her husband was true: that he was as cold and unfeeling as she said. But to wish one's own husband *dead*?

He now saw this woman, for whom he had felt so much pity, in a completely different light. Yet once more she leaned closer to him. 'When he's dead I shall be free. I am well aware that policemen do not earn a great deal but I no longer care about such things. I realize now that it's warmth I crave, James. Warmth and passion – and those are the things I feel for you ....'

The hand which had been grasping his arm slid upwards and caressed his bare neck, and Gordon fought against the images which flashed into his mind. He pulled back from her. 'But your husband is still very much alive, Mrs Scambles. And he has not even faced trial. For all we know a jury might clear him, so it would be improper to dwell on such things.'

She smiled. It was a smile which said she could see into him, and it was disconcerting.

'At this juncture of our lives you and I are made for one another, James. I know it, and so do you.'

Mr Bucket had the faintest of smiles on his face as he approached Peterborough House, number 22 Upper Grosvenor Street in Mayfair, for he had already mentally played out this little scene in advance. He bounced up the immaculately scrubbed steps and rapped on the blue door in which he could see his reflection as clearly as if it were a mirror. After a minute passed he was greeted by the faintly disdainful gaze of the butler Chuddersby – whom Bucket now knew was in fact the criminal – former or otherwise – Alfred Jukes. Bucket also knew that he was both expected and recognized, yet the servant stood before him impassively, looking down his nose as he might to a hawker who had inadvertently come to the front entrance instead of the back. Mr Bucket took the initiative, and instead of waiting to introduce himself he swept past the butler, who followed hard on his heels protesting ineffectually.

'*Sir! But ... sir*!'

'The drawing room, is it?' Mr Bucket said breezily, pausing only to hand over his hat and cane. 'I'll see myself up. I always remember the layout of a house – as I'm sure you do, Jukes. Good day!'

And with that he skipped up the broad stairway. He didn't turn back to watch the gradual transformation of Jukes's expression after the unexpected declaration of his true identity, but he could imagine it.

Lady Rhynde, the wife of the Home Secretary, happened to be already in the drawing room. She was sitting at a writing desk by the window, drawing up her household accounts and she didn't even notice the detective enter, such was his ability to materialize almost supernaturally in a room. Thus, when he gave a polite little cough, her ladyship started somewhat and spun round to face the door.

'Oh, it's you Inspector Bucket. You weren't announced ....'

'Begging your ladyship's pardon,' the detective said with little bow. 'Your butler was attending to my belongings and I thought I would show myself up – not expecting you to be present.'

She sanded off the ink of her recent entries, closed the ledger and came over to shake Mr Bucket's hand. Hers was a slender, distinctly feminine hand, but the detective noticed traces of roughened skin and earth under her nails, which told him that she was not afraid of a little manual labour – perhaps in the garden.

'Have you made any progress regarding the theft of the ferns? I still feel embarrassed that the police's finest brains have to devote themselves to such trifles as this – although it does now appear to be a more common crime than I would ever have guessed. Almost everyone I speak to seems to have suffered the same fate as me!'

'When you say "almost everyone", might certain of those people belong to the society your ladyship is concerned with?'

'I am active in a number of societies, Mr Bucket. One has time on one's hands, and one likes to put it to good use.'

'Most commendable, madam,' he confided, patting her on the shoulder in a way that people don't normally touch the wife of the Home Secretary – but it made her smile.

'There was one very worthy institution I particularly recall.' Mr Bucket's sturdy right forefinger hovered before his face like a conductor's baton. 'It was the National Truss Society for the Relief of the Ruptured Poor.'

'Well, yes, that is one of my—' The light of realization suddenly spread across Lady Rhynde's finely sculpted features. 'Yes, Mr Bucket! There *does* seem to be a significant number of members of that society who have experienced the loss of ferns. Do you think someone with *inside information* knows when we are out?'

'Upon my soul, I do declare that one of her ladyship would be worth any ten sergeants in the Detective!' Mr Bucket exclaimed – but his finger was still waggling, signifying that there was more to the matter than had thus far been exposed. 'Someone who knows when you are out is a definite possibility. But another is someone who knows when your ladyship is *in*.'

'I'm not quite sure what you mean, Mr Bucket. But either way might there be a simple solution? I can hardly believe that any lady who is selfless and compassionate enough to devote her time and energies to good causes would stoop to crude theft. However ... I would not wish to tread on your professional toes, but ....'

'Tread away, your ladyship. I place too high a value on your analytical skills to allow my pride to get in the way of solving the case!'

'Might it be so simple a matter as to ascertain which lady or ladies who belong to the Society have *not* had ferns stolen, and focusing your attentions there?'

'That might be the case if I were investigating a crime committed by one of the lower orders of person, madam. But a lady of discernment and intelligence, even though not versed in the ways of the criminal classes, might not lay herself open to detection quite so easily.'

'Then one of my ladies is a master criminal – how exciting!'

'Do any names spring readily to your ladyship's' mind?'

Lady Rhynde laughed gaily. 'No one, I'm sure Mr Bucket ....' But then her face grew suddenly darker.

'Prey tell me what it is, madam. There's no good in keeping it back.'

'Oh ... it is nothing. A misunderstanding between myself and another member of the Society – but nothing which might lead to something so base as theft.'

'I do believe your ladyship is already enough of a detective to be aware that *anything* out of the ordinary is of interest to an investigator.'

But her ladyship was adamant. 'I'm afraid it is not something I could not bring myself to repeat to another soul, and which, anyway, cannot be relevant to this case. Besides, others who are on far friendlier terms with this person than I have also had ferns stolen.'

'Very well, my lady. I will continue to pursue this matter to the best of my ability and keep you informed of any progress. Oh, but I must ask your ladyship one further question. It is about your butler Chuddersby.'

'Yes?'

'Have you noticed anything different or unusual about his behaviour these last few weeks?'

Lady Rhynde thought for a moment, then shrugged. 'Nothing comes to mind. He does return to his former employer, Baroness Sowerby quite often – he says she is helping him with a little trust fund she helped him set up. He puts a small amount aside from his wages each week.'

'Isn't that something you could easily assist him with?'

'I'm sure it would be if he asked. He seems to prefer to stick with Baroness Sowerby since she is the one whose idea it was and who started the ball rolling.'

'It was her idea? How common is it for a person of her station in life to involve themselves in their servants' financial affairs?'

'It is not unknown, but I suppose it is hardly a regular occurrence.'

'And how often would you say he visits Baroness Sowerby?'

'Not so frequently lately, but for a time it was once a week – sometimes more. Mr Bucket, you have aroused my interest now. Do you read something suspicious into all this?'

'Let's just say it is of interest to me.'

Gordon's meeting with Mrs Scambles not having taken long, he arrived at the area around the Haymarket and Leicester Square, which seemed to specialize in racket courts, gaming houses and the like, and after obtaining guidance from a passing muffin man, his tray balanced precariously on his head while still somehow managing to ring his hand bell with great vigour, he ascertained the whereabouts of Mr George's shooting gallery. Following his directions, Gordon found his footsteps echoing along a long a whitewashed passage which opened out into a dingy, grimy courtyard, and there in front of him was a large brick building bearing the sign: *GEORGE'S SHOOTING GALLERY &c.* The white lettering was weathered and faded, the '*&c*' in particular being in imminent danger of extinction. The court was deserted but for one man in a long black frock coat and a shiny black hat that looked brand new. He carried what Gordon immediately recognized to be a mahogany pistol case under one arm, and he was moving from window to window of George's establishment, peering in. Hearing Gordon approach, he turned.

'Place is quite empty, sir. Gas unlit, no sign of life at all. If you want to shoot I suggest Brady's just a short distance from here – you can walk with me if you wish.'

'Thank you, but it is Mr George himself I came to see.'

'Then I can't help you, sir. If he isn't here some assistant or other usually is. Most unusual. I'm off to Brady's.' He touched the rim of his hat and disappeared into the passageway.

Gordon, too, tried to look through the windows. He could just make out the targets at the far end of the main room: being painted white, they stood out in the gloom. He could also see some swords in a rack, and what looked like boxing mittens on a shelf. But no sign of Mr George or anyone else. There might be a thousand reasons why he had to be elsewhere, but what the man had told Gordon about there normally being some member of staff present, together with some inexplicable instinct of his own, told him that there might be more to this unexpected absence. He tried the door, but, as he had expected, it was locked, and since there seemed no point in knocking he decided there was nothing for it but to pace about this draughty, unappealing yard and await the arrival of Mr Bucket. But just as Gordon turned to begin his second circuit of the perimeter, he almost bumped into a figure standing by his right shoulder, and both parties cried out simultaneously.

'Beg your pardon, sir,' exclaimed a young woman cradling a baby in one arm. Gordon saw an open door across the court and guessed she must have been watching him for some time.

'That's quite all right. I was looking for Mr George, the owner of this establishment.'

'He were here no more than an hour ago, sir, but what's become of him I couldn't rightly say. There's been a number o' reg'lar shootin' and fencin' gentlemen a-knockin' since then. Odd, because Mr George can't hardly afford to lose custom, so they say.'

'And you have no idea where he might have gone, nor when he left?'

'Mr George,' intervened a familiar voice speaking in an unfamiliar tone, 'is in custody in Whitechapel.' It was Mr Bucket, who had materialized in his practised, stealthy manner. But he bore an expression Gordon had never seen before: grim, angry, humourless. It was such a look as to dissuade him from even asking for any further details. But the woman with them was not so easily cowed.

'Mr George locked up? Why, whatever for?'

'For murder, that's what.'

She put a hand to her mouth. 'Why, the man's incapable of it. Mind you, he's a very determined sort. Not the sort of man to be crossed ....'

'Mr George didn't commit no murder, missus, and don't you go putting it about that he did,' Mr Bucket warned her.

'But if he's been arrested ...' Gordon blurted out finally. 'I mean – *who?* Who is he supposed to have killed?'

'Tom Prike. A lad who I've known and looked out for since he was a babbie, and who I promised would come to no harm because of this business.'

'Business? But what *is* the business?' Gordon asked.

'The murder of Edward Mizzentoft.'

'But what can we do? It's not our affair, Mr Bucket.'

'Well, Mr Gordon, *it is now!'*

XIII

M R BUCKET SAID nothing as they made their way to the Leman Street police station in the East End. He walked briskly, jabbing his cane sharply down with each step as if driving it into the body of a fallen enemy. When someone greeted him from across the street – and someone seemed to know him wherever he and Gordon went – he either grunted tersely or even remained oblivious to the hail and pressed relentlessly on. They strode without pausing past people lounging in doorways, shellfish sellers, a row of houses-cum-shops owned by German sugar bakers, past a slop-maker's warehouse and out of a side street into broad Leman Street; about three-quarters of the way down, next door to the Garrick Theatre, they arrived at the station.

It was a dull, overcast, late winter's afternoon, and all the gas lamps inside appeared to be lit and quietly hissed away in the background. A constable was part-leading, part-carrying a drunken woman – almost certainly a prostitute – to the cells. Her mood was perfectly unalloyed by her imminent incarceration and she was giving a spirited rendition of *The Forsaken Gipsy* and encouraging all present to join in. It might have been an amusing scene under other circumstances, but Gordon, even though he had no personal knowledge of poor Tom Prike and had only met Mr George once, had become infected by Mr Bucket's mood and barely heeded this little vignette. They went straight up to the duty sergeant: a gaunt, stiffly moving man with just a streak of white hair on either side of his bald dome. Gordon could scarcely credit that he was not already well beyond retirement age. Just as the sergeant noticed them and was about to speak, Mr Bucket got the jump on him.

'Who arrested a certain Mr George for murder this afternoon? I want to see him – immediately, if you please.'

The sergeant took up a pair of spectacles from his desk and placed them on the end of his nose the better to see his forceful visitor. His tremulous hand only served to accentuate his appearance of advanced age. 'And 'oo might you be?'

'I am Inspector Bucket of the Detective Department of Scotland Yard, *that's* who I am.'

Gordon's superior's voice was not sharp, but certainly a little more strident than usual, and heads turned in their direction. The sergeant seemed to need no further explanation and he called out for a nearby constable to 'go and fetch Charlie'. Within a couple of minutes Charlie, in the person of Constable H27 Gradely, stood before them. He was in his thirties and heavily pockmarked about the face. If he felt any trepidation about being beckoned so summarily, he didn't betray it.

Without any preamble, Mr Bucket said, 'I wants to know why Mr George was arrested for the murder of young Tom Prike.'

'Because he was caught in the very act, sir.'

'You *saw* him killing the boy?'

'He was kneeling over the body with the bloody knife in his hand.'

'Then don't say "in the very act", lad. Don't put that in your report to go before a jury, because that's not what "in the very act" means and you should know that.'

Gordon felt that the inspector was being very harsh with a fellow officer, but thought it better to hold his tongue, for the time being at least.

'Pardon me, sir, but you weren't there, and if you had been—'

'Why were you there, Constable?'

'It happened on my beat, naturally.'

'How "naturally", though? Are you saying you just happened to be walking along and you came upon the bloody scene?'

'Not quite, sir.'

Gordon was impressed with the way the man maintained his poise and nerve under Mr Bucket's quick-fire and rather fierce examination.

'I was a couple of streets away following my normal route when I

109

was approached by a man who had witnessed the knifing himself. He described the culprit and told me where it was taking place. I sprang my rattle and rushed to the spot.'

'And you enjoined him to accompany you – he being a material witness and all?'

For the first time, the constable's air of quiet defiance faltered slightly. 'I did …. At first he ran beside me but he was older than me and not a strong runner, and he began to fall behind a little. By the time I came upon the scene I had to quickly detain the suspect and see to the victim's wounds. Other policemen, alerted by my rattle, were arriving … there was some confusion … and the man was no longer there.'

Mr Bucket could not conceal a slight tutting noise under his breath. The constable's neck stiffened, but he maintained a dignified silence. Gordon could not do so any longer.

'Mr Bucket, it is very unfortunate that his witness was allowed to leave the vicinity, but I'm sure under the same circumstances, when there appears to be a murderer to arrest and perhaps even a life which might still be saved, I might very well have been guilty of the same lapse.'

'That's because you are barely out of nappies as far as police work goes, Mr Gordon, whereas this man is a ten-year veteran and has no such excuse.'

PC Gradely bridled at this. 'Sir, if you have been inquiring into my police record I can assure you that—'

'I don't need to see no paperwork. The slight fraying of his cuffs,' explained Mr Bucket, addressing Gordon, 'and the way the crown has been all but worn away on the brass buttons of his coat indicate several years of service. The faint boot-print on the top of the chimney pot hat he carries under his arm – they use 'em for climbing or seeing over walls, Mr Gordon – indicates a man of some experience. And that make of hat itself is one they stopped issuing even when *I* wore the blue uniform. When you adds it up it comes to about ten years, by my reckoning.'

'Eight and a half, sir.'

'Those boot prints never quite come away no matter how much you rubs at 'em – and I can see you've rubbed mighty hard, lad. Just as well the hat's on your head with the top out of sight when they inspect uniforms on parade, eh?'

'It is, sir,' Gradely, allowing himself the faintest of smiles.

'Describe this vital witness who you allowed to wander away, lad,' said Mr Bucket. His tone was noticeably softer now, and Gordon wondered whether he was recalling some incident from his own days in uniform when he was similarly upbraided.

'He was a very tall man – even a little taller than your colleague here – and well dressed. Like a gentleman, yet somehow I sensed that he wasn't really a gentleman.'

'Why? Put it into words for me.'

'I ... I can't, sir. But I just *know*.'

'Good answer, Constable. Take note, Mr Gordon of that ilk. Always trust that feeling. You're a man that likes to be able to put things into words, that's what *you* are. A lot of what we do can't be put into words, but it don't make it any less suitable for all that.'

Constable Gradely's description of the man struck a chord with Gordon immediately. 'Did this man have long hair – over his collar at the back, and heavily oiled?'

The policeman thought hard. 'I barely glanced at him once he'd conveyed his news. Possibly long hair, yes, but I'm sure I couldn't say whether it was oiled or not.'

'Mr Gordon?' queried the inspector.

'It may be nothing, but this sounds like the description of the man who visited Mrs Scambles' home and caused us to remove her to your wife's sister's house.'

'It may be nothing, as you say, Mr Gordon.'

But Mr Bucket's chunky finger was in action, and Gordon knew, as he directed them to be taken to see Mr George, that he had made some sort of connection of his own, and that all would be revealed in due course.

Beaufort Edwin Scuttle was not in a good mood. The clerk before him was as impassive as a statue in Trafalgar Square. He did not – or would not – accept the gravity of the situation nor the need for a speedy resolution of the matter.

'You would not act to save the good name of a lady?' Mr Scuttle thundered, the cheeks of his fat face quivering. The dramatic effect of his remonstrance was somewhat diminished by the fact that the counter at the Whitechapel Register Office for Births, Deaths and Marriages was so high, and Mr Scuttle so short, that only his mottled red nose and the features above it were on view to the straight-faced clerk. Mr Scuttle's ridiculously tall hat, made of cheap felt for all its ostentation, could only go a little way towards making up for his lack of stature.

'The case is currently under investigation,' said the clerk calmly.

'But a good lady's *reputation* is at stake, sir!' spluttered Mr Scuttle. 'You would not expedite matters? What kind of man would not expedite matters to protect the name of a *lady*?'

'All cases at the Register Office are dealt with in the appropriate order. Always have been, always will be.'

'The government is good at prying into people's private businesses and writing it all down, from the day we're born till the day we die – and everything in between, what with this new Census thing as well. But you're not so quick to give us access to *our own information*! Look, my good fellow, when a man has travelled all the way from Sheffield and cannot remain in the capital indefinitely, when a man's sole object in life is to clear the name of his beloved sister who was cruelly duped by a bigamist – cannot the wheels of bureaucracy be made to move faster? Has bureaucracy no heart? This marriage must be *expunged*! *Annulled* forthwith, I say.'

'The Whitechapel Register Office is impartial in such things, sir, and acts according to due procedure in all cases.'

'Then I shall require your name, sir. I have connections, sir – *connections*!'

An exasperated Mr Scuttle eventually waddled from the Whitechapel Register Office to the Five Bells round the corner where he was reunited with Pikey Pratt, a renowned Sheffield tough who was drinking gin with some newly acquired friends. Mr Scuttle obtained a glass of rum and water and beckoned his companion to a quieter part of the room.

'It's no use, Pikey.' Mr Scuttle sighed as he sank into the chair; his magnificently sprouting and carefully groomed side whiskers seemed to droop in keeping with his mood.

'I *said* thee should'a took me in withee, sir,' said Pikey, shaking his close-cropped head wistfully. 'I'd soon've knocked some sense into them pasty-faced pen-pushers.'

'That sort of thing don't play in places like that.' The watery grey eyes deep in Mr Scuttle's round, piggy face suddenly lit up. *'Not during office hours, any road up!'*

'What's that, sir?'

'We've sorted that bastard Mizzentoft out our own way; perhaps it's time to do the same with the Whitechapel Register Office!'

Pikey rose to his feet. 'Like I said, sir, just leave 'em to me.'

'No, no. You have to play these people at their own game – outwit 'em! All it will take is a page torn out of a book. Mizzentoft himself is no more, and next it'll be as if the marriage between that scoundrel and my sister never existed. You go back and enjoy a drink with your pals, Pikey. But not too much. You're to meet me outside the Register Office at midnight tonight. Meantime, I'm going to have a little snoop round to see if there's a nice quiet back entrance to the place ....'

The cells at the rear of Leman Street police station stank of urine, vomit and various other, less easily identifiable odours. Gordon's eyes took some time to adjust to the darkness in there; there was no natural light at all, the only illumination coming from a couple of gas jets at either end of the narrow space which ran in front of the cell doors. PC Gradely led them along this walkway until they came to a door with a faded number 5 on it. He picked out a key from a bunch on his large, heavy ring, and opened the door, crying, 'Visitors!' He was about to go in first, but Mr Bucket spoke up.

'Would it be all the same to you if we have a quiet parley with Mr George on our own, Constable?'

PC Gradely nodded without hesitation and stepped aside. The cell was nothing more than a dank, whitewashed rectangular room with a straw mattress on the floor and a disgusting pail in one corner. Mr George was sitting on the mattress with his back propped against the wall. He looked up as they entered, but his sombre face registered neither surprise nor pleasure.

'Well,' said Mr Bucket. 'What's all this, eh, George?'

'I didn't do it,' came the disconsolate reply.

'I know that, George. And as from one man to another – and an old soldier likewise, mind you – I shall get to the bottom of this. On that you have my word. But how did such a thing come about, old man?'

'Like I told you yesterday, I had an inkling as to who might be able to tell me where young Tom could be found. This person – who shall remain nameless if that's all right with you, Mr Bucket—'

'It is, George. 'Course it is.'

'This person directed me to a lodging house in the Minories, and I set off this morning to see if I couldn't find him, or at least what had become of him. But when I came out of the court where the gallery is, I noticed a man lounging across the street. There was just something suspicious about him – and sure enough I soon suspected that he was following me. However, I made some sharp turns and deviations along my route and by the time I got close to the house where I was told Tom might be found, there was no sign of him. I went inside, only to be told that Tom had run an errand for someone to earn himself some money. When I came out, I feared I saw out of the corner of my eye the same man who had been following me hasten out of sight at the corner of the street, and my heart sank, Mr Bucket.'

'Don't blame yourself, George.'

'I waited a while, hoping Tom might soon return and I could both warn and protect him. But after a few minutes a feeling came over me that I must act, and I set off in the direction I had been told he had gone. When I reached the corner of Fenchurch Street, the man who had been following me came rushing in the opposite direction, nearly knocking me flying. I couldn't say whether he was chasing or being chased – but my darkest fears were confirmed when I passed an alley near the Royal Mint.' Mr George bowed his head and ran his fingers through his crisp dark hair. 'Poor Tom .... The next thing I knew, I heard the bobby's rattle.'

'The man you saw – the killer, George – he had the quick wit to finger you to a passing policeman as he was fleeing the scene. That's how come you ended up here.'

The poor old soldier made a sound that sounded like a sob. 'I was supposed to be looking out for him, and I led his killer *straight to him*! They might as well hang me – I as good as murdered him!'

'Now, now, George, let's hear no more talk like that. You've been outwitted, old man, that's what's happened to you – and me too, come to that, for if I'd been as sharp as I should have been that man might not have been at liberty to do such a thing. I take it he was very tall, with long, oiled hair?'

The trooper looked up at them for the first time. 'You know who he is, Mr Bucket?'

'I have a good idea, and if all comes to pass as I intend, it should be the key to proving your innocence. But until then, hold fast, Mr George, for I also plan to talk to a good brief I've crossed paths with on several occasions in the past.'

'I can't afford no lawyer, thanks all the same, sir.'

'Don't go a-worrying on that score. That will all be taken care of. And if he's as good at getting *you* let out as he is with folks I wish would stay locked up, then he's your man.'

A cold breeze swept along the banks of the Thames and whistled over the coal wharf at Shadwell. It was a little before one in the morning when the General's bulky outline materialized: a lumbering shape blacker than the blackness of the night, filling the stone pathway along the river like a silent landslide. The tide was high and the stinking water, glinting oily dark, lapped against the wharf. He saw another figure already waiting ahead of him, the outline of his head and shoulders rising above the ugly shape of a moored coal barge.

'That you?' He struck a lucifer, and in its yellow flare he saw his man: a very tall, slender figure.

'You're late.'

'Some business to take care of up Shoreditch way. Couldn't wait.'

A strong gust of wind extinguished what was left of the feeble flame and whipped up a froth on the surface of the Thames.

'Not in trouble, am I?' growled the General, not sounding partic-ularly troubled at the prospect.

'Well, you didn't do the job we agreed, did you?'

'But I provided the information and it was taken care of.'

'You weren't paid to provide information; you were paid to see it through.'

'He was just a slip of a lad! I don't know what you've heard about me, but—'

'Let's not argue about it. My Governor wants to reward you.'

'But ... I only did half the job – and you paid me for that.'

'The boss has been thinking. He wants to make sure the reward really is sufficient to ensure your silence.'

'What's that s'pposed to mean?'

'He's heard that you've been saying things when in drink, General. And that's worrying.'

'I ain't said nuthink, I swears! Mind you, if the Governor wants to give me more money to make sure I keep me trap shut, 'oo am I to complain?'

'Money? There is no more money, General.'

A rat scuttled across the path between them.

'But you said ....'

'I said you would be rewarded. There is only one way to reward a loud-mouthed drunk who puts others at risk.'

The General was a dull, slow-thinking man but in matters of personal survival he was a professor, a renowned authority. He heard rather than saw the muffled movement the tall man made in the darkness, but it was all he needed, and he pounced to take the initiative away from his enemy. What he could not see was the swordstick, nor how close it had already been extended towards his belly.

The worst part, strange to say, was that there was initially hardly any pain. The blade has gone so cleanly through – he felt it pushing the back of his jacket outwards – that at first the General felt almost nothing, just a sort of icy chill in his guts, spreading rapidly down to his groin. He had experienced agonies of all kinds, but this strange iciness was the worst feeling of his life. Yet he was still on his feet. That was the rule. Stay on your feet or you are a dead man. It occurred to the General that he was already was a dead man, but he vowed to himself that he would not be the only one this night. He made a grab for the handle of the sword, but it was even longer than he thought and he felt only more steel, cutting into the flesh of his palm. This *did* hurt, but he ignored the pain and the sticky feel of the blood oozing through his fingers. He stepped backwards suddenly, pulling the sword and the man holding it towards him, then snapped his head forwards with as much force as he could muster. He felt his forehead smash into flesh and bone – maybe a nose, maybe teeth, he couldn't tell. But there was a price. The violence of his attack pushed the sword further through his belly. He felt the hilt pressing against him, and now it hurt beyond belief and he screamed, unable to hide his pain any longer. But he knew his enemy was damaged too. He knew his man wasn't used to such punishment and wouldn't be able to take it, and with a roar which was a mix of agony and defiant anger, he threw a straight right and it hit home with a satisfying crunch. Now it felt as though his insides were falling out, but he had to finish the job. He reached out blindly and grabbed his man by whatever parts of his clothing he could, hurling him over the edge of the wharf and into the freezing water. There was a splash, then silence. No sound of gasping for breath, nor of the desperate thrashing of limbs in the murky Thames. He must have already been senseless before going under. The job was done. But his opponent had kept his hold on the sword, and as he fell the blade had been yanked right out of the General's body, but at a different angle, doing more damage as it exited. An explosion of lights and sounds filled the General's head so that it seemed as if it could only burst. He was unconscious before his face hit the ground.

XIV

'MR BUCKET, I must ask you – are we investigating the murder of Edward Mizzentoft, or at least the guilt or otherwise of Dr Scambles, or are we not?'

It was dark, and there was a chill, damp wind and a threat of rain in the air as they walked west along the Whitechapel Road and approached Aldgate. They had made slow progress since leaving Mr George at Leman Street police station. First, they found themselves offering assistance at the scene of a most unfortunate accident where a deaf, elderly gentleman had been struck from behind by a hansom and had his legs terribly mangled. (Gordon suspected he would not last long after they had made him comfortable and handed him over to the surgeon who had been summoned.) They then stopped to talk to one of Mr Bucket's underworld informants they happened upon at the corner of Goulston Street. Gordon realized full well by now that Mr Bucket had his ways, and very wise and successful ones at that. But the extent to which they were jeopardizing their professional relationship with Mr Stope – a detective equally experienced and as esteemed as Mr Bucket despite his reputation for ostentatious display and a rougher and more ruthless way of dealing with criminals – and also for that matter with their chief, Sir Marriot Ogle-Tarbolton, had been troubling him.

Mr Bucket's stout digit brushed the side of his nose, which Gordon took to be an interesting sign at the very least. 'You are an intelligent man, Mr James Alexander Gordon, and there's no gulling you. Not that I would wish to. But I have a very specific reason to want to keep things under my hat – or at least I did. Now, my old pal Tom Prike has been destroyed and the game has changed. Things will start to happen fast. Just bear with me for a day or two more, Mr Gordon of that ilk, for I say there will be a development ....'

He fell silent, and his ever-scanning eyes had once again fallen on something Gordon had not noticed. 'Just draw off a bit here, Mr Gordon,' he said, guiding him by the elbow towards the corner of an alleyway. They stood silently for a moment, and now Gordon could distinctly hear the sound of scuffling feet and what could have been a door or window being tried. Gordon looked up at the building before them. It was the Whitechapel Register Office, and he considered this a most unusual place for a cracksman to ply his trade. Mr Bucket, his stick raised like a hussar's sword, began to creep forward, motioning Gordon to follow as he did so. It took their eyes a few seconds to adjust to the gloom of the alley, but even before this they began to hear voices just a few yards away:

'Then try pulling up, not down.'

'Nah, still no good. Proper fast.'

'Pikey, can you put that little pane in without too much noise?'

'Aye – gimme thy scarf a second, sir.'

Before any damage could be done, Mr Bucket gave Gordon the nod and moved towards the two would-be burglars.

'We don't want any windows putting in. Makes such a mess!' he announced in his resounding tenor voice.

Gordon heard a scuffling of feet, and saw the taller of the two men make for his superior. They grappled, and since his accomplice didn't seem keen to join in the fracas, Gordon was free to help Mr Bucket. From behind, he thrust his forearm round the neck of the attacker and yanked him backwards. He was very strong and almost wrenched himself from Gordon's grasp, but Gordon had a good hold of him and applied more pressure to his windpipe. It had the desired effect of making him forget about fighting in order to concentrate on the more important matter of breathing. Before things could develop any further the voice of the smaller man rang out.

'Cease, Pikey! No use in all that. I'm certain that once we explain all, these gentlemen will look kindly upon us.'

'I try to look kindly on everybody, sir,' said Mr Bucket good-humouredly. 'But at present I can't look upon you no-how, and I'd be obliged if you and your friend would accompany me and mine into the street.'

So they all trooped back down the alley into the Commercial Road and stood beneath a street light outside the Register Office. 'So, what's all this about, eh?' Mr Bucket inquired.

The small man – who Gordon could now see was *very* small and dressed for all the world like a gentleman – stuck his chest out. 'May I ask to whom I am referring before I go having to justify my activities?'

'You may ask, and I shall tell. I am Inspector Bucket of Great Scotland Yard, and this is my colleague Mr James Alexander Gordon, the Seventh Earl of Drumnadrochit no less – although he might not mention it, not being big on titles himself.'

Gordon had long since given up trying to explain that he was not *yet* the seventh Earl of Drumnadrochit, and remained silent.

'Inspector? What do you inspect, sir, for you do not have the appearance of a policeman, even an off-duty one.'

''E *is* a peeler – I can smell it,' muttered the man called Pikey.

Mr Bucket turned and shot him a piercing look. 'A man who's already in trouble didn't ought to talk to an officer of the law like that. Won't do him any good, and might well make things much worse.' Then he turned back to his accomplice. 'I am from the detective branch, something you might not have heard of if you are recently arrived from Yorkshire as I guess from your accent. The fact is that *I* am a policeman and *you* are a fellow who was attempting to gain unlawful entry to these here premises.'

'Aye – and so would you have been if you were in my position.'

'Very unlikely. But tell me what that position is anyway.'

'It's a long story .... My sister was wedded to a chap named Mizzentoft – or at least she *thought* she was married to that reprehensible—'

Mr Bucket raised his finger and stopped the man in his tracks. 'Mizzentoft? As in, the late Mr Edward Mizzentoft?'

'The very same!'

Mr Bucket placed his hand on the man's shoulder. 'This is not a matter to be discussed in the cold streets. I must ask you to accompany me to Scotland Yard, where we'll be much more warm and cosy.'

*

Gordon hurried through Charing Cross and into Craven Street, just a short walk from Great Scotland Yard, his brain still trying to take in the implications of the sudden turn of events since they had taken Beaufort Scuttle and his henchman Pikey Pratt into custody. The windows of the Ten Bells, the favourite haunt of the detectives, glowed yellow in the gathering fog. Mr Stope was not hard to find, crowded though the pub was. He was leaning against the bar, head and shoulders above most others, his deep, husky but booming voice easily audible above the general hubbub as he ordered another round for his companions; there must have been half a dozen of these, mostly women but a couple of men also. They were gathered around the big man like satellites in the gravitational thrall of a larger body, hanging on his every word, laughing heartily at his jokes. Gordon was already aware that he spent his money much more freely than Mr Bucket did and dressed in a much more flamboyant way. He knew that within the Force his abilities were every bit as admired as those of Mr Bucket, but on the whole he considered himself fortunate to have been placed under the tutelage of the latter.

'Mr Ogle-Tarbolton sends his compliments and asks if you would join him at the Yard, Mr Stope,' he ventured, hovering at the border of his coterie, trying to make himself heard. Gordon was certain he did hear him, and indeed glanced his way with the briefest flick of his eyes. But for some reason he chose not to answer. It was only when Gordon cleared his throat and repeated his request that Mr Stope could drag himself away from the convivial gathering. Before he left, Gordon saw him whisper something in the ear of a gaudily made-up woman; she laughed raucously and slapped him on the back as he turned away.

'What's this about?' asked Mr Stope rather tetchily as they returned to Great Scotland Yard.

'Mr Bucket and I have inadvertently made a discovery which might have a bearing on your murder case – Edward Mizzentoft.' He found himself tensing as he said this, and tried to place a subtle emphasis on the word *your*. And when Mr Stope glanced at him darkly, Gordon quickly added, 'It was quite by chance – we were on our way from Leman Street police station after interviewing an old acquaintance of Mr Bucket, and we stumbled upon an attempted burglary. One of the persons we apprehended claimed to be the brother of a woman Mizzentoft bigamously married. We have subsequently discovered that he and his accomplice had been heard making threats to the wife of Mr Mizzentoft.'

He expected Mr Stope to dismiss this business brusquely. He did, after all, already have his man as far as he was concerned.

'What is this man's name?' he asked finally.

'Scuttle, sir.'

He fell silent, and for the rest of the short walk remained nothing more than a big, dark brooding presence casting its shadow over Gordon.

'Gentlemen,' began Sir Marriot Ogle-Tarbolton. He seemed ill at ease, and allowed himself to become distracted by some papers on his desk, which were apparently sticking out of a folder at an unacceptably irregular angle and needed to be straightened before matters could proceed any further. Gordon also noticed a sort of tic in a left eyebrow – something that his superior had warned him was a sign that their chief's mind was agitated. At the time, this had sounded like one of Mr Bucket's little jokes, but there it was, subtle but clear to see.

'Gentlemen … ' he began again. 'There has been a development in the case of the murder of Mr Edward Mizzentoft – perhaps I should say developments, in the plural, since it is apparent that the events of this evening are only the latest in a number of what, at the time, seemed mere coincidences. But the cumulative effect of these findings has now caused me to think again about this case.'

Gordon surreptitiously looked to Mr Stope's face for his reaction. It was hard to read and yet the very stoniness of it somehow raised the level of edginess in the room. Even Mr Bucket seemed to shift rather uneasily in his chair as they all sat in a semi-circle facing their chief behind his big desk.

Eventually Mr Stope uttered but one word, yet it had the effect of heightening the tension like someone tweaking the string of a violin close to breaking point.

'*Apparent?*'

'Mr Stope?' queried Sir Marriot, his chubby, cherub-like cheeks flushing slightly.

'All of this intelligence about *my* case has become *apparent* to you. How, sir, has it all become *apparent* to you?'

He glared at Mr Bucket, who immediately knew the meaning of what was being asked.

'Now, Billy—'

'No, Bucket. I've been patient, very patient in this matter and the time has come to seek an explanation and a resolution.'

Gordon hated to see these long-time friends and professional colleagues at loggerheads like this. And although Mr Stope's face and posture remained impassive he could sense his profound anger and sense of betrayal lay just beneath the surface like a smouldering volcano.

'Gentlemen, gentlemen … ' Sir Marriot protested ineffectually.

'You forget that *I* know the difference between what you say and what you do,' continued Stope. 'I know how you operate.'

'Honourably always, I hope, Billy,' replied Mr Bucket.

Gordon felt obliged to intervene on his superior's behalf. 'I can assure you, Mr Stope, that Mr Bucket has acted – and has cautioned me to act – only with the utmost professionalism. It's just that our quite separate investigations have brought us into contact with people who have transpired to be in some way connected with the Mizzentoft case.'

'Were you aware,' said Sir Marriot, his left eyebrow twitching quite noticeably now, 'that a Mr Beaufort Scuttle travelled from Sheffield to London only days before Mizzentoft's murder with the apparent intention of avenging his unfortunate sister who had been duped into a bigamous marriage with him?'

'Scuttle is all mouth and no trousers,' growled Stope. 'He ain't no killer.'

'But did you *talk* to him, Billy?' Mr Bucket asked gently.

'My snitches told me all I needed to know.'

'And someone has taken it upon themselves to silence Mrs Scambles in her attempts to prove her husband's innocence,' said Mr Bucket. Then his voice took on a graver tenor. '*And* someone has done for Tom Prike, who appears to have had some knowledge of Mizzentoft's murder. Now, Billy, no one is going to bother doing *that* unless the lad had knowledge of something that has not yet come to light – don't you see?'

'Tom Prike had all sorts of knowledge of all sorts of things that might have got him into trouble. He was always going to end up dead.'

Mr Bucket bridled. 'Well Tom Prike was under my protection *and I shall find whoever killed him and bring them in—*'

Mr Stope rose to his feet. 'If it's directly connected with my case—'

'If looking into Tom's death leads me to someone connected with the Mizzentoft murder then I'll look at that side of things too!'

Voices were raised now. This was the closest Gordon had seen Mr Bucket come to losing his temper, and it even seemed to give Mr Stope pause for thought.

'It is clear to me,' intervened the chief, 'that although there is still every reason to believe that Dr Scambles killed Edward Mizzentoft, there is a chance that we are missing something here. Perhaps he had an accomplice; perhaps he even paid someone else to do the deed for him. I don't know, but I do believe there are some loose ends and so I am instructing Mr Bucket to pursue the lines of inquiry which fate has placed before him. You are free to do the same, Billy. If you believe there is nothing more to be learned then continue with your current case, but if you wish to make any further investigation then by all means do so. But both of you must keep me informed of your progress.'

'That goes without saying,' replied Mr Bucket. His fat forefinger rubbed the side of his nose. Mr Stope saw this, and promptly stalked out of the room, scowling darkly.

XV

G ORDON WAS IN a sombre, reflective mood when he made his way to Great Scotland Yard the following morning. He circumnavigated Whitehall Place to reach their entrance at the rear, pausing only to absently hand a few pennies to an old sailor with one arm begging on the corner. It troubled him that their own delvings into the Montague Street murder, however justified and well-intended, had threatened to breach not only the professional, but also the personal relationship between Mr Bucket and Mr Stope. Their friendship was a long-standing one, and Gordon hated the thought that this was becoming such a serious matter that permanent damage might be done.

From what he had learned of Mr Bucket in the short time he had been working with him, he trusted both him and his judgement implicitly, yet certain questions continued to haunt him. Should they have gone to Mr Stope earlier with their suspicions, their information? And if this all were to lead to a terrible breach between those two respected and long-serving policemen, how much would Gordon personally be to blame? He might have been new to the detective branch but he was no innocent abroad. He was a former cavalry officer with a fair amount of experience of the world and of how professional men who regularly work in close proximity must learn to accommodate one another's feelings and foibles. Last night he had sensed a very deep unease within Mr Stope's breast, one that wouldn't easily or quickly be assuaged.

Just as Gordon was about to go through the big double doors of the police station he was almost knocked over as they burst open and several burly uniformed men came running out, truncheons already drawn. Sergeant Raddle was at the front desk and before Gordon

125

made his way to the office he shared with Mr Bucket he asked him what was the matter.

'A serious disturbance of the peace in among the Thames watermen. Something to do with poaching one another's fares. Very tough and strong in the arm, those watermen.'

Before he could reach the stairs, Mr Raddle called out again: 'Oh, and Mr Bucket says will you meet him down in the holding cells.'

He must have detected Gordon's momentary hesitation – he had not even visited the holding cells yet – because he pointed with his stubby pencil towards one of several highly polished oak doors. It was in the far corner of the foyer, and led directly to another world entirely. The very second he crossed its threshold he found himself in a much bleaker space: a drab, ill-lit stairway along which a mildly dank smell was wafted on a chill draught from below. Gordon's eyes were still adjusting to this darker place beneath the well-lit environment above so it took him a second to recognize the solidly proportioned figure leaning calmly against a wall in the act of lighting a pipe. Apart from Mr Bucket's contented puffing, the only other sound he could hear was a hacking cough from one of the prison cells which lined both sides of this dismal corridor, and the almost incongruous sound of contented snoring emanating from another one further along.

'Good morning, Mr James Alexander Gordon.'

'And a good very morning to you, Mr Bucket. What news of our prisoners of last night?'

'Slept tolerable well, or so I'm told, and ate of a hearty Scotland Yard breakfast. Now it's time for business.'

As he began to seek out the correct key from the bunch he had fished out of his pocket, Gordon tapped him on the shoulder. 'What did you make of the Scuttle connection with the Mizzentoft case, sir? Mr Scuttle certainly had good reason to lose his temper with him if this bigamy charge is correct.'

'And his companion Pikey assuredly seems as though he would be both willing and capable of enforcing any dubious requests from his master. We must look into it,' he said, and added with a wink: 'without giving too much away ourselves.'

They entered the cell and Mr Bucket greeted the prisoners

cordially. 'Trust you had a pleasant night, gentlemen! We do pride ourselves here at Great Scotland Yard in providing a superior form of bed and board for our guests.'

'One o' the best I've come across, all right,' replied Pikey the henchman in all seriousness.

Mr Beaufort Scuttle was not in quite so sanguine a temper. His extravagant side-whiskers were all askew and his ruddy features were so puffy that his little eyes seemed embedded in his face even more deeply than usual, almost to the point of disappearing entirely. He chuntered of indignity, rights and of being confined like a common criminal.

'Well, you very likely would have become a common criminal had not Mr Gordon and myself happened along and saved you from yourself,' smiled Mr Bucket, settling himself down beside Pikey on the wooden bench, which also served as a bed. 'So let us consider it a small price to pay. Even as it is, my sergeant here is seriously considering what the charge is to be: loitering with intent, attempted burglary of Her Majesty's Register Office, attempted fraudulent tampering with official government records. The list is almost endless. Almost a question of sticking a pin in, one might say.'

'It's the *marriage* that were fraudulent,' croaked Scuttle in a first-thing-in-the-morning sort of voice.

'But these things have to be sorted out proper, like. Not by breaking and entering and falsifying official documents. I've often had a yearning to falsify the date my birth certificate, but if we all gave in to such yearnings, why where would the world be then, Mr Scuttle?'

'But I didn't want to *falsify* owt! It was only my intention to *remove* something false, harmlessly and without violence or undue damage. Merely make the record of that monster's sham marriage to my innocent sister disappear. Nobody would have been any the worse for it.'

'I don't know owt about no paperwork, but we sorted that Mizzentoft out good and proper, didn't we!' chuckled Pikey.

Gordon shot a glance at Mr Bucket. 'Sorted him out?'

'Never knew what hit him!'

'Pikey!' barked Scuttle, though with a half-smirk on this chubby face.

127

'Never knew?' repeated Mr Bucket. 'Could it be he never knew because you sorted him out *too* well? Got a bit carried away?'

Scuttle snorted with derision. 'Nonsense.'

Gordon rose and, for effect – or so he hoped – stood over the man, who was a good foot shorter than himself. 'Edward Mizzentoft is dead.'

Mr Scuttle's face was a picture. *'Dead?'*

'Murdered, by person – or persons – unknown,' Mr Bucket added.

Scuttle turned to his thug. 'What the hell did you do, man? You were supposed to break his fingers, not *kill* him!'

'I didn't kill 'im, I didn't! I ... didn't even break 'is fingers.'

'Why not?' Scuttle demanded.

'I tried – but they was all sort of *flexible* ....'

Pikey suddenly jumped to his feet. 'Hey! This is one o' them fit-ups, that's what this is!'

'You'll sit down if you know what's good for you,' Mr Bucket warned him, before calmly taking a drag from his pipe. 'No one's being accused. But put yourself in my position, gentlemen. A policeman asks himself: *Who had a reason to kill the victim? Who were the last people to see him alive?* That's what he asks himself, and then he seeks out that person – or persons.'

Scuttle's face reddened and his flabby cheeks and chins began to wobble. He had woken that morning expecting to face some minor charge if any at all, and the implications of this new development seemed to hit him all at once.

'Well, we weren't the last people to see 'im alive, and that's God's truth!' Pikey shouted in a tone that was half-challenging, half-imploring.

'Pikey!' admonished his employer.

'Of course,' continued Mr Bucket serenely, almost as if he were thinking out loud to himself, 'if we were to find that you gentlemen weren't the last to see Mr Mizzentoft alive. If it transpired to be someone else ... someone with a *name* ....'

'It was!' cried Pikey. 'It *was!*'

Scuttle turned on his assistant, beads of sweat forming on his forehead. 'Don't thee go spinning no yarns and getting us into more trouble. It won't work. We didn't even know he were dead,

Inspector. Surely thee can tell when a man's telling the truth in your line of work.'

'More often than not,' smiled Mr Bucket. 'And I know you are.' But he turned to Pikey and his smile broadened. He didn't have to say anything. The big man shuffled uncomfortably and he stared at his feet.

'Pikey?' queried Scuttle. 'Tell me once and for all – you didn't kill the feller?'

'No. But I knew 'e were dead. Some blokes blabbed about it once they'd had a few pints. And they mentioned a name.'

'Why didn't you tell Mr Scuttle?' Gordon asked.

'I knew he'd think it were me what done it.'

'Why didn't you tell the police – if only to absolve yourself and Mr Scuttle here from the blame?'

'Because they said anyone 'oo snitched on him would end up the same as Mizzentoft. Easiest just to forget it.'

'Oh, for God's sake. All I wanted to do was clear my sister's good name.'

'That will take place in good time and by the proper method,' said Mr Bucket. He rose and placed himself before Pikey.

'Name.'

Pikey shook his head, refusing even to look directly at Mr Bucket.

Gordon expected a battle of wills, but to his surprise his superior turned away with a shrug.

'All the same to me. Any court would convict these two on my word, and as the men with the motive and wherewithal, boasting of how they sorted the murdered man out. I dare say Mr Pike here has made that boast on several occasions in front of his new London drinking buddies, and if so I'll find 'em. If I can't get the right man I'll get the next best thing just as long as I get someone – I'm known for it in these parts, aren't I Mr Gordon?'

Gordon forced myself to maintain a straight face and nodded gravely.

They started to leave the cell, and for a second Gordon thought the ruse was going to fail. Scuttle began whimpering like a scolded puppy, and as soon as Mr Bucket's hand touched the door handle, Pikey cracked.

'The General. They said 'e calls himself the General. Collected debts for Mizzentoft, but something went bad between 'em and they say the General did for 'im. I don't know what 'is real name is, but—'

'Don't matter,' said Mr Bucket. 'We know all about the General.'

XVI

M R BUCKET LED the way back up the stairs. 'The General, eh? What do you make of it, Gordon?'

'I certainly believe him to be capable of it. If this news is true about his connection to Mizzentoft – plus the fact that he withheld it from us when we spoke to him, well ....'

'Well indeed, sir. Now I have Mr George to attend to, so while I'm a-looking into that I should like you to—'

They had just emerged into the relative brightness of the foyer, but there was a shadow cast upon them. It was Inspector Stope. He didn't speak for a moment; he simply blocked their path. His stony countenance, though, spoke volumes. Just as Gordon feared some sort of unpleasant confrontation was about to take place, he uttered two words.

'Evidence Room.'

That was all. He turned his back on them and began to walk away. Gordon looked at Mr Bucket, who nodded for him to follow. The Evidence Room was yet another part of this labyrinthine building Gordon had yet to visit, but he had heard of it. As he trailed after Mr Stope he observed the broadness of his shoulders and his short, thick neck, and the way his heavy step made the wooden floor vibrate as he walked. They followed him along a corridor at the back of the building and through an unmarked door, finding themselves in a large, drab, windowless room. Gordon could just make out in the shadows lots of shelves: fixed ones along all the walls, and large, free-standing ones down the length of the room. Mr Stope took a box of matches from his pocket and proceeded to light two gas lamps on the walls, then a paraffin lamp on a desk, which stood just inside the door. And it was from this light that Gordon first saw the massive safe in the corner behind the door. It was at least a yard high, and looked so bulky and heavy he couldn't imagine how many men it might take to lift it.

Mr Bucket's soft voice broke the silence. 'There's no need for all this you know, Billy ....'

Mr Stope ignored this, and proceeded to turn the dial of the safe backwards and forwards as he fed in the combination, performing with the speed of familiarity. There was a final click, and the door, which was at least four inches thick, swung open silently. He reached inside and pulled out a small wooden box. He carried it past Bucket and Gordon to the table, where he placed it down and opened it as they gathered round him. Under the yellow light of the paraffin lamp he produced a small item wrapped in brown paper, which he carefully opened up. The item he had brought them to see was a silver watch. Mr Stope placed it on the table and stood back into the shadows.

'Now have a look.'

Mr Bucket hung back, so Gordon crouched over the table. At first he hesitated to even pick it up, and just moved it around so that it was in a better light. He could see that it was well made and fairly expensive, but not of the first quality. It appeared to be of silver. But then other things began to catch his attention. The chain was broken – at least half the length it should have been, with the final link clearly wrenched apart by some force. And there were dark spots on the face and edges of the case. At last he picked it up, making sure not to touch the stained areas, and held it closer to the light. There were several more small spots on the back, and one larger one.

'This is blood.' Gordon felt certain he was right, but he glanced over his shoulder for confirmation and saw Stope nod.

And now something else caught Gordon's eye. Beneath the engraved manufacturer's name some initials had been added in a different, extravagantly italic style.

JS.

He straightened up. 'JS. Jonathan Scambles.'

'This was at the scene of the murder in Montague Place, then, Billy? Why didn't you say, old man?'

'Because it's *my case*. Because I never thought there would be any need to prove *my case* to another detective. I'll do that before a jury, and successfully.'

'Mr Stope,' Gordon said. 'Please try to understand that certain things kept coming to light purely by chance as we dealt with other matters. Things that didn't *prove* anything so we didn't feel able to—'

But Stope was already on his way out of the room, leaving them to lock the evidence away again.

Gordon let out a deep sigh. 'Have we handled this in the correct manner, Mr Bucket?'

'I do hope so, Mr Gordon of that ilk. Now you go and escort Mrs Scambles back to her home, something which I know will relieve Mrs Bucket's sister greatly.'

'But won't she be in danger?'

'Not any longer. Off you go. I'll meet you back in the office first thing in the morning.'

Gordon obediently left Mr Bucket, but looked back from the doorway before he departed. The inspector was gazing intently at the back of the silver watch, like a man reading a cipher.

XVII

THE COMMITTEE OF the National Truss Society for the Relief of
the Ruptured Poor met on a monthly basis, the venue rotating
between the homes of the various committee members. This month,
the six esteemed ladies, among the cream of London society, were
gathered at the Mayfair residence of Dame Agnes Bludger. Advance
preparations for the Spring Bazaar were under way. Arrangements
for the fund-raising soirée at the end of February, to which such
eminent personages as Lord Pickance and Admiral Welchet had
graciously agreed to lend their patronage, were all but complete. A
debate on the merits of organizing a raffle – which to some members
had too strong a whiff of gambling about it for it to be considered
acceptable – was interrupted by the arrival of refreshments, and the
ladies took a break from their labours. Lady Rhynde wished to speak
to Lady Bligh about obtaining cuttings from her amaranthus; but
Lady Bligh was already in conversation with Baroness Sowerby, and
Lady Rhynde had certain reasons for wishing to avoid the company
of Baroness Sowerby. She veered away from those two ladies and
found herself gravitating towards the nearest window, where she
gazed down upon the well-wrapped pedestrians, and the steamy
breath issuing from the noses of the horses as they pulled their
various conveyances along the frosted roads.

But her reverie did not last. Mrs Honoria Rusely had spied her
fellow committee member's lack of company, and it was not long
before she had Lady Rhynde pinned into a corner and was subjecting
her to a passionate discourse on the wonders of her pet subject –
phrenology.

'You see, my dear, if *all* of the lower classes might be subjected to
phrenological screening – a perfectly painless and speedy process –

then those with obviously criminal protuberances might be separated out from the rest of society.'

Mrs Honoria Rusely had a disconcerting way of standing uncomfortably close to her captive audience. Lady Rhynde had already backed away as discreetly as possible several times and now she could retreat no further, and had to endure Mrs Rusely's stale breath, and her entire field of vision being filled by the woman's rheumy eyes and jowly undulations.

'Is the reading of lumps and bumps of one's head really to be relied upon to discern criminal tendencies in people?'

'Oh, it is entirely infallible, my dear.'

'But then there might be a large number of such persons. What would one do with them? Particularly taking into account the fact that they would not yet have committed any crime.'

Mrs Rusely swatted away these mere details with the sweep of a fleshy white hand. 'Perhaps not committed any crime *known to the authorities*! They might be allowed to live within special enclosures – perhaps built on ground which is marshy or otherwise unsuited for normal human habitation or cultivation. Or sent to some uninhabited or sparsely populated savage country in the same way that convicted criminals are transported to Van Dieman's Land – with adequate food and clothing, naturally. Such persons are used to having little and surviving on their wits. There can be little doubt but that they should manage.'

'Naturally.' Lady Rhynde looked about the room for some effective yet polite means of escape.

'The problem is, of course, that to get such a large-scale undertaking off the ground would require the backing of at least one prominent public figure.' She placed her podgy hand on Lady Rhynde's shoulder in a conspiratorial sort of way. '*Preferably* one well-placed in the government .... '

This was the moment Lady Rhynde had been expecting and dreading. Her husband's position as Home Secretary meant that she was not infrequently seen as an indirect means of access to Sir Dalton Rhynde by those with plans and schemes for reforming or strengthening the law enforcement or criminal justice systems.

'I believe that the subject of phrenology has been brought to Sir

Dalton's attention in the past, and I have no doubt but that he has given the matter a great deal of thought.'

'But has he heard of the latest theories of Professor Schlumpf of Switzerland? Some of his ideas elevate the whole subject to new levels of perspicacity and sophistication! Allow me to tell you something of his method, my dear ….'

Lady Rhynde scanned the room again, and this time her eyes met those of Baroness Sowerby. Keen though she was to escape the clutches of Mrs Honoria Rusely, she was a preferable companion to the baroness – but that was of no consequence, for Baroness Sowerby was coming to join them.

'Ah, Henrietta! We were just discussing the fascinating subject of phrenology and how it might be made use of to weed out criminal types *before* they have had a chance to transgress.'

'They do say that prevention *is* better than cure, Mrs Rusely.'

'My feelings entirely! Would you care to join our little campaign?'

'I should be delighted to lend my support.' Baroness Sowerby was looking up at the two taller ladies, her sharp features betraying no real enthusiasm. And even though she was replying to Mrs Rusely she seemed to be directing her words more towards Lady Rhynde. 'And with the backing of the Home Secretary, we should in all probability treble our chances of success.'

Lady Rhynde knew this has been said in order to put her on the spot, rather than out of the remotest interest in supporting Mrs Rusely's cause. She maintained a passive expression, determined to deny Baroness Sowerby the pleasure of knowing that her tactic had had any measure of success.

'As I was saying to Mrs Rusely, I'm sure this is something my husband is keeping abreast of, and—'

'I wonder,' interrupted Baroness Sowerby, 'whether this same method is effective in detecting other forms of deficiency of character? Say, tendencies towards immoral or disgraceful behaviour.'

Mrs Rusely was a little thrown. 'Why, I'm sure Professor Schlumpf's technique can reveal all sorts of predispositions. But what sort of thing might you be referring to?'

'Well, let us take for example a case of a supposedly upright woman being unfaithful to her husband.'

Baroness Sowerby continued to look primarily at Lady Rhynde, who still failed to react other than with an almost imperceptible tightening of her jaw.

'I see, well—'

'You see, preventing crime perpetrated by the lower orders is both laudable and increasingly desirable. But there seems now to be so much immoral, depraved behaviour among the supposedly *cultured* orders, those who are supposed to set an example to their social inferiors. I myself have personal knowledge of conduct which, if it were to become public knowledge, would not only create a sensation – but might even bring governments down ....'

Mrs Rusely still did not quite know what to make of this unexpected direction in which her favourite subject was being steered. 'You have certainly opened my eyes to a promising area for investigation. But as regards the *criminality of the lower orders ....*'

With Mrs Rusely back on track and apparently with a new convert to her cause, Lady Rhynde took the opportunity to quietly slip away – aware that Baroness Sowerby's steely gaze remained locked on her as she went.

Mr George crushed the slender right hand of Mr Congreave Burke, of Burke, Gadgeon and Burke of Lincoln's Inn, in both of his own tanned, powerful ones, and shook so heartily that it seemed the latter's shoulder might pop out of its socket. 'Thank you once again, sir. I am in your debt – and yours, Mr Bucket.'

'Now, George. I know you'd do the same for me, and more.'

They sauntered west along Leman Street in the East End. It felt as though it should be a fine, clear day today – albeit a cold one – but the air was very still and a light miasma of mist and chimney smoke hung in the air. Perhaps the hazy sun would burn it off as the morning unfolded. They paused to make a purchase from an oyster man standing at the corner of Leman Street and the Whitechapel Road, and ate their snack straight from the shells as they walked.

'Who would want to kill Tom Prike, Mr Bucket?'

'*Why* is perhaps the question to ask.'

'But you said you had an idea as to *who* the last time you visited me.'

'That I do, Mr George – but it is part of a much bigger matter and I can't say more at present – except that I want but very little to settle the matter.'

'Then you'll get the man who tried to have me hanged for murder? The man who killed poor Tom? Because I can tell you I've a mind to—'

'Don't go a-getting yourself into any more trouble, old fellow. I have plenty on the man in question, but he's only one among others.'

When they found themselves in the shadow of St Paul's Cathedral, Mr Bucket said, 'This is where I must leave you, for I have another matter to attend to. You get yourself back to the shooting gallery. Your regulars will be asking after you, and business is business.'

'I shall. But if you need any help – anything at all – you know you only have to ask.'

Mr Bucket touched the rim of his top hat and nodded, then went on his way.

When Mr Bucket rang the bell of 22 Upper Grosvenor Street he was greeted by a maid and shown in, and after the shortest of waits in the parlour he was led up to the drawing room. Lady Rhynde's usually youthful and healthy complexion looked paler, something accentuated by the darker patches beneath her eyes. She raised a smile upon seeing her visitor, but it did not contain the radiance the detective had seen formerly. There was an envelope in her hand, which she seemed to have forgotten she was holding, because after a moment she glanced down at it then hastily stuffed it into the decorated canvas bag sitting on a little stool beside her.

'Mr Bucket! This is quite a coincidence because I was intending to contact you.'

The inspector nodded towards the bag. 'You were going to Great Scotland Yard?'

She laughed, but it was rather forced, rather sad. 'Oh, no. I think for the Home Secretary's wife to visit the police headquarters might set too many tongues wagging and I'm not sure your commissioners would welcome it. No, I was going into town. I have ... an engagement. You can ride in my carriage and discuss whatever it is you have come to see me about if it's not taking you out of your way.'

'That's very kind. Where exactly is your ladyship heading?'

'I'm going to … I have some business in the Strand. Would that inconvenience you too much?'

'Not at all, your ladyship. Not at all!'

The truth was, it would inconvenience him completely in as much as it would be in completely the wrong part of London for his next port of call.

Lady Rhynde's Landau carriage was drawn by a pair of horses and was, not surprisingly, the plushest, most comfortable vehicle in which he had ever travelled.

'The top can be opened in the summer, I take it?'

'Indeed.'

'This is the type used by the Lord Mayor, I believe?'

'I think so.'

'If Mrs Bucket could see me now!'

'Perhaps she will!'

Mr Bucket withdrew his gaze from the streets and placed his hands squarely on his thighs. 'So, your ladyship, what is it that troubles you?'

'Troubles me?' For a second she looked like a schoolgirl caught stealing from a sweetie jar.

'There was something you wanted to see me about.'

'Oh! Well, there is nothing the matter, exactly. Let us just put it down to the vacillations of a silly woman. Or perhaps it's a lack of nerve. You see, I have decided – and if you are cross with me I shall quite deserve it and you mustn't pretend otherwise – not to pursue the matter of my stolen ferns.'

Mr Bucket studied her impassively. Lady Rhynde glanced at him for a second, then quickly turned her attention to the view through the window.

'You are not a silly woman, if I may be so bold. This is a surprising turn of events.'

'I have wasted your time and I feel most ashamed. But it is only ferns after all and I should hate to think that some person with no previous stain on their character might suffer terrible public humiliation on my account.'

'But how does your ladyship know that the ferns were stolen by some otherwise respectable person?'

'I ... I got the impression the last time we met that that was the direction in which your investigations were leading.'

The carriage rattled along the cobbles of Pall Mall and into Trafalgar Square, where the newly completed Nelson Column dominated the view.

'I didn't see any signs of your butler, Chuddersby, today.'

'He is my butler no more. He left suddenly without working his period of notice – simply told the cook to relay to me that he would not be back. My husband is furious. Still, it means he shall have no references when he next seeks a job.'

'Yet your ladyship still doesn't suspect him of having anything to do with the theft of the ferns?'

'I know he—' She caught herself in mid-sentence. 'His sudden departure is a nuisance, but he had never given me any cause for complaint or reason to doubt his loyalty.'

'Well this is a pity, for I do believe that the solving of this case to be but a simple matter.'

'For a man of your undoubted abilities I'm sure it is. But still, I have reached a decision and would prefer you to act no longer on my behalf. Others will no doubt wish to continue, but I wish my name to be left out of it – and once again I apologize for wasting your precious time.'

'Oh, but it ain't been wasted ma'am, rest assured.'

They rode in silence for a time. Mr Bucket's brows were furrowed. Several times he appeared about to speak, yet each time thought better of it. The carriage came to a halt close to Somerset House. Mr Bucket climbed down first and held out his hand to assist Lady Rhynde.

'Are you sure this is where you wish to be, Mr Bucket? I will be quite happy to instruct my driver to take you anywhere you wish.'

'This is as good as any place for me, your ladyship,' he assured her as he replaced his hat and patted the top so that it sat square and tight. 'Quite close, in fact, to the offices of the *Morning Chronicle*.'

'I suppose it is. It had not occurred to me. Is that where you are bound?'

'No. But I think *you* are, that's what I think. And I only hope your ladyship is not making a big mistake.'

Her face flushed. 'Whatever can you … Mr Bucket, please don't press me on this. I beg you.'

'I caught a glimpse of the address on the envelope before you put it in your bag. Begging your pardon, ma'am, but ladies such as your-self don't normally go a-visiting newspaper editors in person. And they don't normally drop charges of theft when the case is almost done. It all adds up to something not right, that's what it adds up to. Crime or no crime, I find myself deeply concerned on your lady-ship's behalf.'

'Mr Bucket, I am most grateful but still I implore you—'

'Now, I have half an idea as to what's behind this, and no doubt you could tell me the other half if you thought it might benefit you. My duty, as I see it, is to persuade you that it *will* benefit you. And I say that not as a police officer but as a man, and a man of honour, at that. You see, if the half of an idea I have is right, then I see this as something which will be forever hanging over you if left unchal-lenged, whereas I feel confident I can take care of it in a way that will put an end to it permanently – *and no one will ever know.* Don't you see? No one. Ever.'

Her searching eyes held his for a second, then she took him by the arm. 'Please come this way, Mr Bucket. There is a place where we may talk in private.'

XVIII

GORDON WAS EXPERIENCING not a little apprehension at the thought of having to chaperone Mrs Scambles from Mr Bucket's sister's house in Camden Town to her own home in Bloomsbury. Several irreconcilable feelings jostled to gain the upper hand in his mind. He could not forget his distaste for Eleanora's sudden cold and mercenary attitude towards her husband once she discovered that he – and by the same token, she – was in debt, nor his shock at her unashamed and explicit advances towards him. And yet.... Her husband had seemed such a cold and intimidating man – and still possibly even a murderer – that perhaps her lack of feeling for him was at least, in part, justified. And Gordon would have been fooling himself not to admit that her great beauty, her physical and personal allure, presented a challenge to his resolve. He was after all, to put it crudely, in the invidious position of a man with normal desires, yet one who was without female companionship at an age when most men were married and settled.

Mrs Scambles, who had been forewarned by Mr Bucket, was ready for him. As soon as he saw her distant figure from the hansom window, dressed in a lustrous green skirt and matching tunic-like top which was tailored to accentuate both her slender waist and full-bosomed figure, bags at her feet, Gordon experienced that same strange mixture of stimulation and wariness bordering on intimidation as on other occasions. Yet when she drew closer he was surprised to see a rather subdued expression on her face.

'Good day, Mr Gordon.'

She smiled, but she had insisted on them addressing each other by their Christian names when they last encountered one another. Had

Mr Bucket said something to her? Had she been crushed by Gordon's previous rebuff?

'Hello, Mrs Scambles. I hope you are well and looking forward to returning to the comfort of your own home?'

'Oh, I have been most comfortable here, sir. I am used to a larger house but the warmth and hospitality I have received have more than made up for it.'

'Oh. Right ... well, then—'

'Shall we go?'

'Of course. Allow me to carry your bags.'

She made no attempt to speak to him as the carriage got under way, and his own efforts – as always in such circumstances – were not of the most adept kind. She was neither unfriendly nor antagonistic towards him, merely quiet in a resigned sort of way. Gordon soon felt himself in the strange position of shifting from being offended by Mrs Scambles' blatant advances to feeling like the guilty party for apparently having hurt her feelings. She was a lady in a strange and frightening situation, and one with normal feelings and desires yet which fate had prevented from being satisfied. Even if he had acted correctly, had he done so in a harsh and unfeeling manner?

The staff at her house in Russell Square also seemed to have had advance warning of her return, since as soon as their hansom hoved into view they all paraded out and lined up along the pavement in front of the building like soldiers on parade. Mrs Scambles removed a lace handkerchief from her pocket, and Gordon noticed that a tear was trickling down her cheek.

He gently touched her arm. 'You are obviously well liked by your servants!'

Instead of placing her hand on top of his as she almost certainly would have done on previous occasions, she simply continued to gaze out at the scene before them, dabbing at her eyes. 'One would like to think so. I must say, it is very affecting.'

When they entered the house she spent some time looking all about her as if seeing everything for the first time, and it brought home to Gordon how disturbing this business must have been for her. One's home is normally a place of refuge, the place to which one can retreat and escape from difficult times, and Eleanora Scambles had been denied that basic source of comfort for a number of days now. While the rest of the staff went about their business, a maid was sent away to arrange for some coffee. He and Eleanora settled in the drawing room.

There was an awkward silence for a while, which Gordon eventually felt compelled to break.

'So, it must be good to be home, Mrs Scambles!' He immediately admonished himself for uttering such a feeble statement.

'Yes. Very heartening, thank you.'

Eleanor was sitting on the edge of a chair some feet away from him, perfectly upright and with an admirably straight back. In a way, the downcast look in her sad blue eyes and the slight but curvaceous pout to her lips made her look more attractive – perhaps in a more vulnerable sort of way, even, than usual.

'And you are sure you were well cared for at the home of Mrs Bucket's sister?'

'Very well indeed.' She still didn't look at him, and now Gordon began to feel like an intruder.

'Mrs Scambles ... Eleanor. If I spoke in such a way as to offend or hurt you at our last meeting, then I really do hope you will accept my sincere—'

'It is I who should apologize. I let my womanly feelings rule over my intellect and placed you in an impossible position.'

'But if you don't mind my saying so, you seem troubled, preoccupied. If it was not my words which caused it, perhaps sharing your burden would be of some help?'

She looked directly at him for the first time, then rose from her chair in a decisive way. 'I take it that returning me to my home is a sign that the danger is past, that an arrest has been made?'

'Not an arrest yet, but Mr Bucket believes that one is imminent.'

'And this is in some way all tied up with my husband's incarceration and the murder of Mr Mizzentoft.'

'I believe so, yes.'

'Then ... then I have something to say which may make you and your chief alter your thinking.'

Gordon was so caught unawares by this sudden pronouncement

that he didn't reply immediately. And just as he was about to do so, the maid came in with the coffee and a tray of little cakes.

'Beggin' your pardon, ma'am, but Cook made the cakes special – to welcome you home, like.'

Gordon saw Eleanora smile for the first time that day, and it seemed to light up the room. 'Thank her from me, Lily, and tell her I am very pleased to be back among my people. But now I have important matters to discuss with this police officer, and I am not to be disturbed on any account. Is that clear?'

'Yes, ma'am. Very good, ma'am.' Lily gave a little curtsy and left the room.

As soon as she had gone, Eleanora went to the door and locked it. Gordon's heart began to beat a little faster.

She dropped the key into a pocket, then leaned with her back to the door, her head bowed.

'It will be better if you tell me what ails you,' Gordon ventured. 'Get it off your ... get it out into the open.'

'Will it?' she sighed almost inaudibly. 'What I say will change lives – might even cause one to be destroyed. Will it make me feel any better? *Oh, James, this is much harder than I expected.*'

She began to sob, and he rushed to her side and escorted her to the sofa. Still crying, she pressed her face against his chest. 'It's to do with my husband ... and it is very serious,' she whimpered. 'Very grave indeed.'

She was by now virtually in a state of collapse, and Gordon had to support her soft, wilting form. 'You must tell me. Keeping some-thing so painful to oneself can only make matters worse – you will make yourself ill!'

She grasped his hand with both of her small, warm ones, but at the same time pulled slightly away from him and straightened her posture in a way which seemed to represent some new inner resolve. She pointed to a door at the far end of the room.

'Mr Gordon, through that door is my dressing room. On the smaller of the two tables is a dark coloured hairbrush with ivory decoration on the back. Would you be so kind as to fetch it for me?'

'Of course.'

He thought nothing of entering that room. Being an innocent in such matters, to him it was just another room in the house like the parlour or the drawing room, albeit a smaller and more private one. But as soon as he took in his new surroundings he realized how naive he had been. Lilac hangings decorated with lace covered the walls, against which hung numerous dresses of all type and colour, and there were silk and tuile curtains of a rich pink. The scent of lavender hung in the air, presumably one of the perfume bottles on a shelf above the larger table, among which other items that one might expect to find in such a room: a horse-hair toothbrush, toilet water, other perfumes, and arsenic – which, Gordon had been told, was good for the skin. But it was what was draped over both the table and two chairs that demanded his attention most of all. There were white calico drawers neatly laid out and smelling of a scent he had detected on Eleanor herself .... Cream and white chemises with lacy trimmings, which seemed to billow as if still containing her full figure .... Corsets, loosely open and with their laces splayed about as if the owner had only just removed the garment .... And garters. Black garters of lace and ribbon. For a moment he was almost over-come by a sense of shame and guilt, as if he were some type of depraved intruder. But he reminded himself that he had been sent here by the owner of these normally private, concealed garments. And did ladies normally leave everything out, arranged in this manner? It was almost as if they had been placed so deliberately ....

He found the brush, which had been placed upon a corset made of some sort of silken, azure material, left the room and closed the door behind him. When he turned to face Eleanor, all became clear.

She was standing in the middle of the drawing room completely naked.

She had unfastened her hair, and it cascaded down her back like a waterfall of honey, framing her delicate, doll-like features and flowing over the edges of her voluptuous breasts. And as she came towards him, those perfectly formed globes swayed, clashed gently together and quivered. Gordon knew he should not stare, but he was helpless. He had witnessed many things which most people never have or would; but that was a socially cloistered military exis-tence, and in truth he had led a life sheltered from the real world. Before him was a sight he had never seen, a physical perfection he had never touched, and it was being offered to him freely. An over-whelming maelstrom of revulsion and desire, of the chill of fear and the heat, quickened the surge of blood in his veins, threw his mind and body into utter chaos, and he could only stand there with his back to the door, wanting to turn away from the mesmerizing sight before him yet completely and pitifully unable so to do.

'Do I disgust you, Mr Gordon?' Her expression was open, unfath-omable, yet a tear rolled down her rose-hued cheeks. It was almost as if she did not *want* to do this, but *had* to.

'Not disgust....' He *had* thought it disgusting, but it now was impossible to experience such an ugly sentiment towards such a beautiful, alluringly pathetic creature.

'Then let me make it easier for you to express it – because I don't hesitate to say that I sicken *myself.* I have only ever known the company of a cold, uncaring man. Then, in my hour of need I met a strong yet kind, understanding one – but the Almighty saw fit to make it impossible for us to decently enter into any kind of union. But is it so bad, so wrong to wish for solace just once in this cruel life? A fleeting moment of comfort and succour against the cold real-ities of the world?' She moved again until she was right before him. Her breasts pressed lightly against his chest, and he breathed in that same fragrance he had detected in her dressing room. She gazed up at him through moist eyes, and began to speak in a tremulous whisper.

'Mr Gordon, while I was away I read an article about the detec-tive force by Mr Dickens. I learned that sometimes detectives pay for confidential information. I have information you cannot ignore. But you will have to pay, Mr Gordon.'

Another tear welled then rolled down her cheek, her voice wavered, and Gordon's heart reached out to her just as strongly as did his baser desires.

Gordon could not say whether she threw herself at him or whether it was a mutual moving together, for he was no longer thinking clearly, if at all.

XIX

THE COFFEE HOUSE of Simpson's in the Strand was quiet. A city gent sat at a window seat the more easily to read his copy of the *John Bull*, and two respectable-looking young ladies, both in crinolines of matching shades of green, chatted gaily at the table closest to the kitchens. In a dimly lit corner well away from these customers, Mr Bucket of the Detective and Lady Rhynde, wife of Sir Dalton Rhynde the Home Secretary, leaned confidentially close to each other across the table, speaking in low voices.

'My dear Mr Bucket, I know you have already guessed that there is an ulterior motive for my abrupt and peculiar change of heart. I know I can trust you. More than that: I value your knowledge of the world and of the people in it, because that makes it easier for me to reveal what has happened recently.'

She stooped towards her bag on the floor beside the table and pulled out some sort of writing book or journal. What the book was did not matter – what was concealed among its pages did. It was a piece torn out of a newspaper. She handed it over to Mr Bucket, who flattened it out on the table before him and examined it. At first all he could see was advertisements: Professor Grandle's Famous Brain Tonic; Coffin's pills for Oppression of the Stomach, Nervousness and Constipation; and a Galvanic Belt for Irregularities of the System caused by Want of Electricity – testimonials free on receipt of one stamp. Then his roving eye picked out personal advertisements: a quiet home is urgently required for a seventy-nine-year-old lady who will not abide children and must be treated firmly. Beneath this appeared to be a publisher's advertisement – but it was not. It was a privately placed notice, and the wording was very singular:

SHORTLY TO BE PUBLISHED
Original Letters from a Gentleman to a Lady
~ both PUBLIC FIGURES of some note ~
Revealing
Matters touching on the Honour and Integrity of same.
Any interested party should contact the Editor of this
Journal before the 20th Inst.

Mr Bucket issued a snort of derision. 'Blackmail. Plain and simple for anyone to see. How could any editor of a self-respecting paper even consider—'

'This appeared in one of the more sensationalist publications which now seem to abound,' Lady Rhynde explained. Seeing the detective's quizzical look, she smiled wryly and added, 'It was brought to my attention by a third party.'

'Mrs Bucket has been known to peruse the pages of such journals,' Mr Bucket grumbled, half to himself. 'She maintains that one must make oneself aware of the depravities of society in order to combat it, whereas I maintain that I won't have such rubbish in the house. Much good it does me.'

Lady Rhynde laughed unexpectedly and brightly, and Mr Bucket seemed pleased to have lightened her mood, if only for an instant. But his face soon took on a more sober appearance. 'The *substance* of this matter is no concern of mine. What we must do is—'

'I had an abortion last year.'

'Your ladyship—'

'I had an affair with a man I loved very much .... In fact we are both very much still in love, but now we have seen sense, even though it is very hard. I am not a naturally deceitful or disloyal person, Mr Bucket ....

'Of that I am quite sure. Madam, there really is no need for you to explain—'

'But my marriage is, and has been, completely lacking in any physical, emotional or intellectual connection almost from the beginning. I was resigned to my fate. I considered it my duty to make the best of my lot. But then ... to experience a meeting of minds, a meeting of hearts for the first and only time ... I was overwhelmed. Anyway,

149

in short, I one day found I was with child. My husband and I have no children and I thought I was medically barren, which obviously proved not to be the case. Recently – after the theft of the ferns – some very personal letters were stolen. Hence the reason we are here today.'

'Have you any idea who took them – the letters, I mean?'

'No. None at all.'

'Well it doesn't matter, because I believe I have worked it out.' Ignoring her look of astonishment, he continued. 'This ... procedure. It was carried out by Dr Jonathan Scambles?'

Lady Rhynde's eyes widened further. 'Mr Bucket – have you been secretly investigating *me*?'

'Perish the thought, your ladyship. No, but other unrelated matters have meant that several things have become rather entangled, shall we say. To some extent your butler – your former butler – Mr Chuddersby is involved in all this.'

'I must confess that after your earlier hints I am not as surprised as I once might have been.'

Mr Bucket's fat forefinger glided towards his nose. 'His real name is Jukes, by the way, not Chuddersby. Our paths have crossed professionally in the past.'

'My God.... To think I trusted him completely.'

'He is very convincing, your ladyship.'

'Then, do you think he is behind the theft of the letters ... *and the ferns*?'

'I have little doubt but that he has some close connection. But there is more to it than that. I take it you heard about Dr Scambles' arrest for the murder of Edward Mizzentoft?'

'Of course. Oh, dear – should I have mentioned—'

Mr Bucket waved her self-reproachment away. 'Irrelevant. Your, ah, *treatment* at the hands of the doctor has no bearing on things.'

'But Chuddersby, Mr Bucket – you surely don't think *he* rather than Dr Scambles murdered Mr Mizzentoft?'

'Before his butlering career he led what you might call a colourful life, your ladyship. While I can't say he was the man that wielded the knife, let's just say his testimony would be of interest to the police.'

Lady Rhynde shuddered. 'To think he lived under the same roof as me ....'

'Think back, ma'am. You mentioned that he was often away from his duties visiting Baroness Sowerby. Mr Mizzentoft was killed in the evening of the eighth of this month. It was a Monday and it occurred at a house in Montague Place, hard by the British Museum. I must press you – is it at all possible he was away ostensibly on one of his visits on that day?'

Lady Rhynde thought hard, pressing her hands to her temples and closing her eyes, but she shook her head. 'So much has happened since then ... I really don't know. If I attempted to guess I should in all probability mislead you.'

'It's only to be expected, and you've already been most helpful. As for the – *ahem* – other matter, I intend to visit Baroness Sowerby and—'

'Oh please no, Mr Bucket. I beg you.'

He leaned closer in a conspiratorial way. 'I ask you to trust me when I say that there shall be no exposure as regards any personal affairs of your ladyship's. Bear with me for a little time longer. Discretion shall be my watch-word.'

Her drawn, pained face softened. 'Your ability to know things which ought to be unknowable are disconcerting – do you realize that, Mr Bucket?'

'I depend upon it! Mrs Bucket remarks upon it frequently – though not in such a flattering manner as your ladyship. I fear I must make for a difficult and trying companion in life.'

'No, sir. I have believed everything you have told me thus far, but not that.'

There was a twinkle in Lady Rhynde's steady gaze – and just the merest fleeting hint of pinkness to Mr Bucket's cheeks.

XX

NORMALLY, A LACK of cloud cover, cold temperature and a certain humidity in the air would result, perhaps, in a low-lying mist and cold but brilliantly starry skies. But this was London. Overcrowded, over-industrialized London. Nature's water droplets and smoke from the homes of two million people and the chimneys of untold factories and smaller places of work combined to form a choking, dirty sea of fog, which her inhabitants must drift through with watering eyes and blackened phlegm. Mr Thomas Jones proceeded from his temporary lodgings in Gravel Lane to the Welsh Trooper public house on the south bank of the Thames near Reddin's Wharves, Bankside. He clasped a rather ragged scarf of indeterminate colour to his mouth and nose to combat the effects of the fog, having had weak lungs since birth. Despite the conditions he was in a buoyant mood, for several reasons. First, he was no longer Alfred Jukes, an identity that had proved to be a burden from a legal point of view almost from the time he had learned to filch a handkerchief from a gentleman's coat-tail pocket, which itself had not been so very long after he had learned to walk. Secondly, neither was he any longer the butler William Chuddersby, whose name had sadly also become too hot to handle, despite it providing him with the greatest status, the most material comfort and the most regular income he had ever known in his thirty-seven years of life. Even having all that – more than he could ever have envisaged or hoped for – still there had been *opportunities*, and for a man from a back-ground like the present Mr Thomas Jones, opportunities were simply too hard to resist. It seemed almost morally wrong to let an opportunity go to waste.

So now, with the net closing in – something he sensed rather than knew – it was time to move on. The only thing left of William Chuddersby was the broken nose bequeathed to him by the General, but even that had healed quite nicely and had left him with a pugilistic appearance that might give future potential adversaries pause for thought. He was now an itinerant potman who, when the work could be found, wandered the streets south of the river selling jugs of porter and stout from a specially constructed frame hanging by straps from his shoulders. He was currently residing in a doss house with Long Liza, a dollymop with one set of clothing, a hair brush with a missing handle and seven-and-a-half teeth to her name. But he was not downbeat. He had cadged a couple of shillings off Liza; he was going to enjoy a glass or two of gin at the Welsh Trooper and he was going to make friends, establish useful contacts and move on. Ever on.

But even though he was separated physically and even culturally by the Thames from his usual London haunts, and even though the capital was a city of countless souls and larger than all the other major towns and cities in England put together, the city was still, oddly, like a large village. People knew each other, their business, their movements ....

The newly created Thomas Jones's evening was enjoyable and productive. He inveigled himself into conversations, was bought drinks and was quickly co-opted into some minor criminal scheme, for the execution of which he was to meet Greek Harry outside the Old Mint at midnight two days hence. He left the pub at around 11.30 p.m. and again used his scarf, despite its reeking of stale alcohol and tobacco fumes, to keep out the noxious fumes hanging in the bitterly cold air. Shadowy figures flitted about in the night fog like ghosts. At least, most of them flitted about. One had been motionless, waiting. As soon as Thomas Jones's half-covered face was illuminated by the feeble street light outside the hostelry, this particular shape became animated, moving towards the former butler to Lady Rhynde.

Thomas Jones could make out very little of this person. Not the clothes, not the hair and certainly nothing of the facial features. Yet he knew who it was straight away. The bulky shape was enough.

Yet it couldn't be. *He was dead.*

Thomas Jones had to consciously tighten his thigh muscles before his failing knees gave way beneath him, and the sudden hammering he could feel against his ribs, even reaching up into his neck, was surely more than any human organ could stand for more than a few seconds. It wasn't that he believed in ghosts – though he did. No, this was far worse than a ghost. The figure lumbered into the light and Thomas Jones received his final confirmation. It was the man he ran through with his sword; the man who fell into the swollen Thames, his spurting blood mingling with its contaminated, icy waters.

The General.

Jones glanced surreptitiously about him for an escape route. At their last encounter he had both a sword concealed in a stick and the element of surprise on his side, yet still hadn't managed to finish off the former prize-fighter. Things weren't looking good, except ... he *knew* he had grievously wounded him. Surely the General would not be capable of out-running him?

'Fancied a change of scenery, did yer?'

'What do you want?'

'You tried to carve me up good and proper, but I don't take it personal. No doubts you 'ad yer orders. But it's bad fer business if a man like me don't settle 'is scores. See – nuthin' personal!'

He inched a little closer to Thomas Jones. One of his hands was in his jacket pocket, and it occurred to Jones that the General would probably expect him to be armed. He would come prepared this time. While the General had been speaking he had been assessing the lie of the land. There was a dead-end to his right. There was an alley across the road which looked promising – but the General's wide frame was between him and that route. The main road to the left, at the end of the street they were standing on, was by far the best bet, and it was a dash of only about thirty yards. But the General clearly knew his game. He had been very slightly edging to his right and angling his body so that he was at least half-covering that way too. An image sprang, out of the blue, to Thomas Jones's mind. It was something he had witnessed seven years ago. He had seen a lot of things that day, but this particular scene lasted no more than a few seconds. A melee in a beer house. The General dispatching a man with a tickler to the lower ribs, which doubled him up, teeth clenched, breath whistling through them like the air being slowly released from a toy balloon. Another man grabbing the General by the throat from behind. The General reaching backwards, grasping the man's head in his great paws and spinning them both round in a sudden, violent motion. The unearthly click of the attacker's neck breaking. His body on the floor, twitching like a puppet controlled by a man with a severe nervous tick, then flopping back down, lifeless.

Jones snapped himself back to the present – suddenly he saw a course of action clearly in his head. He had no idea where it came from and he wasn't expecting it, but he impulsively grasped at it.

'I can dodge you and I can out-run you and you know it. If you were to make a sudden move I could run back in there and out through the rear, or I could simply skip round you and leg it down the road. Either way you'd never catch me.'

'I reckon you'd've already done that by now if you wuz so sure of yerself.'

'We can help each other. You've got things on me; I've got plenty on you. But so have others. Together, we can look out for each other, cover each other's tracks. There's things that need to be covered up good and proper so they can never come to light. I know about you and Mizzentoft– and I'm not the only one.'

Even in the fog and the dim light, Jones saw the General's face grow darker.

'And 'ow can you look out fer me, might I ask?'

'I can take care of anyone who knows things that could bring you down.'

'In case yer didn't know, I'm pretty good at that sort o' thing meself. Why do I need you?'

'Take Mizzentoft. I know people who know things. I know who they are and how to get to them. You don't. There is more to this than you know. You were purposely only told what was necessary. But I know it *all*, and that's my insurance policy. That's why you need me.'

The General's shoulders seemed to relax. He removed his hand from his pocket and let it fall to his side. A grin spread across his face. 'I told yer it weren't personal. Just business. It's *always* just business – and that sounds like good business to me!'

The General sidled up and patted Thomas Jones on the shoulder. 'Come back inside – I'll buy yer a drink to seal the deal.'

Jones nodded, but then suddenly grimaced and bent forward with a hand in the small of his back.

'I didn't 'urt yer, did I, friend? Sometimes I don't realize I—'

'No, no. It's my old back. Lumbago.'

'A drop o' rum, that's what you need.'

As the General spoke those words, Thomas Jones, still bent over, whipped out the thin-bladed knife tucked into his boot. He straightened up and thrust it in one swift movement, the blade glinting dully in the gaslight as it arced towards the centre of the General's chest. He was cool, totally focused on executing a lightning, perfect strike. Which was why he did not even see the shorter, broader blade that the General had been palming since taking his hand out of his pocket.

At a glance it looked as if the General had punched Thomas Jones, knocking him to the ground with the sheer brute force of the blow. But a closer inspection would reveal a knife buried to the hilt in the taller man's neck. And there was arterial blood spurting from the wound. It looked black under the artificial lighting as it splattered into the gutter and quickly began to spread and pool. The General was keen to leave while no one was about, but he was not going to waste a perfectly good knife. He put his boot on the rapidly fading Thomas Jones's head for leverage and yanked the weapon out, causing a sudden extra-strong gush of blood, which narrowly missed his trousers. He wiped the blade clean on the unconscious, dying man's coat. Then, with the clump-clump of his heavy-footed tread, he was swallowed by the fog.

XXI

O<small>N THE MORNING</small> after Gordon's meeting with Mrs Scambles, he was more nervous, as he crossed the floor of the Back Hall and climbed the stairs to the detective offices, than he had been when he had arrived to begin his first day in the post. The encounter itself he had simply been unable to put out of his mind. Various details: subtle smells, physical sensations, sighs, whispers – all jumping into his consciousness unbidden like a series of photographs, yet in vivid colour, flashing before his eyes, one after another. It was both wonderful and terrible, but now, in the cold light of day a multitude of possible consequences dogged his every footstep like a spiteful, taunting rabble of street urchins. How much should he say, how much should he hold back? Not only was he not accustomed to lying or deceit, but this was *Mr Bucket*, not some ordinary acquaintance who might swallow a convenient falsehood without a second thought.

The said Mr Bucket was leaning back in his chair, puffing thoughtfully on his pipe, and gazing out of the window.

'Good morning, sir.'

'Morning.'

Gordon struggled to discern his mood. Was he merely cogitating on something – or did he even *know*? How could he know? It was impossible. No one knew. But – he was Mr Bucket!

'Foggy again,' Gordon ventured, removing his hat and great coat and hanging them up on the stand.

'A veritable pea-souper, as they say. And like to stay so for a good while yet, according to Mrs Bucket. How did it go yesterday?'

'Very well ....'

'And Mrs Scambles was completely satisfied?'

Gordon gulped. *'Satisfied?'*

'That it was safe to return to her home.' He took another puff on his pipe, and brushed away a little ash from his maroon waistcoat, the buttons of which were straining somewhat against his ample girth. Gordon noticed for the first time a mourning ring on his little finger. On reflection he felt sure it had been there since their first meeting, yet he had failed to spot it. What sort of detective was he?

'She appeared to be perfectly content. What about you?'

'Me? *I'm* perfectly content. What did she have to say?'

'No, I mean did you uncover anything interesting after we parted? Has Mr Stope said anything else?'

'Billy has kept himself to himself, but then that's his way. I had a very interesting interview with a lady, but certain things were discussed which appertain to that lady's reputation, and so I'm not free to share them with anyone else, not even you. Leastways, not those parts which have nothing to do with our case.'

Gordon guessed he was referring to Lady Rhynde. He was so discomfited that he was barely registering what Mr Bucket was saying, yet he was keen for his superior to continue in the pathetic hope that it would distract him from asking any more questions about his meeting with Eleanora – even though Gordon knew he *had* to tell him what he had discovered. 'But this lady was able to provide you with some useful intelligence?'

'To be sure. So, did she have nothing useful to tell you?'

'Who?'

'Well I'm not a-talking about the Queen of Sheba, Mr Gordon.'

Gordon forced a laugh. 'Quite! As a matter of fact, yes – she did have something very interesting to relate.'

Mr Bucket removed his pipe and sat up straight. 'Go on, then.'

'Mrs Scambles says … that her husband *did* kill Edward Mizzentoft.'

'She thinks, or she knows?'

'She states it as a fact.'

The plump right forefinger began to perform. 'The last time you spoke to Mrs S she turned on her husband because she had discovered he'd ruined them financially and was greatly indebted to Mizzentoft. How can you be sure she's not just saying this out of malice?'

'Do you recall when we first saw the General at the beer shop in Seven Dials?'

'It was a distinctly memorable kerfuffle, Mr Gordon of that ilk.'

'He bore various scars—'

'He was a prize-fighter, man!'

'But there was a fresh scar. A distinctly recent one on his right cheekbone – did you not notice?'

'I did not, sir. Why, Lord bless your soul: you really do have the makings of a detective! And that would have been just days after the murder.'

'There is more. Dr Scambles *bested the General in a fight*! The General was employed as a debt collector of the brutal sort by Mizzentoft and was sent to apply pressure to make Scambles pay back what he owed. Things became heated; the doctor lost his temper and by all accounts turned into some sort of wild man and completely overwhelmed our surprised pugilist friend. Then, still in an uncontrollable passion, he sought out the man who had sent the General to him – Mizzentoft – and did for him.'

'What about the knife?'

'What do you mean?'

'Mizzentoft was stabbed. We are to believe that Scambles lost all self-control – yet such a state can only be maintained for so long before the blood begins to cool and the likely consequences of one's actions begin to come to the surface. It must have taken some time to obtain the knife.'

'He was a doctor – he must have had easy access to all manner of sharp implements.'

'I take it the fight with the General did not take place while Dr Scambles was with a patient?'

'I don't know for certain, but I don't think so.'

'Then he may well not have had his bag with him. The mere act of returning home, probably having to speak to servants, to his wife, having to pick out the best instrument for the job – all of these things would allow the fury to dissipate and the intellect to intervene. I'll grant you, we got a fine example of the fellow's temper when we paid him a visit in Coldbath, but I see Dr Scambles as being a flash-in-the-pan sort of a man. Flares up, then just as quick dies down. Likes to be in control of himself, that's what *he* likes. Bet he's never been drunk in his life!'

'I agree up to a point. But according to El— Mrs Scambles, he is capable of seeing through a vendetta to its end, no matter how long it takes.'

Mr Bucket left his desk and went over to the window, not that he could see much, what with the fog outside and the condensation on the glass. But Gordon knew he was looking inward, not out. 'It don't take much imagination to see him committing the ultimate sin, that much I do concede. *But,* was Mrs Scambles being truthful, or merely vengeful? Did she offer up this information freely?'

Gordon was glad Mr Bucket had his back to him. 'Not entirely....'

'Oh?'

'There was a price. I would just like to state —'

'There's always a price for intelligence as prized as that. That's the way we work. You'd better put in an expenses claim.'

'A what? Oh, I see, yes.'

'I realize she is now a needy woman. How much did it cost?'

'She is a needy woman, and it cost ... a lot. Look, Mr Bucket ... she attempted to barter with me by using ... *intimate* methods. If I had been foolish enough to succumb, how serious a matter would it have been? Purely for future reference.'

'More of an embarrassment than a sacking offence, I'd say.'

'But I'm not talking about internal discipline. If something like that came out at Dr Scambles' trial, it may adversely affect the case. I mean, for a detective officer to admit to intimacy with a material witness—'

'She didn't witness anything, so don't go using police terms till you know what they mean, Mr James Alexander Gordon.'

Gordon felt as if a great weight had been lifted from him. But Mr Bucket had not finished.

'Supposing you had succumbed to Eleanora's – begging your pardon, Mrs Scambles' – wiles, I doubt whether she would want to get a fine, good-natured man like yourself who has shown her only kindness into trouble. But one day you will come up against someone who *would* use it against you, yet you'll find it hard to tell the difference. Very hard.'

He extinguished his pipe and knocked the ash into the metal bin beside his desk, then picked up his coat.

'Where are you going?'

'*We* are a-going to see Baroness Sowerby, that's where we're a-going.'

But once they had left the building and had entered Great Scotland Yard itself, they had barely walked five paces when they encountered Mr George coming towards them.

'How do, Mr George! What brings you here?' said Mr Bucket.

'I hope I'm not wasting your time, gentlemen,' the old soldier began, 'but I've just had a conversation with a person in my shooting gallery that I thought you might want to hear about. It's all second-hand tittle-tattle, I'm afraid, but when I heard the name Mizzentoft—'

'Bless your heart, Mr George. I'll be glad to hear what you've got to say – can't have too much information in this game, and it's easy enough to discard what don't matter.'

'The man who came to shoot is a solicitor from Tooting, and he's also a member of the Chandos Club in Langham Place. It seems that Edward Mizzentoft also happened to be a member, and the two were vaguely acquainted. Sounds as if, although Mizzentoft had money and acted the gentleman, most of the members saw through him and guessed there was something a bit off about him. Who he really was and how he came by his wealth was the source of much gossip at the club, and all sorts of rumours abounded. The one which caught my attention was that he was something of a ladies' man, and that among others he was said to have consorted with the beautiful wife of a doctor acquaintance of his. No names were given, but adding two and two together....'

'Mrs Scambles?' Gordon couldn't help blurting out.

'That's for you gentlemen to decide,' Mr George replied.

'Well, she does have that way about her,' said Mr Bucket, giving Gordon a knowing look. 'That's very much appreciated, Mr George.'

'But there's more, Mr Bucket. It was rumoured that Mizzentoft was living in fear of her – having got wind of a story that she paid to have a former lover done in!'

Mr Bucket glanced at Gordon again. 'Sounds like a dangerous woman to know, this Mrs Scambles.'

'If indeed it *is* her,' Gordon countered.

'He was an elderly landowner called Digby whom she bewitched so completely that he wrote her into his will – whereupon she approached a known tough and offered him money to bump the old man off. But in the meantime the man's family got to know about the liaison and intervened, threatening her with exposure if she did not disassociate herself from him.'

'Do we know if Mizzentoft left a will?' Gordon wondered out loud. 'If he did, and he left money to Mrs Scambles ....'

'Quite, Mr James Alexander Gordon of that ilk!' said Mr Bucket. 'This is something that might turn our whole investigation down a new path. Something that needs investigating.'

'Mr Bucket, I think that owing to my previous contact with Mrs Scambles—'

'So off you go! I have matters to discuss with Mr George here over a glass of brandy and water in the Ten Bells. We shall meet again at three at the home of Baroness Sowerby.'

Approaching the Russell Square home of Eleanora Scambles, Gordon's heart was pumping so forcefully that he could feel his ribcage quaking rhythmically inside his heavy coat. The last time he had felt this way was before battle, yet this time, despite the new information they had received from Mr George, his fears weren't to do with any danger he might be in. It was simply ... *her*. No other human being he had ever met had possessed the power to send his mind into such a state of chaos and confusion. Even possessing this new information about her – which still may or may not be true – Gordon wasn't sure whether he was afraid of being bewitched by her again, or of the possibility that perhaps he *wanted* to be. He told himself that the latter wasn't true, but in reality he no longer trusted his rational judgement in the matter.

As Gordon was being shown in he endeavoured to scrutinize the maid's face for signs that she was aware of the previous intimacy between himself and her mistress, and that she assumed that his current visit was of the same nature. Servants had a way of gleefully letting one know these things subtly even while still deporting themselves in the correct manner. But the dull-featured Polly seemed incapable of such artful behaviour. She led Gordon not to the parlour but directly to the drawing room, even though Mrs Scambles was not there to receive him. He was about to sit on the sofa, but then thought better of it and switched to the relative isolation and safety of an armchair. Despite avoiding the sofa, as Gordon cast his eyes around the room he could not avoid the memories of his last visit. He perched uncomfortably on the edge of the chair, as if not wishing to sully himself further by any more physical contact with this room than was necessary.

He expected that, once she heard his name announced, she would arrive very quickly. But the longer Gordon waited and fidgeted, the more another thought began to take shape in his mind. He recalled his last visit, and the sight he had encountered when re-entering this room after emerging from her dressing room. Was she taking so long because she was 'preparing' herself for him? *Might she even be doing so in that dressing room right now?* He stared at the door and listened carefully, but could hear nothing.

Gordon found he could no longer sit still; he rose from the chair and walked over to the window, where he gazed down at the horses' hooves and the iron-rimmed wheels of the vehicles rumbling over the damply glistening cobbles below. To him, everyone seemed to be miserable: heads bowed, caught up in their own little worlds. He was tiring of winter in London. Was it always like this? His mind was drawn back to days not so long ago in leafy Hampshire, when—

'You look ill at ease, Mr Gordon.'

Gordon spun round sharply, like a child caught stealing. 'Mrs Scambles – you startled me.'

'So I see!' She drew closer to him, and looked out at the same scene that he had been watching. 'Last year we fled to Greece to escape the cold and rain. Everything was different last year ....'

'And for me, too.'

She grasped his arm and looked up at him with those captivating blue eyes. 'I'm glad you decided to come back to me. Everything could be different again next year, you know.'

He tensed and pulled back from her a little. 'I'm afraid I come on police business, Mrs Scambles.'

She recoiled as if he had slapped her. '*Mrs Scambles?* Does our previous meeting mean so little to you?'

'What happened ... should not have.'

'But it *did* mean something to you. A woman can tell that much, James. What we did was wrong in the legal sense, but was it in a natural way? Soon, Dr Scambles will be no more, and I shall be alone and in need of a companion. I know of no other man alive with whom I would rather—'

'Your husband will soon be released.'

'I – *what*? But he ... but I know he murdered that man! You see, I probably should have told you, but I was also acquainted with Edward Mizzentoft....'

'I know now that you were *acquainted* with him, Eleanora.'

'Oh, please, James, don't look so accusingly at me. If you only knew what my life has been like.' She took both of his arms this time, pulling herself to him. He could feel her breasts against his chest and smell her perfume – *that* perfume again – and he felt the familiar surge of passion rising within him, threatening to overwhelm all reason. Gordon knew now that she was a manipulative woman – but he also saw beyond that a sad, needy creature whose life really *had* been miserable and loveless. It seemed an offence against God that such a thing of beauty and warmth should suffer such a fate, and he found it hard to condemn her pathetic attempts at employing what-ever tools nature had endowed her with in order to gain some little consolation. With a supreme effort of will he prised himself away from her.

'Eleanora, I have learned that you were at one time on intimate terms with a Mr Digby, but that you eventually made plans to pay a third party to take his life so that you could inherit at least part of his estate. You must see that that, added to your admission of a relation-ship with the late Mr Mizzentoft, is, at the very least, suggestive.'

He expected her to deny the former accusation, so her reaction took him by surprise. The radiance faded from her eyes for a moment, and they began to fill with tears. She sank to her knees, weeping uncontrollably.

'*I was a wretched, foolish child then … I dreamed up and said foolish things,*' she spluttered between sobs. '*But like a child, I soon regretted my words. You must believe that it was merely words, and that I would never have made good my threats. Where would I find the kind of person who would carry out such an act?!*'

Gordon had to admit to himself that it did seem unlikely, and also that Eleanora was pouring her heart out to him in a truthful way. 'What of your association with Edward Mizzentoft?'

She slid off her knees to the floor so that she was slumped with her back against the wall, then placed her elbows on her knees and buried her face in her child-like, soft white hands. She looked so pitiful that Gordon felt guilty for even posing the question, as if he were deliberately prolonging her torture and humiliation. He squatted down beside her. 'I hope you understand that these are questions I *must* ask.'

'Of course. It's nothing less than I deserve. My husband told me that Mizzentoft was a patient – I had no inkling of the financial dealings between them, and needless to say certainly not that Jonathan was deeply in debt to him. I met him a couple of times in the presence of my husband, and then one day he came to call when he must have known Jonathan was working. You may find this hard to believe, James, but Edward Mizzentoft seduced *me*. I did not find him an attractive man in any way; in fact he was rather ugly and arrogant. I suppose it was a way of punishing my husband. Even though he never knew about it, I gained some warped personal satisfaction from the knowledge that I had been unfaithful to him with a mutual acquaintance. God, how you must loathe me now!'

He placed a hand on her shoulder. 'I loathe you *less* now.'

She reached up and cradled his face in her hands, her eyes imploring. 'James….'

He took her hands and gently but firmly placed them back in her lap. 'I cannot, Eleanora. I hope you understand. But I do believe in your innocence in the matter of how Edward Mizzentoft was killed, and I must report back to Mr Bucket.'

Gordon felt as though ten strong men were holding him back as he straightened up and moved away from her. He could still hear her heart-rending sobs as he walked out of the room and left her crumpled on the floor by the window.

Mr Bucket didn't seem surprised when Gordon met him in Belgrave Place, outside the home of Baroness Sowerby, and told him of his certainty that Eleanora Scambles was innocent of the stabbing of Edward Mizzentoft.

'There was never a possibility that Mrs Scambles was the killer.'

'Then, if you don't mind me asking, sir, why did you send me to interview her about the matter?' Gordon tried not to let the irritation show in his voice, though knowing Mr Bucket's powers of perception, he doubted whether he had succeeded.

'All loose ends must be tied up in an official investigation, Mr Gordon. And besides, all loose ends must be tied up in *life*, too.'

'Well, I'm not sure that they were, Mr Bucket.'

'Ah well, where murder's concerned there's always a right and wrong conclusion, provable by cold fact. That's what I like about murder. In life things ain't always that straightforward. But you're your own man, you are, and that's all a matter for you to decide.'

XXII

'HER LADYSHIP IS not at home, I'm afraid, sirs.'

'Well, we'd like to see her anyway if it's all the same with you.' Mr Bucket replied cheerfully and tapped the tip of his stick rhythmically on the floor to the beat of some unheard tune that was apparently playing in his head.

The maid blinked uncomprehendingly at him. 'No, sir, what I mean to say is, she's *out*. Perhaps you'd like to leave your card?'

Gordon fidgeted and struggled to keep his silence. It was common practice and considered perfectly acceptable in polite society to use the excuse that someone was out if they did not wish to entertain a visitor for some reason. Surely even Mr Bucket was aware of this? It assuredly was *not* considered good form to press the point as he seemed intent on doing.

'And what I mean to say, madam, is that I *intend* to see her. I have seen her carriage standing horseless round the corner, I have seen the lady herself at an upper window and I shall not withdraw until I have seen *her* in person! Tell her it is Inspector Bucket of the Detective and Sergeant James Alexander Gordon, Seventh Earl of Drumnadrochit. Tell her it is to do with ferns, and more particularly, tell her it is to do with nasty notices in the *Morning Chronicle*. I believe she will see us.'

Gordon felt sorry for the poor girl, who was little more than sixteen and only trying to do her mistress's bidding in the face of Mr Bucket's irresistible powers of persuasion. Gordon had quite forgotten the business of the ferns – something which seemed not only trivial but even inappropriate to be dealing with now that the Mizzentoft case was officially theirs to look into. Quite what he meant by 'nasty notices' Gordon had no idea.

A couple of minutes later the maid returned and sheepishly ushered them straight up to the drawing room where Baroness Sowerby was to be found. She was standing by the hearth, stiff and erect, glaring at them from afar. The fire had recently been built up; it spat and crackled, and in complete contrast to Baroness Sowerby the room was invitingly cosy after the dank chill of the streets outside. There were to be no formalities this time.

'Say what you have to say, Bucket.'

She uttered his name like someone spitting a disagreeable morsel of food out of their mouth. Her manner was defiant, yet also strangely resigned, like a defeated general reluctantly offering his sword to the victor.

'It's an honour and a privilege to be invited to share your ladyship's company again,' Mr Bucket said most affably. 'Mr James Alexander Gordon and I are most grateful to you for making the time in your busy schedule to see us – are we not, Mr Gordon?'

Since he had no idea what his chief was building up to, Gordon had little choice but to go along with his approach. 'Very grateful, my lady.'

Baroness Sowerby had not moved from her position at the hearth. She tipped up her chin haughtily and said in a low, harsh voice, 'State your business and leave, sir.'

'I shall indeed state my business, ma'am. But first, perhaps your ladyship would care to sit on that sofa over there and make herself more comfortable? It is my aim to be as quick as I can about this matter, but one can never tell how long these things are likely to take.' He still smiled warmly and spoke as if to an old friend, while the sense of barely concealed animosity emanating from their reluctant interviewee was almost palpable. What puzzled Gordon was that she could have ordered them to leave at any point, an order they could only have disobeyed at the cost of their careers and reputations as gentlemen. In fact, she could have refused to have even let them set foot over the threshold in the first place, despite Mr Bucket's harrying of the poor maid who had answered the door. What was going on here? Gordon was torn between anxiousness and fascination as the scene unfolded.

Baroness Sowerby's only response to being invited to sit on her own sofa was to remain standing imperiously and defiantly by the fire like one of a pair of iron dogs that go with many fireplace sets.

'Now, it's like this, your ladyship. Myself and my colleague here, Mr James Alexander Gordon of that ilk – a sergeant of no little potential in the detective force – have been investigating this business about the ferns, and we have reached a conclusion.'

'Really?' Although she maintained her air of condescension and disinterest, Gordon could sense a certain uneasiness.

'Yes, your ladyship. But that's where it starts to get a bit complicated, for in the course of making inquiries into the disappearance of valuable ferns from several households, I have discovered that one thing leads to another, as Shakespeare possibly once said. One thing – being the ferns – led to the unearthing of another crime: the theft of some personal letters and a consequent attempt at blackmail. Whether the press or society in general would consider one crime more serious than the other I have given some thought to and I confess I can't quite reach a definite conclusion.'

'Neither can I, Inspector. Nor is it of any interest to me.'

But Gordon knew by now, and Mr Bucket undoubtedly did too, that she was very interested indeed, even if she would rather not be listening to what he had to say.

Mr Bucket raised his forefinger and his face lit up as if he were regaling a friend with a fascinating yarn. 'Ah! But that is not the end of it by a long chalk, ma'am! For I then became aware that those two matters were in turn connected – however loosely – with a third and yet more serious felony: that of *murder*!'

Gordon was as fascinated by this battle of wits as one in the audience of a superior mystery play, and was watching Baroness Sowerby's face intently. There was a sudden draining of colour at the mention of murder, and an almost imperceptible movement as if her legs nearly gave way beneath her. But he couldn't help but admire the way in which she instantly recovered her composure. She quickly gathered herself, and let out a disdainful snort.

'Mr Bucket, this has all been very entertaining but not only have I not the slightest idea what all these riddles mean, they most certainly have nothing to do with me and I must now ask you to leave. I have a luncheon date with The Honourable Mrs Jessamine Cranson Wight and I do not intend to make her wait for me.'

Mr Bucket's response took Gordon quite by surprise. He gave a brief nod and turned on his heels, walking towards the door. 'Then I won't take up any more of your ladyship's valuable time. Mr Gordon and I are also busy men – warrants to prepare and the like. I just hope this all doesn't get into the press too quick as is sadly so often the case in these more sensational cases.'

Gordon followed him, having quickly worked out that this was a bluff on his part, since despite his inexperience he knew they didn't need a formal warrant in order to arrest someone against whom there were sufficient grounds and evidence. Which he fervently prayed there were....

They were in the act of crossing the threshold of the room when the call came.

'Mr Bucket....'

Her voice was weary, empty of its former sense of superiority. They turned to face her. Baroness Sowerby's face and posture retained some of their former boldness but it was little more than pride, and her eyes told a different story. That's why what she said next took Gordon quite by surprise.

'If you arrest me it will cause me great inconvenience and humiliation, but the case would never come to court no matter how much proof you have. I am a first cousin of the Earl of Runnymede and distantly related to and on friendly terms with the Duke of Wellington himself. There are people who would not let this proceed. My reputation might be tarnished, but yours – and your career – would be destroyed utterly.'

'Arrest, your ladyship? Why, who said anything about an arrest?'

'You … you spoke of a warrant.'

'A warrant to search the premises – that's what I was referring to. To enable me to locate certain concealed items of a fern-like nature, as I am sure would be found within a very short space of time. My sergeant would remain here to make sure no such items were surreptitiously removed from the premises while the warrant was being obtained.'

'Not only is this preposterous and an outrage—'

'Now, now, madam! What *you* want is for this matter to be sorted out quickly and quietly, not all drawn out and painful. *You're* a woman of intelligence and knowledge of the world and its ways, that's what *you* are. You know what I know and I know what you know, and there's no sense or pleasure in playing games with words any longer. Now you go and sit down upon that sofy and allow me to reveal my hand in plain terms.'

To Gordon's amazement, Baroness Sowerby meekly obeyed. She left her post at the fireside and settled on the sofa – though she perched herself on the edge in a tense, uneasy posture. The detectives drew up two chairs and sat opposite her.

Mr Bucket clapped his hands on his thighs and launched into the case he had against her without any preamble. 'Your ladyship, overcome by jealousy or some womanly emotion to which I'm not privy, took it upon herself to relieve a member of the Society for the Relief of the Ruptured Poor of a fern or two from their, perhaps, over-large collection.'

Baroness Sowerby opened her mouth to interject, but Mr Bucket raised a finger and waggled it till she thought better of her plan. 'Now, I never suggested that your ladyship personally performed the deed … although I do wonder whether the very first occasion might have been simply a moment of weakness or opportunism when your ladyship was alone for a moment. But no, I believe an intermediary was used for the most part. The type of person I'm more used to dealing with is motivated by want or greed, but in this case I suspect it was at least in part a sense of illicit adventure which led to further such escapades. And I'm as sure as eggs is eggs that the aforesaid intermediary went by the name of Alfred Jukes.'

Again Baroness Sowerby attempted to speak, but again she was cowed into submission by that stern forefinger. 'Alfred Jukes is the name in the parish book, if his appearance in the world was ever recorded in such a sacred volume in the first place, but he would be known to your ladyship by the name of Chuddersby. This Chuddersby left your employ and found himself a position with Lady Rhynde. One thing I'd be interested to know is whether this was by chance, or part of a grand design on madam's part.'

'It suited my purposes,' she replied with a shrug of indifference.

'There you are, Mr Gordon – foresight! Resourcefulness! That's what that is, Mr Gordon. But then, in the specific case of Lady

Rhynde, you took things further – too far, as if what you'd already done wasn't bad enough. You discovered, no doubt through some freelance prying on the part of the man you knew as Chuddersby, that that good Lady—'

'She is neither good, nor a lady in the *purest* sense of the word!' hissed Baroness Sowerby, finding a target for her spleen at last.

Mr Bucket was unmoved. 'Let he who is without sin and all that. Anyhow, some weightier matter came to light that you knew could be used against her. And this intelligence suited you admirably because you feared that Lady Rhynde knew or had guessed that you had something to do with her own missing ferns. Thus you had something over her to ensure her silence. And that's what I believe them who knows bigger words than the likes of me call *ironic*. Because having interviewed her ladyship I'm quite certain that she originally had no inkling of any impropriety on your part nor even any suspicions regarding Chuddersby.'

Gordon noticed the first crack in Baroness Sowerby's facade. At the news that her risky and – presumably – illegal enterprise had all been for nothing, she winced briefly and he thought he detected a sudden paleness to her complexion. But then she seemed, after an internal struggle, to reach a decision.

'You are a very shrewd and clever man, Mr Bucket. Far more so than I would have credited for someone in such a lowly station in life. So now it is time to lay our cards on the table. You believe I am responsible for stealing ferns from certain ladies in London, and of....'

At this point she glanced in Gordon's direction as if she had only then remembered he was present and felt constrained to choose her words carefully. The fact that his own chief and this apparent crim-inal, however well regarded in society she might be, appeared to share a secret to which Gordon was not privy made him feel like a child being protected from grown-up matters by his parents. He had little choice, though, but to silently go along with their game and listen to her pronouncement.

' ... Of attempting to embarrass Lady Rhynde. But I also suspect that you cannot, nor never will be able to, prove any of it – and since I certainly shall not own to any such improprieties I don't see that you have any choice but to quietly let the matter drop.'

'These are not improprieties, madam, but *crimes*. Don't you see? Offences for which people go to gaol if convicted. I spoke of warrants earlier, and what if I were to obtain one that permitted me to examine every nook and cranny of this splendid residence, eh? What do you think I might find – plants which might be identified by bereft owners? Copies or originals of incriminating letters? Perhaps, if your ladyship is as meticulous as I suspect she is, even accounting ledgers showing unusual payments to certain former butlers known to associate with the criminal fraternity.'

'You would never be granted such a warrant, Bucket.'

'It is my job so to do, your ladyship.'

'But I am not a common criminal. I am the widow of Sir Langley Sowerby. I have only to say the word to ensure not only that any warrant sought by you is refused or rescinded, but that your future in the Detective is a very short one.'

Mr Bucket stuck his thumbs in his lapels and considered this for a moment. 'Well, now; I see I shall have to lay my cards on the table too. It is only Mr Jukes – Chuddersby to you – as I'm interested in from a criminal point of view. Does he still keep a room here?'

'*Keep a room*? May I remind you, sir, that this is not a common lodging house.'

'No it is not. But I suspect that he has some sort of temporary base here – perhaps his old room still contains some of his possessions?'

'We have plenty of spare rooms and it has not been cleared out.'

'And when he visits – as I know he does – he makes use of this room?'

'He has been known to – but I can assure you that you will not find him there now or at any time in the future.'

'I can quite believe it. But I believe him to have involved himself in other enterprises – ones with which madam would *certainly* not want her name to be associated. More to the point, I suspect that an item purloined by him, which would have a great bearing on this grave matter, can be found in this house. Will you not reconsider your decision to prevent us from inspecting the premises?'

'Good day, Inspector.'

'That is a shame. The other things that have been alluded to can be put right and then forgotten about. Earlier, I mentioned laying my cards on the table and speaking of cards, madam seems to delight in gambling for high stakes – and believe me, these are high stakes for a person of your station. Maybe you could stymie my inquiries, and yes, even get me the sack. Maybe not. I ask very little of you, and the consequences of denying me could prove to be disastrous for *you*. I could obtain new employment – but could your ladyship get her reputation back so easily? I'm sure a little time for reflection will make madam come round to my way of thinking! I have other matters to attend to, so my colleague and I shall bid you good day.'

Without further ado Mr Bucket gave a slight bow, and they proceeded to show themselves out. Out in the street, the fog had cleared somewhat and a weak, hazy sun shimmered over Hyde Park.

'Could she really get the case stopped, get you dismissed?'

'There's no maybe about it, Mr Gordon. She risks exposing her own underhand dealings, and after we've let her stew awhile she should see sense. But she's a pig-headed woman when all's said and done, so what *we* need is an insurance policy.'

'What do you mean?'

Mr Bucket stopped and rubbed his chin as if the plan were still solidifying in his mind. '*If* some minor calamity were to befall number 6, Belgrave Place in the middle of the night, which prompted her ladyship to rush *out*, and some brave officers of the law forsook all thoughts of their own personal safety and rushed *in....*'

Gordon broke into a grin. 'Such as a burglar who makes a lot of noise yet manages to slip through our hands!'

'Or a fire....'

He raised his eyebrows. 'You did say *minor* calamity, sir. Much as I detest Baroness Sowerby I shouldn't wish to see her burn to death.'

'Upon my soul, not a bit of it! But if some deranged criminal mind could engineer a small, contained blaze in an uninhabited area, creating a lot of smoke without causing much damage ....'

'The consequences if your plan should be discovered ....'

'Why, I might just as well get sacked for one thing as another!'

Gordon couldn't argue with that – and besides, the idea of

Baroness Sowerby getting her come-uppance in such a deliciously devious plot appealed to his sense of natural justice, if not to his professional one. 'I believe it would have to be tonight, and that someone should keep the house under surveillance in the meantime to prevent her from disposing of the evidence.'

'Why, Lord! It's mighty selfless of you to volunteer for such a tedious task,' beamed Mr Bucket.

'Thank you; but I wasn't exactly—'

'Such enthusiasm shall be noted in your record, *that's* what shall be done! In the meantime I need to see a man about a fire.'

'You have someone in mind?'

'I do indeed – a trustworthy and intelligent fellow who will be perfect for this job – none other than our friend Mr George!'

XXIII

A FIGURE LEANED against a wall near the corner of Belgrave Square and Belgrave Place, unhurriedly refilling his pipe. He was well away from the nearest street light, his head covered by a broad-brimmed felt hat so little could be discerned of his features; but he was powerfully built and despite his casual posture there was something of the military bearing about him. He had some sort of workman's canvas bag slung over his left shoulder, which looked bulky and filled to capacity. It was coming up to 2.30 in the morning, and the presence of a man loitering at this hour might arouse suspicion in other towns and villages; but this was London, a place where idlers and workers alike haunted the streets and alleyways at all times of the day and night. A police constable turned the corner of Eaton Place and strode slowly towards the man just as the newly lit tobacco in his pipe began to glow brightly in the darkness. Even though it was common for the constable to see people out and about at this hour, the man's bag and loitering presence might well have prompted a brief comment or inquiry – but the policeman walked by and didn't even look in the smoker's direction. In fact, Belgrave Place was not even part of his normal beat.

Soon after the policeman had passed, another man came into view. He was wearing an expensive silk top hat, and tapped the pavement with a silver-tipped cane. This man was quite fat, and the hint of unsteadiness in his gait showed that he had enjoyed a long and pleasantly bibulous evening with friends. When his eyes fell upon the pipe smoker, a scowl darkened his face.

'What are you about?' he growled.

When no reply was forthcoming, he stopped and glared at the

idler. 'I ask again, sir – what are you about at this hour? There have been burglaries in this area!'

A contented puff of the pipe was the only response from the man in the shadows, which only served to inflame the fat man further. He banged his cane down and lurched towards the object of his suspicions. But before a confrontation could develop the constable who had passed by only moments earlier returned.

'Nothing to worry about, sir. Let's not cause a fuss and go waking folks up.'

'But ... ' spluttered the fat man, pointing his cane in the pipe smoker's direction.

'This fellow is known to me,' said the constable calmly but firmly, 'and there is no cause for concern at all. Kindly move along.'

The fat man did reluctantly get under way again, occasionally glancing back over his shoulder at the mysterious, silent presence leaning against the wall. Once he had gone, the constable gave the pipe smoker what almost looked like a wink before returning to his patrol.

Belgrave Place fell silent once again. The pipe smoker removed his pocket watch and struck a match so that he could read it clearly, then he glanced both ways, straightened himself up and walked briskly towards Eaton Place. This narrow thoroughfare ran at a right angle to Belgrave Place, and a little way along it was a gap between the buildings that led to the rear of number 6 Belgrave Place, home of Baroness Sowerby. He disappeared from sight, and when he reappeared approximately twenty minutes later, his empty bag flapping loosely with each step, the man pulled the brim of his hat down low over his eyes and headed away from Belgrave Place towards the east of the capital.

The policeman conveniently reappeared at this point and retraced his steps along Belgrave Place. As he passed number 6 he glanced up. All seemed well, but he stopped and waited. Within two minutes, black smoke began to seep through an open window at the top of the building, and the constable immediately sprang his rattle and twirled it energetically.

'*FIRE! FIRE!*'

Within seconds, the windows of numerous houses were lowered

and servants' heads emerged. Raised, muffled voices began to seep into the streets, and lights come on. Almost as if they had been waiting for this moment, two men came running out of Wilton Street and made for number 6, where the constable was, by now, hammering on the door and shouting urgently. The glow of lighted candles flitting quickly past upper windows could be seen from the street below. Soon there was a rattling of bolts and locks, and the door was thrown open. By now, smoke was billowing from the top floor window. The constable entered the house yelling for everyone to leave, and as the two men – a rather portly one of average height and a taller, more athletically shaped figure – approached the steps, two women were in the act of leaving, the younger of the two supporting the other on her arm. Both were still wearing night-clothes and had blankets wrapped around their shoulders; the woman being supported was short, wiry and elderly. Physically she looked frail, yet signs of an inner strength could be seen in her eyes: she was not a person easily given to panic or fear. When her gaze fell upon the two men coming up the steps, her countenance darkened considerably.

And when the stouter of the two men touched the rim of his hat as he brushed past her, saying, 'Fear not! We shall ensure everything is taken care of,' rage flared across her features, but he and his companion were already in the house before she could raise her voice.

XXIV

A T FIRST IT seemed odd to be charging into someone's property in the midst of such pandemonium about a fire, when on the lower floors there was no evidence inside the building of any conflagration whatsoever. By the time Gordon and Mr Bucket reached the first floor landing they encountered their accomplice, Constable Garmory, bringing up a pail of water from the kitchens below.

'No rush, Constable,' said Mr Bucket now that they were out of sight of the house's normal inhabitants. 'Mr George knows what he's about. There'll be no danger from *that* fire.'

But the policeman still beat them to the top floor. As they climbed after him up the narrow stairs to the servants' quarters, they could at first smell and then see the smoke. Gordon was surprised, then, to hear laughter from above.

'Why, old George decided to make life easier for us!' Constable Garmory exclaimed when they joined him. And there, positioned neatly outside the door under and around which the smoke was emanating, stood a large pail of water.

They joined in the constable's mirth, and Mr Bucket picked the additional pail up and handed it to Gordon. 'You can play the fireman!' he grinned.

Garmory opened the door cautiously and they waited a moment to let the initial rush of smoke escape. Through the smoke Gordon glimpsed tongues of orange flame, no more than a foot high, in the centre of what looked like a little-used storage closet with bare floorboards and just a dust-coated cupboard inside. The constable advanced towards the fire and emptied the contents of his pail onto it. This in itself appeared to have doused the fire completely, but Gordon followed suit just to be sure. He could now see that to

179

protect the floorboards the fire had been made on a few house bricks, and appeared to consist of some kindling at the bottom with green shrub-like leaves and wet branches placed on top.

Mr Bucket produced a sack from the pocket of his great coat. 'Here, Garmory. Once it's a-cooled down all safe and sound you'd better place everything in here and take it away for ... eeh ... scientific examination.'

'Very good sir.'

Then, turning to Gordon, Mr Bucket said, 'Let's look sharp, Mr Gordon! You take her ladyship's private rooms. Ferns and letters!' he urged. 'Collect up all the ferns, and then look for letters – private, incriminating letters. But don't you go a-reading 'em! I'm going to the servants' quarters.'

'But what if they're Baroness Sowerby's own ferns?'

'If they're hidden away, chances are they're *all* a-pilfered, Mr Gordon. We shall work on that basis, anyhow. Bag 'em all, or at least as many as you can. Any inconsistencies can be sorted out at a later date, but I doubt whether her baronesship will press the point.'

He dashed off to inspect other rooms in the attic while Gordon hurried down the stairs, wondering quite how he could identify incriminating letters without reading their contents.

Moving quickly along the landing, he soon located what could only be Baroness Sowerby's bedroom. This was spartan in the extreme, but otherwise looked perfectly normal; there was a door leading off it, which he assumed must be her dressing room, so he turned his attentions there. As soon as Gordon opened the door he felt as though he had entered a jungle. The room was full of ferns in containers of all shapes and sizes. He took from his pocket the hessian sack he had been instructed to bring along, and began to carefully fill it. Once this was done, his eyes fell on some sort of bureau, which had previously been hidden by the mass of foliage. The first drawer he tried was locked, but before he could try any others Gordon heard an urgent clatter of footsteps on the stairs. He went out onto the landing and was confronted by two men in the uniform of the Fire Brigade – and Mr Bucket, who had moved swiftly to intercept them.

'Bravo, gentlemen! A swift and timely response – you are a credit to your insurance company. I am Inspector Bucket of the Detective, I am, and let me assure you that no further professional intervention is required, as the fire is quite put out. My colleague and I – Mr James Alexander Gordon, the Seventh Earl of Drumnadrochit, no less – just happened to be patrolling these streets in search of Lenny Boyle the notorious cat burglar when we were alerted to the fire by the constable's rattle. Turns out it was a conflagration of small and harmless proportions, easily extinguished. Perhaps you might explain that to her baronesship on your way out?'

The would-be firefighters seemed only too happy to be able to return to their beds, and trooped back the way they had come.

'I have found a locked bureau, Mr Bucket.'

'Lead on!'

The detectives went back into the dressing room, where Mr Bucket bent down to examine the locks on the drawers of the desk for a few seconds. He then reached into his pocket and drew something out – Gordon could not see what it was, but he soon heard a great deal of fumbling and scraping for a minute or two, followed finally by a distinct metallic click. He heard Mr Bucket let out a little grunt of satisfaction, before pulling the top drawer open and rummaging around inside.

'*Bingo!*' he cried, and waved a bundle of letters in the air like a trophy. They were tied together with a black ribbon, which Mr Bucket quickly undid, picking out one of the letters at random and inspecting it. 'Yes, just as I thought,' he said rather enigmatically, slipping the letters into his pocket.

He then reached into another pocket and took out a piece of paper and a small, rectangular, silver box, ornately decorated – no doubt his prizes from Jukes's old quarters.

'Lookee here, Mr Gordon!'

'Is that the snuffbox taken from Dr Scambles' room?'

'I'm willing to wager my career on it. Come to think of it, I *am* wagering my career on it. Better make sure then!' He opened the box and sampled a generous pinch. 'Yes. Good quality, that. Too rich for Alfred Jukes's pocket – sure to have belonged to Dr Scambles. Care to join me in a pinch?'

Gordon shook his head. 'It's not something I indulge in, sir. So,

Jukes was the person who broke into Mrs Scambles' house. I can't help thinking that it must be linked to the murder of Mizzentoft – yet I can't think how.'

'Oh, I'm *sure* it is linked, Mr Gordon of that ilk. But not in the way I once suspected – if *this* is to be believed.' He held up the piece of paper which he had also retrieved from Jukes's room.

'What does that signify?'

'It is not what I expected to find, and that's a fact. But what it signifies, sir, is that one of our prime suspects for the murder of Edward Mizzentoft is an innocent man – all things being relative, of course, and just so long as the account contained within it proves an accurate one and this here legal company turns out to be equally legitimate ….' Mr Bucket's usually alert eyes clouded over and darkened for a moment in a way Gordon had not seen before. 'It also signifies that my worst fears are one step closer to being confirmed.' He let out a troubled sigh, then pulled back his shoulders in a determined fashion. 'Be that as it may. Napper and Narkin of Lincoln's Inn, Mr Gordon. Pay them a visit tomorrow and try to confirm their dealings with Alfred Jukes.'

He held the document closer for Gordon to examine, and he saw that it was an affidavit; the name *Alfred Jukes* was prominent in capital letters at the top, and again at the bottom, where a spidery 'X' was scrawled beside it.

'No time to peruse at length now,' he said, stuffing it into a pocket with the other items before making for the door.

'Might I ask what those other letters are? Are they to do with the stolen ferns?'

Mr Bucket shook his head. 'No. Not directly, at any rate. These epistles were never intended for anyone's eyes other than a certain lady, and I shall be destroying them at the first opportunity. Now let us return to our homes and get some kip, Mr Gordon. There is work to do tomorrow!'

Inevitably, they encountered Baroness Sowerby as they exited the premises. Two constables who had been alerted by PC Garmory's rattle were standing guard at the door and the baroness reminded Gordon of a little terrier straining against its leash as she waited to return to her home. The look on her face when she spotted them was worth a thousand words, and he was certain that she had discerned the truth of this whole charade. Mr Bucket smiled affably and raised his hat.

'Madam will be pleased to know that all is now safe and well! I'm sure she will wish me to pass on her thanks to the policeman whose sharp eyes saved her home and belongings from certain destruction, and I shall be happy to oblige.'

He made to leave, but her sharp tones cut through the night. *'What has he there? What has he in that sack?'*

'Nothing but a few plants, singed and wilted beyond saving, sadly. Don't worry – Mr Gordon knows exactly how to dispose of them. Oh, and certain letters also perished in the inferno – but they looked like the sort that needed a-burning anyway. Now everything's squared away and I feel sure our paths will never cross again. Good evening, ma'am!' He touched the rim of his hat again, and they strode away feeling her glowering stare boring into their backs.

'So, what next?' Gordon asked Mr Bucket later when they emerged from Great Scotland Yard and prepared to retire to their own homes.

'Once you have been assured of the veracity of that there affidavit, I should like you to pay a visit to Dr Scambles and discuss its contents with him. I have other matters to attend to.'

The drama of the fire had caused Gordon to quite forget about Mrs Scambles' husband locked away in Coldbath Prison awaiting trial for murder – not least the fact that she was accusing him of the crime.

'Perhaps we should wait until we have further investigated Mrs Scambles' accusations before we say anything about it to him. After all, we have no proof – it is merely the word of a woman scorned, as you might say.'

'But we do have proof, Mr Gordon. Proof of his innocence!'

'*Innocence?* What about Dr Scambles' bloodstained watch that Inspector Stope showed to us? His watch, his initials engraved upon it – found at the murder scene!'

'His wife's claims, as you indicated, are nothing but the cater-waulings of a bitter woman. The watch? Yes, the watch …. It *will* lead us to the real murderer, but it is not Dr Scambles. We have this case all but tied up and Dr Scambles is not our man. Bear with me. I have one more matter to attend to, and then we shall make our move.'

XXV

THE OFFICES OF Napper and Narkin were situated within the ornate red-brick building of Lincoln's Inn Hall, and after locating their office and waiting for a few minutes in an outer room, a clerk summoned Gordon into the presence of Mr Narkin. He was a much younger and less solemn man than he'd expected. Of wiry build and fresh complexion, he came bounding towards Gordon with his hand outstretched.

'Mr Gordon? Pray take a seat, and I'm sorry to have kept you waiting.'

'It was hardly any time at all, and I'm sure you're very busy.'

He pulled a face. 'I wish we were ... but that's of no consequence to you and I'm only too happy to help the police in the course of their duties. I've read about the detective force in the newspapers and I must say I find it all very fascinating!'

'As a matter of fact I'm new to it myself, and so do I!'

'Would you like me to send for drinks, Mr Gordon?'

'Thank you – but I have an urgent appointment as soon as I leave here. I only wish to ask you about one Alfred Jukes, who I believe visited these offices a few days ago. He's a tall man, with—'

'Oh, I remember Jukes!' grinned Narkin. 'Very strange affair. He wanted me to draw up an affidavit – without telling me what it was about!'

'Can you describe it? I only wish to confirm that it is a legitimate document.'

'Not much to describe – a single sheet of paper bearing our seal. Jukes himself is illiterate, so he scrawled an "X" beside his name.'

'That certainly sounds like the document we found.' Gordon had accomplished this particular mission, but since Mr Bucket had

185

chosen not to divulge its contents to him, he couldn't help asking more. 'Are you at liberty to tell me what the affidavit was about?'

'Ah, you put me in an awkward spot, Mr Gordon – confidentiality is paramount in our business, of course.'

'Does the fact that Mr Jukes is dead make it any easier for you?'

'Dead? Well, I suppose he couldn't sue me! All I will say, sir, is that it was very brief and cryptic. The strangest thing I've ever had to deal with, in truth. He wanted me to write that he was being coerced into committing certain criminal acts against his will. The cause of this was that a particular person had some sort of hold over him, and the consequences of not obeying this person were too dire for him to contemplate – he even feared for his life. Quite rightly, as it turned out. He did name the individual, but working on the assumption that he isn't also dead I'm afraid I would be exceeding my remit if I named him.'

'That's quite all right, Mr Narkin. You have been most helpful.'

As Gordon was walking away beneath the skeletal, leafless trees of Lincoln's Inn Fields, he tried to make some sort of sense of what he had just heard. Could Jukes's fear and accusations regarding the controlling influence of this shadowy figure indicate that Mr Bucket and he had missed something? Was it possible that there was a Mr Big who had so far not figured in their investigations? A puppet master who had concealed himself so well that they weren't even aware of his existence?

It was a thing Gordon should have thought impossible, but the Coldbath Fields House of Correction looked even grimmer and more foreboding than it had the first time he had laid eyes upon it. Then, the temperature had been freezing but at least the skies had been blue and bright. Now, it's ugly bulk could be half seen through a thick, dirty, choking fog of the sort Gordon had only ever encountered in London and which emphasized its sinister grimness. Once he had gained entrance he was led again past the giant treadmill and the rows of hunched and broken men silently oakum picking until he came to the interview room in which he and Mr Bucket had first encountered Dr Scambles.

'We offered to move him to a nicer part of the prison, sir,' the warder who was guiding Gordon said. 'Thought he might like to help out in the clinic, him being a doctor and all. But he refused.'

This didn't surprise Gordon. Dr Scambles might not be a murderer – although until Mr Bucket could prove otherwise he still hadn't completely dismissed the idea – but that didn't make him any more likeable as a man. Mrs Scambles' stories about his coldness rang true, and Mr Bucket and he had witnessed the power of his sudden wrath at close quarters.

'Let me make something clear, Mr Gordon,' said Scambles once they were seated opposite each other in the cold, drab office. 'The only matter I shall even entertain discussing is my innocence and how you can prove it.'

His icy gaze was unnerving but Gordon made himself hold it, and he realized it was his anger on Eleanora's behalf that, in part, fuelled his determination. 'I have been instructed by my senior officer to tell you that we believe we do indeed have evidence that might secure your release.'

This was enough to dissolve even Dr Scambles' cold-blooded demeanour. Now, Gordon saw a new Dr Scambles – one with his seemingly fixed, harsh, cold exterior suddenly breached. *'New evidence?* What? Pray tell me what it is? When shall I be out of here?'

Gordon raised his hands to calm him. 'All is not decided yet. Mr Bucket is, as we speak, looking into things and frankly I know no more than you do at present. But I can tell you that *he* believes in your innocence ....' He fought back the urge to say *even if your own wife does not.* 'And that there are other strong suspects. I must also add that your connection with the unfortunate Mr Mizzentoft and your financial predicament has come to light. It would have been better if you had revealed this earlier.'

'Ha! In order to furnish you with even more evidence against me?!'

'But that might have led us more quickly to others who had dealings with him – such as the man known as the General.'

'Was it him? Is he the real killer?'

'That I cannot say at present. But it is true that you fought with him shortly before Mizzentoft died?'

'I will not be bullied by any man.'

'Still, it was relevant to the investigation to discover the real killer. Do you know of anyone else in debt to Mizzentoft who might have had reason to murder him?'

Scambles gave a sardonic snort. 'It's a little late for that, isn't it, Sergeant?'

'Do you mean to say that you were never asked when you were originally arrested?'

'The big brute of a detective who arrested me merely informed me that I as good as had a rope around my neck, and I never so much as saw him again. And now I come to think of it, I assumed from what you said at our last meeting that you and Mr Bucket were *not* investigating the murder at all.'

'That was true at that time. There has been a change of circumstances.' Gordon answered rather absently because the news of how Mr Stope, an experienced and supposedly successful policeman, had dealt with this case had puzzled him. 'Getting back to my question, do you know of anyone else who might have been angry with Mizzentoft?'

'*Anyone* who is heavily in debt is liable to become angry at the exorbitant interest rates he charged and the methods he used to ensure payment was made, Sergeant. *I* was not angry with him, however. I was only angry with myself. We all knew what his terms were when we turned to him. I do recall that the General didn't work alone.'

'What do you mean?'

'I met him on more than one occasion, and I saw him in various places at other times. Mizzentoft employed him simply as a thug to get the money he was owed. But I occasionally saw the General in the company of another man, someone who also seemed to provide him with work of some, no doubt, dubious nature.'

'A tall man with long, oily hair?'

'He was very tall, yes. Do you know him?'

'He has cropped up several times during the course of this investigation.'

'Another suspect! Things are looking better for me by the second!'

XXVI

THE FOG WAS so thick outside that Sergeant Raddle had to light the lamps in the Back Hall even though it was almost noon. He knew it was almost noon without even looking at the big clock on the wall by the staircase because of the hollow growl coming from his stomach. Soon, Constable Hacker would be here to relieve him and he could then repair to the Ten Bells for a spot of lunch. Just as he was tidying his belongings away, the double doors flew apart and two people arrive enveloped in a swirl of fog like some sort of Biblical manifestation. But as the vapour cleared, Sergeant Raddle's heart sank. He could see that it was not two but three … *beings* that had entered the foyer.

Constable A43 Lush.

A man with a small body and an over-sized head topped with a ludicrously tall hat.

And a monkey.

Sergeant Raddle cast his face into an impenetrable mask to hide his dismay and coughed to drown out the urgent and alarmingly prolonged gurgle emanating from his belly. The small man in the constable's clutches had a strong chin. A jutting chin, which spoke of determination, of indomitability. It was the look of one who Knows His Rights. These were attributes that would add many minutes to this encounter; Sergeant Raddle knew it. The mere presence of the monkey added incalculably more. He sank into his chair, trying to maintain a straight back.

'A dip, Mr Raddle. Witnessed in the very act,' announced Constable A43 Lush.

'Why 'ee says *dip?*' the small man with the annoyingly large head and the monkey on his shoulder loudly demanded to know, in an accent which the worldly Sergeant Raddle identified as Italian. '*I* no dippa da pockets! Why 'ee says *dip?*!'

The small man possessed an unconventional shape in every way. His ever-moving, oddly angular limbs seemed to jerk about in a variety of eccentric directions, which, in Sergeant Raddle's opinion, they simply should not. In fact, he found the newcomer's limbs inexplicably offensive.

'Now, now, sir. Let us be calm and orderly about this and we'll have it sorted out in a jiffy.' Sergeant Raddle couldn't help twitching his eyes to the clock again. 'My officer here saw you picking the pocket of an innocent—'

'Not me, sir, Mr Raddle.'

'But you said—'

'A *witness*, Mr Raddle. "Witnessed in the very act". '

'Then who saw it?'

PC Lush's stiff, white fingers fumbled with the brass button securing a deep pocket of his uniform and produced a small, damp, black notebook with curled corners. 'Mrs Emily—'

'*Amelia! Amelia!*' spouted the arrested man, waving his angular arms in – to Sergeant Raddle's mind – a preposterously extravagant Latin manner. 'I knowsa da woman. She a watercress girl in da Charing Cross. *Amelia!* She got it in for me because-a da money I owes her papa! *Amelia!*'

'It says "Emily" here,' the constable asserted defiantly, tapping the black cover of his notebook, 'so *Emily* it is.'

Sergeant Raddle tried to expedite the matter and extracted his own much larger black book from the desk drawer. 'So, we have a witness to this gentleman picking the pocket of an innocent—'

'Not *this* gentleman, Mr Raddle.'

The mask of official inscrutability cracked for a moment and an agonized grimace fleetingly distorted the weary sergeant's features.

'*Who*, then, Constable? *Who* is your dip?'

'Pippo, sir.'

'Pippo?'

Constable Lush aimed the finger of indictment at the bored, fidgeting monkey perched beside the overly large head.

Sergeant Raddle ran a finger between his neck and the stiff, high collar of his uniform. 'The monkey stole something.'

'A pocket book, Sergeant Raddle, sir.'

'So the animal, surreptitiously and with intent, removed a gentleman's pocket book, handed it to this gentleman, and the witness then—'

'Not *him*, sir.'

'"Not him" *what?*'

'The pocket book wasn't handed to this gent, sir.'

'Then *who?*'

'To a dog, Mr Raddle, sir.' Sergeant Raddle didn't even hear the clock chiming twelve times. His mind was in a deep, dark chamber of mortal cries and groans. He straightened himself up with an effort of will.

'The monkey gave the pocket book to a dog.'

'A Norwegian elkhound, sir. Which I know for a certain fact because my sister's fiancé used to have one. Run over by an 'ansom, sir. 'Orrible mess. The said dog – this gent's, not my sister's fiancé's – proceeded in an easterly direction towards Craven Street in … ' the constable read from his notebook, '… a *determined yet shifty manner*, sir. With the pocket book in its mouth.'

Sergeant Raddle slowly opened his big book. There was nothing for it – this was an incident which protocol dictated must be officially recorded. He produced a pen from his desk drawer, dipped the nib into the inkwell and prepared to write. It was a picture which captivated both Constable A43 Lush and his prisoner, for Sergeant Raddle was not a natural man of letters by any stretch of the imagination. He was poised with moist nib held aloft and his singular countenance, although actually one of supreme effort and concentration, was the frozen mask of one who had just been stabbed in the back by an unseen assailant. Constable Lush looked at his felon, and the felon, who feared that the man before him had entered a state of apoplexy, returned the glance.

But a new development saved the day. The double doors opened again and in walked Inspector Bucket. The lower half of his face was protected by an emerald coloured scarf from the noxious fumes pervading London's streets, but it was definitely Mr Bucket. And then, from a different direction, came Constable Hacker. Since Sergeant Raddle was in the middle of dealing with Lush and his detainees, strictly speaking he should have completed the task before handing the reception desk over to Hacker. But Mr Bucket had unwittingly provided him with a way of escape.

'Hi – Mr Bucket sir!'

'Yes, Sergeant?'

'I have some very important information to relate to you.'

Mr Bucket unbuttoned his coat and shook it, as if trying to rid it of the clinging noxious vapours. 'Yes?'

'Constable Hacker, if you would be so kind as to deal with PC Lush and his prisoners while I speak to Mr Bucket on a most important matter ....' Without waiting for an answer, Sergeant Raddle moved swiftly from behind the desk and ushered Mr Bucket to a quiet corner of the Back Hall.

'What's the to-do, Mr Raddle?'

'A message from Inspector Stope, sir. He says there has been a development on the Mizzenmast case, and would you be so kind as to join him in questioning an informant at Execution Docks: the Imperial Spice and Tobacco Company at 2 p.m.'

'The *Mizzenmast* case, no less!' Mr Bucket echoed with the hint of a twinkle in his eye. 'Still, plenty of time. Meanwhile, I think I shall—'

'Not necessarily, I'm afraid, Mr Bucket. Sir Marriot Ogle-Tarbolton is at the Southwark Mortuary where lays a body he feels you might like to see.'

'Well, there goes my lunch break then, Raddle old man!'

'Yes, sir. Shame,' replied Sergeant Raddle – but he was wearing a half-smile and had one eye on Constable Hacker, who was being harangued by both the man with the large head and his monkey.

'A stabbing, Mr Bucket,' pronounced Sir Marriot Ogle-Tarbolton, the Commissioner of Great Scotland Yard.

'Evidently,' said the detective, looking down at the naked, blue-tinged, lanky body with a deep purple, congealed slit in the left side of its neck.

'He has been identified by his lodging housekeeper as Thomas Jones.'

'Really?'

'And then by an acquaintance as William Chuddersby, a former servant of Lady Rhynde.'

'And now by me as Alfred Jukes!'

'I beg your pardon?'

'That's his real name. But I'd rather know the name of the man that killed him. *That* would suit me very nicely. Begging your pardon, sir, but what brings the Commissioner of Police to a common mortuary?'

Sir Marriot shrugged. 'Everyone seemed to be out on other cases, and I realized this was to do with her ladyship's stolen ferns.'

'And a lot more besides.' Mr Bucket's right forefinger traced the outline of his sideburn, before pushing the rim of his hat up a little.

'What? Do you refer to the *Mizzentoft* case, Inspector?'

Now, the wandering finger briefly touched the side of his nose. 'Things are coming to a head, sir. If the Commissioner will indulge me a little longer, I have every reason to believe I shall be able to deliver not only a full report to him, but the true killer!'

'So it *isn't* Dr Scambles?' Mr Bucket shook his head, and the Commissioner groaned quietly to himself. 'He'll no doubt sue us.'

'I doubt that, sir.'

'Billy Stope won't be very happy, either.'

A shadow passed over Mr Bucket's face. 'No, sir. He won't.'

Sir Marriot nodded towards the corpse. 'And I suppose it was not he who killed Mizzentoft?'

'No, sir. It wasn't him neither.'

A bulky man was loitering in a doorway near the church of St George the Martyr in Southwark. Even though the street lighting was unequal to the dense fog, he was clearly visible to passers-by and nearby shopkeepers, and he looked suspicious. But he was big, shaven headed and scarred about the face, and as long as he stayed away from them and their property, no one was going to approach him or trouble to involve themselves with what he might be up to.

When Mr Bucket left the mortuary, he pulled up his green scarf against the fog and, ignoring the main roads, took the most direct route towards Westminster Bridge through the side streets. The bulky man who had been lurking nearby stirred himself and followed, much to the relief of those who had been keeping a nervous eye on his presence. Now he was someone else's problem.

The General kept in step with the detective, but some yards behind; that, and the dampening effect of the fog meant that he was able to follow in virtual silence. He continued to do this for some minutes, until Mr Bucket crossed busy Waterloo Road and took yet another quiet, narrow street which would take him toward Westminster Bridge Road. As far as could be seen through the sickly miasma, this thoroughfare was deserted, and the General quickened his step; as quietly as possible at first, then, when he was just a few paces from his objective he launched into a sprint, which was surprisingly swift for a big man. As Mr Bucket twirled round, the General was already upon him. He grabbed the policeman by the lapels and yanked him into an alley with such sudden force that he was powerless to resist. He was pinned to the wall and his arms were trapped against his sides by the General's mass pressing against him.

'You've got to help me, Mr Bucket!'

'It don't seem like you're a-needing much help from *me,* General.'

The bruiser sheepishly relaxed his grip and took a step back. 'Things 'as got out of hand, Mr Bucket. I'll stand up to any man – any two or three if it comes to it. But this is diff'rent. This is too big for me. But I swear I ain't goin' to the gallows, Mr B.'

'The Montague Place business?'

The General nodded. 'The finger's startin' to point my way and I know it – but I swear it weren't me. I didn't even know about it till after it'd 'appened.'

'Then why might you think you're in the frame? We've already got a man locked away in Coldbath for it.'

'Aw, come on Mr B – you're in on it like the rest of 'em. Everyone knows that doctor's going to walk. Now Jukes is dead, you'll be coming after me – and I swear I'll take one or two of you to 'ell with me afore ye get the bracelets on me, so I do!'

'Now, now, General. No need for that sort of talk.'

'I break heads, Mr Bucket. I don't do people in – except the odd time in self-defence.'

'Naturally.'

'I *know* 'oo killed that man – but I can't tell yer or I'd be signing me own death warrant anyway.'

'There's someone even the General is a-feared of?'

'Not in *that* way ....'

Mr Bucket reached out and placed a hand on the General's shoulder. The big man tensed, since this was the way arrests were made; but the detective merely gave him a couple of heavy, reassuring taps.

'I know you didn't kill Edward Mizzentoft, General. And *you* know I'd never send an innocent man to the gallows.'

'I do, sir. I do that!' he replied in an almost pathetic manner, like a guilty dog hoping to avoid a beating from its master.

'And I believe I know who *did* do it. But what I need from you is to confirm it – and you may well need to stand before a court and tell everything you know.'

'Grass someone up in court? There's my reputation, Mr Bucket.'

'It's the only way, old fellow. You've already said you fear for your life one way or the other, and I might not be able to help you if you don't help me. Together, we can make sure the real murderer goes down and then you can stop looking over your shoulder. Why, you can soon restore your reputation by breaking a few more heads.'

The General half turned away. His big paw of a hand rubbed back and forth across his bristly scalp while the internal struggle went on.

'Will you make me say 'is name, Mr B?'

'*I* will say his name. You don't have to say anything. If you turn and walk away, I know I'm right – and you can swear before the good Lord and on your mother's grave that you never named anyone to the law.'

'But my mother ain't dead, Mr B.'

'Well, your grandmother or your great-great grandmother. It's all the same, and it is the best way, don't you see?'

The General did see. Mr Bucket looked him in the eye for a moment until he was sure he had his full attention, then he named his man.

The ex-prize-fighter shuffled awkwardly, checking all about him for any sound or hint of someone lurking in the fog. Then, he cast

Mr Bucket a knowing look and walked briskly away. Mr Bucket himself did not leave immediately but remained rooted to the spot, gazing at the back of the figure as the curtain of mist quickly closed behind it. In order to solve one slaying he had to turn a blind eye to another. One involved important people, the other a mere street urchin – that was the simple fact of the matter. Because in order to avoid jeopardizing his case Mr Bucket had to allow the killer of Tom Prike to walk free.

XXVII

'How has my wife been taking all this?' asked Scambles. 'She hasn't visited me in a while.'

Gordon thought he felt a warmth come to his face and feared he had reddened slightly. He hadn't expected Scambles to mention Eleanora, since he had shown no signs of caring about her or her plight before now.

'She has had her ups and downs. I assume you are aware she has been staying with my superior's relative for a while since the burglary at your house?'

'Yes.'

'Well, we now have deemed it safe for her to return home.'

'Does she know everything?'

'If you mean your financial predicament, yes, she does.'

He gave a bitter smile. 'And I can imagine how she reacted. I can no doubt look forward to a warm welcome if, as you say, I am soon released from this place.'

He turned that piercing, unwavering gaze on Gordon again. 'You think I'm an unfeeling man, don't you, Sergeant.'

It was a statement rather than a question and he was momentarily knocked off balance by it. 'I ... it is not my business as a detective officer to make personal judgements.'

'Oh, come, sir. It is *exactly* your business! You must decide whether the people you interview are truthful or liars, wicked or harmless. I know I am not a man of great personal charm or warmth, Mr Gordon. I keep my own counsel and I care not for what the world thinks of me. For my part I don't think much of the world, so what it thinks is of little moment to me. But *she* is far worse than I! I prefer to remain aloof and trouble no one. She is an actress, a beguiler. She has beguiled many men, Sergeant. Has she beguiled you? It's a question which intrigues me. I cannot quite decide whether you are weak enough or greedy enough to allow it.'

Gordon believed he did know the answer, and enjoyed his discomfort. He hated Scambles then more than ever – and he was determined to answer without telling the truth yet also without lying. 'I am well aware that the air of innocence and vulnerability she presents to the world is a facade.'

To Gordon's surprise he threw his head back and laughed. 'Good answer, Mr Gordon!'

He was greatly relieved when they were interrupted by the door opening and a prison officer thrusting his head round it.

'Dr Scambles, your lawyer is arrived.'

'Already?' He removed a watch from his pocket and looked at it. 'He is a good half hour early – but who am I to complain? He had arranged to visit me to discuss the trial, yet now it seems that we can talk about my imminent release!'

'Dr Scambles, I pray you do not build up your hopes too—' The doctor was in the act of returning his timepiece when it hit Gordon, and he cried out, *'Dr Scambles, pray do not put that watch away.'*

'I beg your pardon?'

'Is that new? Perhaps one your wife bought while you have been in prison to replace the one you lost?'

'Lost? I have not lost a watch, Sergeant. This watch was given to me by my father as a twenty-first birthday present.'

'You did not perhaps own another which has gone missing?'

'What is this? No, sir. I own only one watch, and it has never been lost.'

Gordon could feel the skin on the back of his neck tingling. 'A watch bearing your initials was found at the murder scene – a blood-stained watch. May I see yours?'

He handed it over. At first it appeared that it was not personally engraved the way the one in the evidence store at Great Scotland Yard was – but Gordon snapped open the case and there on the inside he saw an inscription:

To JWS from his father

'*JWS?*'

'My full name is Jonathan Webster Scambles. An ancestor married into the Webster family of Dorset and the name has been perpetuated in the naming of the first-born male in the Scambles family ever since. I always go by the full name Jonathan Webster Scambles, never simply Jonathan Scambles.'

'Then neither you nor anyone else who knew you would use the initials *JS* when referring to you or inscribing any of your property?' Gordon's heart was beginning to pound as the enormity of this discovery's implications sank in.

'Certainly not. Anyone who knows me is well aware that— *Oh, but wait a moment!*'

'You have remembered something?'

'When you first came here to meet me it was about a burglary at my home. Something was missing from my desk and no one – including myself – could recall what it was but now I have it! It *was* a watch. My footman's watch was in need of repair, and tinkering with mechanical and other such devices being a little hobby of mine I offered to look at it for him. He gave it to me shortly before I left the house on the day of the murder at Montague Place.'

'What is his name? The initials engraved on the watch found at the murder scene were *JS*, so it was assumed ....'

'His name, Sergeant, is James Strachan. I don't wish to play the detective, but it appears to me that since the theft took place *after* the murder, whoever stole it did so in a deliberate attempt to bolster the case against me after the fact, mistakenly assuming from the initials on the watch and the fact that it was on my desk that it must be mine. Quite who that could possibly be—'

'But what about Strachan himself?'

Scambles snorted derisively. 'Not only does he know nothing of my dealings with Mizzentoft or anyone else and so would have no motive to kill him, but he is simply not capable. The old boy has bad lungs and suffered a minor stroke last year, and he could barely lift a knife, let alone kill someone with it.'

Gordon was on his feet before Scambles had finished. He had never really believed it would have been Strachan anyway, but asked the question because the alternative was too terrible to contemplate. There was surely only one man who it could possibly be – even though the very idea seemed utterly appalling and unthinkable ....

XXVIII

Mr Bucket gazed out of the cab window at the Tower as the horse struggled up Tower Hill – or at least he gazed in the direction of the Tower, since all that could be made out was an indistinct, vaguely portentous mass which appeared to alter shape and hue as the lightest of airs off the Thames constantly rearranged the polluted vapours that enshrouded it. And it was because of the choking, lung-clogging fog that he had gone against his usual habit of walking and had opted for public transport to take him to the Imperial Spice and Tobacco Company at Execution Docks. To the detective, the city had the appearance of one that had had its population ravaged by a great plague and been abandoned by survivors. The folk of the capital were undoubtedly there, but the fog had dampened all sound and hidden from sight those who had ventured out; they flitted briefly in and out of view, hunched, faceless souls, like ghosts seeking a resting place.

Leaving the cab at the top of Old Gravel Lane, Mr Bucket tugged up his emerald green scarf so that it covered his mouth and nose, despite the fact that by now the garment felt damp and cold against his skin. He turned up his collar, pulled down the rim of his hat and embarked on the short walk to his destination. He passed not a soul on Old Gravel Lane, though it was lined with the houses of seamen, shipwrights and dock workers, and as he neared its end he could just hear the lapping of the water on the banks of the river and catch a glimpse of the odd mast in the distance as the fog drifted and eddied. From somewhere nearby he heard a man cry out a greeting, then a muffled reply; from another direction came the weary clip-clop of a horse. It was as if he were in a playhouse: the auditorium was in darkness, but the curtains were still drawn even though the performance was under way.

At the end of Old Gravel Lane Mr Bucket turned into Wapping Street. Even without being able to see clearly he knew that lining the river were wharves and small shipyards, and that some of the taller shapes on the shoreline were wooden cranes for unloading the ships that arrived here from all corners of the world. He also knew that he was now in the vicinity of Execution Dock, which was in the jurisdiction of the Admiralty and until recently a place where pirates and mutineers were hanged and their corpses left to be disposed of by the tides. The locals said that Captain Kidd met his end in this place.

The lack of visibility and difficulty in locating landmarks was disorienting, but when Mr Bucket caught a glimpse of the spire of St Mary, Rotherhithe he knew he was getting close. And sure enough he soon found himself looking up at the warehouse of the Imperial Spice and Tobacco Company. The sign was in surprisingly good condition, for the building itself was derelict. The last time Mr Bucket visited this area it had been, he felt certain, a thriving business; but now it was abandoned. The door leading to the offices was shut and barred, but the great barn-like doors through which goods were once moved were lying drunkenly apart, and the detective barely had to duck his head in order to slip through the gap between them. Mr Bucket could sense the cavernous space around him even though the area was in total darkness and the breached entrance and numerous broken windows had allowed the fog to enter as freely as if it were one of the streets or lanes surrounding it. He took a few steps towards what he calculated to be the centre of the warehouse floor, then stopped and looked unseeingly about him, listening, waiting.

So this is where it was to end. A friendship and working partnership of decades; a bond of brotherhood. But *how* would it end?

Mr Bucket walked again, and kept walking till he reached one wall of the building; then he proceeded to feel his way methodically around the inner perimeter. Distinguishable from the acrid vapours seeping in from the outside world, he could make out the musty smell of rotting timber and the pungent signs of rodent infestation. His sturdy boots crunched on broken glass and wooden splinters. Rusting nuts, bolts and assorted detritus were scattered about with every step, and small animals scurried from his approach.

And then he stopped suddenly. He had heard a different sound, something far above his head. It was not repeated, but he believed he had pinpointed its location, and when his perambulation brought him to an alarmingly decrepit-looking set of stairs, he began to ascend, placing his feet with great caution at every step. The flimsy stair rail – the only thing between him and the floor below - was leaning at an alarming angle, and moved several more inches when he put his hand on it. The treads beneath his feet were rotten, holed, loose and occasionally missing completely. But it had to be possible to negotiate this path, because he knew another had recently done it before him. Just before reaching the top, the detective took a step and the timber beneath his boot crumbled away, pitching him forwards and down. He instinctively grabbed for the banister even though he knew it was useless. It buckled and splintered, and Mr Bucket stumbled towards the edge, praying that the step his hands were about to make contact with would bear his weight. It did. He winced at the jarring of his wrists and shoulders on impact; his hat rim struck the bridge of his nose, bounced onto the stairs, then was swallowed by the darkness. There were a couple of seconds of silence, then it could be heard clattering onto the floor below. There was a searing pain in his knees where they had struck sharply against the splintered edge of the stairs, but the stinging was nothing to him at that moment. He had avoided plummeting to the warehouse floor below, and now there was undoubtedly a greater challenge to be faced.

The fog was much thinner on the landing, and Mr Bucket could see that this floor consisted of a long corridor with numerous rooms leading off it. The doors to most of the rooms were ajar, as if only temporarily vacated by the staff who once worked here. There was no sound, no movement; which room had the noise Mr Bucket heard come from? He proceeded stealthily, listening, looking. Then he heard something like the shuffle of a single foot against bare floorboards and paused, fixing his eyes on a door to his right a little way ahead. He edged towards the room until he was within reach of the door, then waited, listening intently. He could only hear the sound of his own breathing, but his stout forefinger moved to a spot just in front of his nose and hovered there; he sensed a presence behind this door. His hand moved away from his face until his palm rested against the door. It moved easily but noisily until it was half open, when the bottom became stuck fast against an uneven floor.

Across the room he could see daylight – such as it was that grim day for not only had a large window been smashed from its frame, but a jagged section of wooden wall itself had gone, too, leaving a gaping hole in the side of the building. Silhouetted against this grey glimpse of fog and sky he could just see the spire of St Mary's, Rotherhithe. But there was another dark outline beside it. This one was within the room, and was topped by the shape of a tall hat. The bell of St Mary's chimed two o'clock; the sound was dampened by the heavy, dank atmosphere, as if the church itself was in awe of the drama being played out.

'Afternoon, Bucket. Right London Peculiar out there.'

'Terrible choker. Even worse than yesterday, and that was bad enough. They say it will clear up tonight, though.'

'The Chief has been in a bad mood today. Don't know what's got into him.'

'He's just discovered his mother-in-law is a-coming to stay for the weekend. They've never quite seen eye to eye, as you might say.'

Stope laughed gruffly. 'Well that wouldn't be an easy thing to accomplish because I saw them together at a function a couple of years ago and—'

'—She's a good foot taller than him!' Mr Bucket finished the sentence for him, joining in the subdued mirth. 'That was just after we'd rounded up that gang of forgers from Essex. *That* was a good job, all right!'

'Nobody else in the Detective could have got to the bottom of that but you and me, Bucket. And what about the Mizzentoft case? How does that go?'

'That's nearly all squared up, Billy.'

'Thought as much. That's why I thought I'd have a little chat with you ....'

'No, old friend. You've got more than *that* in mind. If you'd wanted a little chat we could have done that at the Yard. You have something more significant planned.'

The dark, broad-shouldered outline remained as static and solid as that of the church in the background. A finger of fog spiralled into the room through the yawning wound in the side of the building and formed a translucent barrier between the two men.

'I knew it would come to this. For God's sake, as soon as you started nosing around I *knew* it would end like this.'

'I never made it my business to interfere in your case, Billy. I promise you that as one man to another. It was just circumstances. First, Mrs Scambles comes to me and tells a convincing tale. Then I get involved in the stolen ferns business – quite by chance, Billy. Just happened to be passing one of those swanky houses off Drury Lane. That led me to Jukes – though he was calling himself Chuddersby. It took me but a little time to remember him. It took me quite a bit longer to remember that when we were in uniform he used to sell scraps of information to you. It was him, wasn't it?'

Stope nodded curtly.

'From what Mr James Alexander Gordon and I have picked up along the way, I guessed he had stolen the watch from the Scambles home.'

'You've got it. After Mizzentoft died I needed someone to run the General to keep everyone in order. That made me two removed from things and harder to be fingered.'

'That was good thinking. But, Lord, Billy – *why kill Mizzentoft in the first place?* That's not you, that's not.'

'I turned into a greedy man, that's what it was. That's what I became.'

'A greedy man, a flash man – but not a murderer. It don't add up, old man.'

'How many times have we heard someone claim it was all a terrible misfortune? *There was a scuffle, and it was an accident, Officer.* Too many. Well, that's how it was. But I knew how that would go down, especially when it came out that I owed Mizzentoft a lot of money and I'd made certain threats in order to keep him quiet. Empty threats, but people knew of them. He must have thought I was coming to make good my promises, and he pulled a knife on me. I grabbed his wrist, we wrestled, fell over a footstool, and I landed on top of him. My weight forced the knife into his chest.'

'Well there you are, Billy! You're not a common criminal but a respected officer of the Detective. Your word will carry weight with a jury. You've let things get into a mess through greed and bad thinking, but *you're* a man of the world, a man of sound sense, that's what *you* are, Billy.' Mr Bucket began to move towards Inspector Stope. 'What *you're* going to do is—'

Stope also advanced, but in a much more menacing fashion. 'That line won't wash with me the way it does with others! We both know it's the hangman for me if I don't vanish.'

'Duty is duty, Billy, and you know what I must do.'

'You can tell as well as any man I've known when someone is lying. You know I didn't set out to murder Mizzentoft – that it was an accident. I could just disappear, run for it. You tried to catch me, but I got away. You never were a fast runner, Bucket – it was always me as caught the dashers.'

'You could always out-run me for sure, but now is not the time for running. *You* can judge when a man is a-telling the truth every bit as well as me, my friend, and you know I have to take you in.'

Mr Bucket took another tentative step into the darkness of the fog-shrouded room, his tentative feet searching out hidden obstacles.

Stope stayed where he was – but his hand reached into his pocket. *'God help me, Bucket – I won't be taken.'*

XXIX

G ORDON BURST THROUGH the big double doors of Great
Scotland Yard, sending an unfortunate middle-aged civilian
couple reeling backwards and landing in a heap on the floor.
Ignoring their indignant cries and those of others who had witnessed
it, he raced straight up to Sergeant Raddle at the front desk. He was
in conversation with Sir Marriot Ogle-Tarbolton.

'Where is Mr Bucket?'

'Why, Mr Gordon – what has come over you?' Sir Marriot
demanded.

'I must see Mr Bucket immediately. And where is Mr Stope?'

'Really, Mr Gordon—'

'Mr Bucket has gone to meet Mr Stope in Wapping,' Sergeant
Raddle stated. 'Must be a serious matter, since Billy requisitioned a
revolver from the armoury.'

Gordon groaned. 'Did Mr Bucket also?'

'No, sir.'

'Pray calm yourself, sir,' said Sir Marriot, 'and tell me why you are
acting in such a manner.'

'It was Billy Stope who killed Edward Mizzentoft!'

The two men exchanged bewildered glances. 'Have you gone
completely mad?' asked the Chief.

'The primary piece of evidence against Scambles is supposedly his
watch. I have discovered that this is *not* his watch – and anyway
could not have been at the murder scene as Mr Stope claimed since
it did not go missing till *after* the murder. There are other things.
Mr Bucket knows more than I, but you must believe me! *We must
assume that Mr Stope intends to silence Mr Bucket!*'

Sir Marriot's eyes widened and his mouth opened and closed
indecisively.

'Sergeant Raddle – tell me exactly where Mr Bucket was to meet Mr Stope.'

'Execution Dock, sir. The Imperial Spice and Tobacco warehouse.'

Gordon turned sharply on his heels. 'Then I must go there.'

'Wait for me, Gordon!' called Sir Marriot.

'Don't you want pistols, sir?' came Sergeant Raddle's voice.

'No time,' Gordon replied without looking back. He'd never had cause to requisition a weapon since joining the detective branch but he knew they had to be located, unlocked and signed for and every moment counted. Gordon was soon out of the building and racing into the fog with no thought as to whether or not Sir Marriot was keeping pace with him – when it occurred to him that he had not the slightest idea where Execution Dock was. Then he heard the Chief hailing a cab.

'It's a long way, Gordon. This will be quicker.' The Chief's disembodied voice came through the fog. He wasn't sure whether he really meant it was too far for *his* little legs to carry him at such a pace, but he had little choice other than to run back and join him as he was boarding the hansom and barking instructions to the driver.

'And get us there as quick as you can. You'll be paid treble your fare if you do!'

The driver yelled at his horse and cracked his whip, and the cab lurched into action, the driver lashing at the animal and uttering short, sharp imprecations. It was the most terrifying journey of Gordon's life. They could see no more than ten yards ahead, and if any unexpected obstacle had presented itself they should have had no chance whatsoever of stopping. Several times the two-wheeled vehicle tilted so crazily as it raced round corners that Gordon felt sure they should tip over completely; and every few seconds shadowy figures loomed out of the fog, running or jumping for their lives as they flew over the cobbles like a coach from hell with the Devil at the reigns. But a greater fear than all that weighed on Gordon's mind as he fretted over the fate of Mr Bucket. He was sure he must now suspect Billy Stope, but they were long-standing friends. Perhaps his heart would prevent him from admitting to the obvious conclusion. There had always been something about Stope that made Gordon slightly uneasy, and as far as his character went it now fell into place and he felt sure that the inspector would stop at nothing to avoid arrest. If Mr Bucket had gone to the rendezvous unprepared for what Billy Stope had in mind ....

The cab thundered noisily down a narrow street, and as it turned a sharp corner at the bottom, the right-hand wheel clipped the wall and jolted them so violently that Gordon's head cracked against the stiff rim of Sir Marriot's hat. The Chief ignored it, and continued to peer outside earnestly.

'This is it, Gordon,' he muttered, leaning forward and beginning to swing one leg over the side even before the vehicle had slithered to a halt on the wet cobbles.

Gordon could barely make anything out of where they were, but the distinctive stench of the river told him they were close to its bank. He jumped down to follow Sir Marriot, and in doing so held on to the handle of one of the great brass lanterns attached to either side of the cab. Then an idea occurred to him. He put both hands on the body of the lamp, ignoring the burning pain from the hot metal, and after a few wrenches this way and that, lifted it out of its fitting and carried it by its cooler stem.

'*Oi!*'

'This is a serious police matter. Wait there and you will be hand-somely rewarded.'

Sir Marriot Ogle-Tarbolton had reached the door of the ware-house only to find it locked, and was barging his shoulder against it. Gordon joined in, kicking at it with the sole of his boot. He soon heard the sound of splintering wood, and between them they forced it open. It was only after they had passed through two rooms of a large office and emerged into the warehouse space itself that Gordon saw a feeble patch of daylight, which told him that the goods entrance was gaping open and would have allowed them easy entry. But by now this was the last thing on his mind – for he could hear voices from above. He hissed to Sir Marriot to stop.

'*Listen!*'

The words were indistinct, but to his great relief Gordon felt certain that one of the speakers was Mr Bucket.

'*Look,*' said the Chief. '*Stairs. Let us proceed silently and cautiously. If Mr Bucket is in danger we may be able to catch Billy off guard.*'

Gordon nodded, and they crept towards the stairway as quietly as the debris-strewn floor would permit. The stairs themselves were in a parlous state and they had to take extra care both to avoid too much creaking and for their own safety. But all that changed in an instant. The subdued conversation they had been listening to suddenly rose in intensity, followed by a series of crashes, bangs and shouts, which spoke of a sudden eruption of violence. They quickened their pace, stumbling, but still managing to keep their feet. When the unmistakable sound of gunfire rent the air, all attempts at stealth were forgotten and they stumbled and raced to the top of the steps, finding themselves in a long corridor. The shots seemed to be coming from a room near the end, and they ran towards it. But then the firing had stopped, and Gordon heard voices again. They both instinctively slowed, and resumed their silent advance.

'*Easy there, Billy,*' Mr Bucket could be heard saying. He sounded somewhat shaken and breathless, but Gordon was relieved merely to know that he was still alive.

'*I don't care any more, don't you see?*' Despite Mr Stope's deep growl, there was a catch in his throat as he forced out these words. He sounded like a man close to breaking point.

Gordon could now see that there was a second door to this room further down the corridor. He positioned himself by the first one and gestured to Sir Marriot to go to the other. Gordon intended to show himself to attract Billy's attention, in the hope that the Chief would have an opportunity to take him by surprise. Sir Marriot nodded, and tiptoed towards the far door. Once he was in position, Gordon slipped in through his door, deliberately placing his feet down heavily so that he would be noticed in the darkness. He shone his lantern about the room until, finally, it illuminated the face of Billy Stope. The eerie light fell on his heavy brow and cast his eyes in deep shadow, making him look more fearsome than ever.

'That you, Mr Gordon?' came Mr Bucket's voice from the darkness.

'Yes, sir. Are you all right?'

Gordon turned the lantern in the direction from which his voice had come, and saw that Mr Bucket had somehow managed to snatch the revolver away from Billy Stope and was aiming it at his erstwhile friend. It was a relief – yet something felt dangerously wrong about this scene .... By the time Gordon realized what it was, he was already too late. Mr Bucket's back was to the other door. Sir Marriot suddenly came crashing in shouting for everyone to stand still, but in the process sent Mr Bucket flying into a table in the middle of the room. One of its legs fractured and it collapsed beneath him. He went sprawling, the revolver hit the edge of the table and went off. Gordon instinctively threw himself to the floor, and in the same instant heard the bullet ricochet off some metallic object and then embed itself in one of the walls. In diving for cover, the large hansom lantern Gordon had been carrying was knocked from his grasp and clattered along the dusty floorboards. It must have spilt nearly a full load of oil, because a streak of flame instantly flared into life and rapidly began to spread. Scraps of paper, wood shavings and other scattered rubbish combusted in a chain reaction, and by this light Gordon could see that the fire was spreading towards a big old sofa.

Worse still, he could see that Mr Stope, on the other side of the fire from the three of them, somehow now held the revolver. It was levelled at Mr Bucket.

'Would you, Billy? Even now – even after it's come to this, would you shoot me in cold blood?'

'My blood ain't cold.'

'Then it don't look good for me. I know you're a crack shot 'cos I recall the time when that American fellow had me cornered with his Colt against my noggin. Shot him in the temple with an old flint-lock from ten yards, you did – remember that, Billy?'

'Yes.'

'*I* do, because I felt the ball whistle over my shoulder. Just past my ear, it went. Still sets it a-ringing just to think of it. That was when we were still in uniform. Long time ago.'

'You mean when I was a good copper.'

'That ain't what I'm getting at. You're still a good copper – you've just succumbed, that's all. Could happen to any of us. You see, Mr James Alexander Gordon of that ilk, he ain't always been flash, our Billy. I saw the signs, but I ignored them because he's my colleague – my friend. Even now, deep down, he's the salt of the earth – *that's* what Billy Stope is. Me and him have always looked out for each other. But they don't pay us much. We have to put up with a lot of nonsense from folk every day and risk our necks. We deserve more, and Billy decided it was time to get what he could. Any man might do the same.'

'Not you, though.'

'Who can say what a man might do ....'

Stope took a step forward with the gun outstretched. 'STOP IT! I KNOW WHAT YOU'RE DOING AND IT WON'T WORK!'

At the same moment the sofa suddenly burst into flames. It looked like a scene from hell as the red and orange tongues of fire instantly leaped to the height of Billy Stope's head, the shadows playing across his contorted features. Very quickly now, other items caught light: a single curtain beside what was once a window, the broken table, a basket of some unidentifiable material in a corner. The heat was so intense that Gordon had to step back, towards the door.

'Billy!' cried Mr Bucket, his voice choked with genuine fear and compassion. 'You must give yourself up to me now before this here fire traps you good and proper. Forget the damned gun – there's three of us and only one bullet left by my calculations so you would only be shooting me out of spite before you got taken, and I know that ain't you.'

The fire whooshed and leapt like a wild beast now. The heat was barely tolerable and the angry cracking of wood and the roar of the unpredictable flames and was a sound both terrifying and sickening. Billy Stope was almost completely encircled, with only his head visible, yet he didn't flinch for a moment.

'No, that ain't me.' He had to raise his voice over the noise of the conflagration, but a grim smile played on his lips. Then, he slowly raised the gun until it was level with his own temple.

Gordon was frozen to the spot, but Mr Bucket charged into the flames. *'FOR GOD'S SAKE, BILLY – NO!'*

There was a sharp *crack* the instant before Mr Bucket hit Billy Stope and bundled them both to the floor. Gordon dashed through the only ever-narrowing gap in the circle of flames, feeling his hair singeing and his throat and lungs burning with every breath. Mr Bucket was on top of Billy. Blood and brain matter covered the side of his head, and the back of his coat was on fire. Gordon quickly grabbed him by the ankles and dragged him back through what was left of the break in the barrier of fire. He was conscious but a dead weight, as if he could not bring himself to let go of the corpse of his friend.

The next thing Gordon knew he was slumped against the door frame and Sir Marriot was patting the top of his head furiously. Only then did he feel the stinging, scorching sensation on his scalp and catch the smell of singed hair. He began to cough and choke so violently that his lungs seemed to go into some sort of spasm. He saw his own black phlegm adding to the ghastly pattern on Mr Bucket's body, and suddenly felt like a drowning man. After that, everything went black.

XXX

THERE WERE EARLY signs of spring in the air as Sergeant Gordon and Inspector Bucket cut through St James's Park on their way to Mayfair and the home of Lady Rhynde. This was the third successive day of cloudy but bright and mild weather; snowdrops and the odd crocus provided a splash of colour here and there, and a robin was chirruping merrily from the branches of a tree ahead of them.

It was the week after the funeral. During the course of his duties, Inspector William Joseph Stope had been tragically killed in a fire despite the best efforts of his colleagues to save him. That was the official story. Mr Bucket would not break the law to save his friend from justice, but now that justice had been done in an unforeseen and terrible way, he could at least do that much for the memory of his old comrade. Not that Gordon's chief had explained this to him. He had not raised the matter nor even mentioned Billy Stope's name since Gordon had recovered from the damage done to his lungs by the smoke and heat and returned to work, and he had no wish to press him. Sir Marriot Ogle-Tarbolton was fully behind this version of events, but Gordon knew that it must have originated with Mr Bucket. Dr Scambles was free and reunited, as least for now, with Eleanora. Jukes was dead and the General had disappeared, said to have gone to sea. The only hint Gordon had heard of the whole affair was a remark from Sir Marriot that although Mizzentoft had died at the hands of Billy Stope, it truly had been a tragic accident. This too, must have come from Mr Bucket and so Gordon believed it implicitly. There was nothing to be gained by destroying Billy Stope's family and making the full truth of the case public. As for the mysterious matter of the ferns, Sir Marriot was happy in the belief – again no doubt acquired from Mr Bucket – that they had been stolen by a mad gipsy woman who had since fled London leaving her haul behind her to be safely reunited with their owners.

They were soon admitted to Lady Rhynde's house and shown up to see her. But when they entered the room Gordon sensed tension and apprehension in her. The reason for this became apparent when her husband, Sir Dalton Rhynde, the Home Secretary, stepped forward. He had been sitting at a writing desk with his back to them when they had entered, and Gordon had failed to notice him. He was a very severe-looking, snowy-haired man who appeared to be a good ten years older in age and even more than that in his manner than his attractive wife. Whatever troubles Lady Rhynde had experienced went far deeper than mere ferns and Gordon could easily guess that it was something she would not want raising in front of her husband. What Gordon knew – and was sure she did too – was that Mr Bucket had brought a batch of letters written in her hand. They were the same ones he had removed from Baroness Sowerby's house, and were currently nestling in an inside pocket of his coat.

'My husband was due to be at a reception for Leopold, King of the Belgians, but we hear that His Royal Highness is indisposed this morning and the function has been postponed until tomorrow,' her ladyship reported with rather forced lightness of manner.

The Home Secretary ignored Gordon and approached his superior. There was an unnatural stiffness about both his gait and the way he held his head and neck, as if all of his clothing right up to his collar was made of wood.

'You're Bucket?' His voice had a gravelly, grunting quality to it, as though speaking to people below his rank – which was most of the population – required more effort than it was worth.

Gordon's chief gave a formal nod. 'Mr Bucket of the Detective at your service, sir.'

'I know why you're here.'

Gordon's heart leapt a little, and he noticed a sort of fleeting wince disturb Lady Rhynde's face.

Mr Bucket remained as unaffected and affable as ever. 'Really?'

The politician held out a bony claw of a hand. 'I wish to thank you for putting my wife's mind at rest regarding this business with the ferns.'

He didn't smile, yet Gordon realized to his astonishment that this was the closest he came to displaying warmth.

'My pleasure, sir,' replied Mr Bucket.

'I know it's a damnable business, calling upon senior members of the Detective to deal with such a trivial matter, but you know what women are like.' He spoke as though his wife were not present. 'I feel particularly embarrassed at getting you tied up in all this, since it has come to my attention that you have had a far graver matter to occupy your time, and indeed that a valued colleague of yours lost his life during the course of that investigation. So on behalf of my wife and myself, let me once again thank you.'

He gave the slightest of bows, then turned his back on them and went back to his writing desk leaving Gordon, Mr Bucket and Lady Rhynde standing looking at each other rather awkwardly for a moment.

'*Pteridomania*!' said Mr Bucket suddenly, his left thumb tucked into his lapel and his stout right forefinger raised.

'Mr Bucket?' frowned her ladyship.

'The term for avid fern collecting is pteridomania. I have it on good authority. No less than Mrs Bucket, who is herself a pterido-maniac like your ladyship. Pardon me if *that's* not the correct term, ma'am. Don't sound exactly flattering when said like that.'

Lady Rhynde recovered something of her former brightness of spirit. 'No – but unfortunately is probably quite correct!'

'Mrs Bucket has managed to grow them out of doors – in the humble back yard of our little home in Pimlico. Has your ladyship had any similar successes?'

Gordon now saw where he intended this to go – as, evidently, did she. 'I have indeed. Perhaps yourself and Mr Gordon might like to step outside with me to see them?'

'Why, it is an opportunity not to be missed! I might even pick up some ideas for Mrs Bucket – though I promise to take only *ideas* back home with me ....'

Gordon found it heart-warming to see Lady Rhynde's face light up as she chuckled at Mr Bucket's quip. She led them through the house – which reminded Gordon of a hotel more than a family home – and out into the garden.

'There,' she said. 'I dare say it is no larger than your own "humble back yard" in Pimlico.'

'Only a little – but the *setting* is far grander.'

Indeed, Gordon was surprised at how little space she had. The houses of Upper Grosvenor Street, though certainly imposing, were much taller than they were wide and were closely packed together, leaving little space at the rear. But, this being the residence of the Home Secretary, there was a gardener at work at the far end, tending to a little bonfire. And ferns there were: some growing in flower beds, others under little glass cloches about the size of a dog's kennel. To Gordon, as ever they all looked like drab green foliage, and he could barely differentiate between them; but Mr Bucket listened intently as Lady Rhynde picked out and named her prize specimens.

'Upon my soul, your ladyship has been most informative and kind,' said Mr Bucket at last. Then he glanced in the direction of the gardener and lowered his voice a little. 'But there is one further matter which needs to be discussed.'

She nodded. 'Jackson – could you leave us please? I'm sure if you go to the kitchen Emily or Mrs Porter will soon have some refreshments ready for you.'

The gardener touched the rim of his hat and went indoors. Mr Bucket watched him go, then slipped a hand into his coat and pulled out the bundle of letters. Gordon was sure that she had known for some time that they were in his safe keeping, yet still the sight of them caused a tremor to run through her slender body.

'Mr Jackson's fire is dying,' said Mr Bucket. 'Shall we help it along a little?'

'Yes, please,' she replied in a barely audible whisper.

'Would your ladyship care to do the honours?' He held the letters out to her but she recoiled from them, so he went to the fire and threw them in. As it flared up and crackled, a shadow seemed to dim his eyes and he gazed for a moment. The sounds, the heat, the smell of the smoke ... Gordon felt something stir in his own breast at the same moment.

'Sometimes, Lady Rhynde, letters and other things must be burned out of necessity.' Mr Bucket was still staring into the fire as he spoke. 'But that don't necessarily mean that bridges must be burned ....'

'I take your meaning, Mr Bucket. Thank you.'

Gordon wasn't privy to the significance of this message. But equally, he knew she could not possibly have understood fully the meaning it had for him as the orange flames reflected in his distant gaze. Then, as if a spell had been broken Mr Bucket suddenly straightened up, and all signs of melancholy had vanished from his countenance. He raised his hat. 'Well now, your ladyship. That appears to conclude our business!'

She stepped towards him, beaming and holding out her hand. Instead of allowing him to shake it, she pressed it upwards towards his face, and he kissed it lightly. She did the same with Gordon.

'There concludes the amazing *Mystery of the Ferns*, Inspector! But pray bear in mind that my position does have its advantages. My husband is, ultimately, your employer and there might come a day when I can repay you in some way. You must promise that you will not hesitate to ask if you are ever in need of some *divine intervention*!'

Mr Bucket removed his hat and bowed at the waist. 'Your ladyship is most kind.'

They were sauntering through Charing Cross on their way back to Great Scotland Yard, talking about this and that. It was actually Mr Bucket who was doing most of the talking, since Gordon's voice was still painfully husky from the fire. The detective told Gordon a little of his days in the army before joining the police, and of the adverse and suspicious public reaction towards himself and the other members of the new detective force when it commenced operations only a little more than two years previously. But when the tales began to stray towards exploits that involved the late Mr Stope, this line of conversation soon dried up and Mr Bucket quickly changed tack.

'Do you know what the best thing about getting out of the blue uniform was, Mr Gordon?'

'Pray tell me.'

'No longer having to wear them damnable collars, *that's* what it was. Well, not so much the collar, but the leather stock we wore inside of them. And do you know what the reason for that was?'

'I really can't imagine, but it does sound very uncomfortable.'

'It was to prevent garrotting, Mr Gordon! It was in case someone crept up behind us and attempted to strangle or garrotte us. Now, never in all my years in uniform did I hear of a single attempted garrotting, yet we still were made to—'

But Gordon's attention had been diverted away from Mr Bucket's undoubtedly interesting story towards a scene he had spotted before the railings surrounding the statue of Charles I. A man in a filthy hat with a badly frayed brim was selling songbirds in wooden cages in front of the monument, and a respectable-looking gentleman with what looked like his son were inspecting them and conversing with the bird-seller. Nearby, an idler lounging against the railings was casually looking all about him as if watching the world go by – but his gaze kept coming back to the man studying the birds, who had his back to him. To Gordon's mind, it was a calculating gaze.

'Hold a moment, Mr Bucket ....'

'What's that?'

'Let us stand here a moment.' Gordon positioned his back to the little group of people beside the statue. 'Look over my shoulder to that thin man in the grey jacket by the railings – but don't make him aware that you are observing him.'

Mr Bucket scowled at his sergeant. 'I do know my job, Mr James Alexander Gordon of that ilk. Now, let's have a look-see. No, don't recognize him. Could be just .... No, hang on. Prepare for action, Mr Gordon! Hold – not yet, sir .... There he goes, shuffling closer ... going for the coat-tail pocket I'll be bound. NOW!'

Mr Bucket took off like someone in the hundred yard dash, and Gordon turned sharply to follow. He veered away to the right so that he would come up behind the would-be pickpocket. Sure enough, as soon as he saw Mr Bucket charging towards him he spun round to head in the opposite direction – straight into Gordon's arms. The man cursed and struggled but he was so slightly built as to be almost emaciated, and Gordon had no trouble in restraining him without Mr Bucket needing to intervene; his only fear was that the gentleman whose pocket had almost been picked and who was now advancing upon them with a face like thunder might launch an attack on his prisoner. But Mr Bucket had descried a policeman on his beat walking up the Strand, and summoned him. Their captive was grasped firmly by the collar and led away.

'Most commendable, Mr Gordon. You are becoming quite the finished detective.'

'I am fortunate in having a good teacher.'

'I was thinking we might repair to the Ten Bells.'

'I won't argue with that, Mr Bucket.'

'But then it occurred to me that you have some paperwork to deal with.'

'I do?'

'Well, there's your expenses form to fill in, at least.'

Gordon searched his mind. 'Expenses?'

'Yes. On the occasion when you last met Mrs Scambles you informed me you had to *pay* for the information given to you. So we had better get a form for you to fill in. Don't want you out of pocket.'

Was that a twinkle in his eye, or Gordon's paranoia? 'I ... I am in no need of recompense for that, Mr Bucket ....'

'Ah! Feeling flush, are we? The drinks are on you then, Mr Gordon. Mine's a brandy and water, if you please.'

Glossary of Slang Phrases

Aris – backside

Barney – fight

Bawdy Houses – brothels, low lodging houses etc.

Beak – magistrate

Beershop – private house selling beer

Bit Faker – maker of counterfeit coins (also "coiner")

Black Maria – police vehicle for taking prisoners to gaol

Bob – shilling

Bounce – swagger

Bullies – bouncers on doors of brothels, lodging houses etc.

Bull's-eye – lamp carried by a constable

Bunter – woman who takes lodgings then absconds without paying

Cad – omnibus conductor

Claret – blood, esp. from a fight

Crack a case – burgle a house

Cracksman – more professional type of thief than an opportunist

Crown and Anchor – gambling game

Dip – pickpocket

Dollymops – amateur, opportunist prostitutes

Dollyshops – unofficial pawnbroker, often receivers of no-questions-asked stolen goods

Double-eye-glasses – hand-held spectacles which can fold over one another. The folding action differentiates them from **lorgnettes**. When folded, could be used as single lens of double thickness.

Doss House – lodgings

Drag, a – three-month prison sentence

Dragsman – thief who robs carriages/cabs by climbing up behind and taking luggage from roof

Fan – to fan someone: to feel someone's pocket for something worth stealing

Fustian – [Also called **bombast**] a heavy woven mostly cotton fabric

Game – brave

Grass – informant

Growler – type of cab, larger than hansom, for up to four people. (Actual name: Clarence cab)

Gull – to cheat or con

Irish Row – a fight; when a row spills over into a fist fight. Esp. a faction fight

Ivories – teeth

Jug – prison

Kidsman – trainer of child thieves

Life-preserver – form of cosh consisting of leather strap with heavy metal ball on the end, also covered in leather

Lorgnette – spectacles with handle for holding to eyes

Lucifer – a match

Magsman – an inferior burglar; conman, street swindler

Maltooling – picking pockets on a bus

Mother's Blessing – laudanum or other mixture to keep babies quiet

Mudlarks – scrabblers for discarded materials on river-banks

Napper – head

Palanquin – a covered litter carried on poles by four men

Peace warrant – arrest warrant

Peterman – safe breaker

Phizog – face

Physic – medicine

Plucky – courageous, "a plucky one"

Quodded – imprisoned

Ragged schools – establishments for educating street children

Rookeries – slums

Scarletina – alternative name for scarlet fever

Smasher – utterer of base coin

Swell mob – conmen and pickpockets dressed as gents who worked theatres, race meetings and other gatherings